Spring House

R. Christian Crabtree

Cover artwork and tree illustration by Sandy Crabtree

Designed and produced by:
Maine Authors Publishing
12 High Street, Thomaston, Maine
www.maineauthorspublishing.com

Printed in the United States of America

*For my wife and family, for all their love and support,
and in memory of my great-grandfather, Herman Jules,
who grew up on the farm that inspired this book.*

Chapter 1

Conner Williamson woke with a jump, his right cheek peeling away from the tan leather headrest like masking tape. He ran his hand across his face and through his hair. It felt warm and matted. He was coming out of one of those periods of sleep that are reserved exclusively for long car rides. You are not entirely awake nor completely asleep, but drifting aimlessly in a sweaty nether region where dreams hijack sounds from the real world and incorporate them into your dream story. Thick misty-green vegetation rushed by in a blur, and he wondered how long he had been out. He looked over at his father, who didn't seem to notice he was awake. Old Dad was focused on the real world, staring ahead at the road, his jaw set in carved stone.

Conner turned his gaze to white lines on the road slithering beneath the tires of the car. It was almost dark, and he could make out the headlights shining faintly on the black tar.

The situation was unbelievable. Conner had finished up an uneventful eighth-grade year and was getting ready for a languid, hot Virginia summer of hanging out in the icy air-conditioning on the couch, watching endless on-demand shows and movies, swimming in the community pool, and blowing away terrorists in his video game alternate universe. Then, without any warning, his happy plan had turned into debris and chaos.

Break up; separating; need some time apart; we'll see what happens; it's not your fault. We both love you very much. It's best if you go and spend some time with Gramp this summer. You'll have fun. You haven't spent any real time with him. You'll get to work on the Farm and go fishing and maybe even hunting.

It's for the best. Trust us; it's for the best, you'll see.

It was as if his parents had consulted the "We're Going to Ruin Your Life with a Divorce" manual to get the lines they had recited to him with a deliberate if somewhat dramatic tone as they all sat together in the formal living room of his house. Conner always hated the place. The walls were a soft lime-green color, and the end tables and two chairs were overly ornate and uninviting. The long couch was a stiff, uncomfortable thing adorned with embroidered flowers and vine patterns. Conner always felt like he was sitting in some royal function whenever he was in the room, which was usually only when visits by friends and family demanded it.

It was *not* for the best, not *his* best. It could only be for *their* best, if that were even possible. They were only thinking of themselves, not him. Not what this could do to him, to his life. He felt guilty for a fleeting moment, thinking this probably wasn't easy for them either, but it quickly passed, and he dove right into some unabashed self-pity. He couldn't understand it. They didn't fight, there were no big house-thundering arguments between them, and the cops never showed up. What could have happened that they suddenly, seemingly out of the blue, decided they didn't want to be married to each other anymore? It just didn't make sense.

"Where are we?" Conner asked, stretching his back and chest out to the limits of his seat belt.

"We just came into Massachusetts," Marcus answered.

Great, Conner thought. He had been tortured with Early American History for the past two months before school ended. Massachusetts, home of pewter, candle-making techniques, tea parties, muskets, and revolution; that was what this last week had felt like to him—the first shots fired of what promised to be a long and bloody conflict.

"Can we stop somewhere and get something to eat?"

"Sure…let's just get on the Mass Pike, and we'll find a rest stop."

Conner laid his head in the shoulder sling of the seat belt and looked back out the window of the SUV. The air-conditioning hummed steadily out of the vents, numbing his bare knees. He could not believe this was happening to him. Sure, divorce was nothing new among his classmates; it seemed like every other kid had two sets of parents, two Christmases, two birthdays, two Thanksgivings. The lucky ones were shuttled directly back and forth by amicable co-parents between their two parallel universes, avoiding the embarrassment of swapping out families at some sketchy convenience store. His friend Nathan described his exchange location as the "neutral zone."

"My parents won't even look at each other," Nathan said to him once. "They pull up next to each other, and I get out of one car and into the other; it's like a hostage exchange. I should be wearing a bag over my head." Conner remembered he had felt sad for him, one of the unlucky kids caught in the middle of never-ending conflict. Some barely saw their fathers at all, and then only for a week or two each year—what a hard existence. So now his life was destined to be the same as one of theirs, and there was nothing he could do about it.

Conner looked down at his wristwatch: 7:52 p.m. It was a heavy gold Omega Seamaster Cosmic 2000, oddly out of place on his thin, fourteen-year-old wrist. The watch had belonged to his grandfather, his mother, Evelyn's, father, and his grandmother gave it to him after he died. There were no numbers on it, only hash marks showing the time by the positioning of the hands. There were two small windows on the right side of the watch face showing the day, abbreviated in three capital letters, and the date. For the first few months, it didn't run, stopped dead at 12:36 a.m., but one day when he was trying to figure out how to take it apart and change what he assumed must be a battery in it, he gave it a couple of shakes and it just started to run on its own. Weird, but it had run perfectly ever since, as long as he shook it a few times a week. That was almost two years ago.

Marcus put his turn signal on and drove the car into the bright rest area parking lot, maneuvering through the zombie hordes of people dressed in their sagging T-shirts, weather-beaten sandals, and flip-flops. Summer was definitely upon them. They parked, climbed out of the car, and stretched their backs in unison, looking like an adult and adolescent version of the same person, and headed to the welcome center. It was still hot and humid despite the early evening hour, the air lying heavy over their heads. Wordlessly, Conner opened the doors, and they walked into the babbling entryway, looking around at the various mini-restaurant food options. Burgers, pizza, some Asian cuisine place that had no line—the usual uninspired fare.

"Do you need to use the restroom?" Marcus asked.

"Sure, I guess so."

They headed through the tight right-left turns of the bathroom passageway, quickly enveloped by the disinfectant and freshly used urinal smell that plagues all public bathrooms. Conner headed toward the back to seek out one of the less trafficked stalls—using the urinals wasn't even a remote option. Standing next to some balding fat guy with his glancing eyes peeking over and down as you try to go, thinking you won't notice; no thanks. There were perverts everywhere.

Conner entered the last stall in the back, the one accessible to wheelchairs where he felt less claustrophobic, and closed the door. He didn't touch the black horseshoe-shaped seat, opting to lift it with the tip of his white sneaker. Conner hitched down the front of his hiking shorts, stood back, and released a fast stream, trying to keep his aim to the center of the bowl. Wearing shorts while going was not ideal because no matter how careful he was, he could always feel the disgusting tiny splatters of water hitting his bare legs. Gross. He had to assume the same splatters hit long pants the same way, but at least there was no persistent reminder of that grim fact.

Conner kicked the silver flush knob behind the toilet with the sole of his sneaker and then used its tip to hook the lid down with a loud plastic *clack*. He exited and walked over to the nearest unoccupied sink and squirted some of the foam they try to pass off as soap onto his hands. The mirror was silver and pockmarked, casting a distorted reflection. He had dark circles under his eyes like he used to get when he was younger, and his light-brown hair was sticking up in shocks on the top of his head like little wheat bundles in a field. He pressed down on the water knob, which never stayed on long enough to wash and rinse his hands thoroughly, shook them off with a wet snap, and headed for the exit, bypassing the sanitary blow dryers that made his ears throb.

Marcus was already waiting for him on the outside, having perfected over his forty-five years the art of getting in and out of public bathrooms with military-like precision.

"What'll it be? Shall we grab some greasy burgers?" Marcus asked with a slight smile.

"Okay, sure," Conner replied in the mumbled whisper that all teenage boys employ.

They ordered up the standard go-to food, a fried chicken sandwich meal with a diet soda for Marcus, and the double cheeseburger meal and root beer for Conner. If his mother had been there, it would have been the salad or grilled chicken sandwich for Marcus, his weak attempt to meet her rigorous health standards and to avoid remarks on his modest but undeniably present and ever-expanding gut. More likely, they wouldn't be eating this stuff at all, Conner thought. It would have been pack lunches: wheat bread and some dry, organic sliced turkey overloaded with lettuce and tomatoes. Standard off-the-shelf mayonnaise did not exist in his mother's world; rather, the sandwiches would have some veggie spread on them that looked like it had grass clippings in it and tasted even worse.

Conner and Marcus sat down with the tray and started to dig through the bags for their food, scooping out the runaway French fries from the bottom. The napkins unceremoniously stuffed into the bags were already grease-stained, a sure sign of unhealthy food fare if there ever was one.

They ate in silence; what was there to say? Conner was being sent off to his grandfather's place without his feelings mattering in the slightest. His grandfather lived in northern Maine in some little smudge of a town called Morgan that from what he had seen during an internet search only had one real street running through it. He had visited his grandparents with his family during the summers for as long as he could remember when they lived in Connecticut, but after his grandmother had died, his grandfather had sold the house and moved up to the old farm where he'd grown up. Fresh pine air, cold streams to fish in, thick woods to explore—"You'd love it," Gramp had said while thumbing through a photo album with him.

In some ways, Conner felt like he had already been to the "Farm," as Gramp called it. The fading photographs of the white house and connected barns, and Gramp's stories about growing up there told over and over, almost to the point Conner could anticipate the next words out of his mouth with startling accuracy. Details sometimes changed with each telling, but Conner didn't mind. Once, when they were raking leaves, his grandfather told him about a bear encounter when he was a boy.

"One day," Gramp said, "me and my sister Livie were sitting on the fence in the barnyard when up the road came old Wilbur Bump carrying a beat-up old bolt-action .22 rifle he liked to tote around with him everywhere like it was an extra arm on his body. He got about twenty yards from us when he just froze quick and looked down over the bank, down the road to where we couldn't see. Old Bump drew up that .22 and fired off a round, then started working that bolt just as fast as he could, cracking off shots like a madman down the side of the bank. He must have fired off five shots, just as fast as he could manage. Livie and I were startled at first, but then we started laughing, figuring he was putting on a show for us. Bump was always doing crazy things like that. After he stopped shooting, old Bump just stood there with a dazed look on his face, rifle slung low in his hands, shoulders hunched over, staring down that hill. Livie and I hopped off the fence and ran over to him. You might not believe it, but down that hill and not ten feet from Bump's clodhopper boots was the bloody nose of a black bear slumped dead on the ground with its front paws stretched out like it was reaching out to try and tear him to shreds. We heard a scurrying sound in a tree a bit further down the hill and saw two bear cubs glaring at the three of us like we had just murdered their mother, which I guess Bump just had, but he didn't have a choice. That old bear saw Bump as a threat to her young, and she was only doing what nature programmed her to do.

"I felt sad, though," Gramp continued. "We watched those cubs for a good fifteen minutes, then they just climbed down and vanished into the brush. I don't suppose they had any chance of surviving, but I hoped they would, and were somehow able to forgive old Bump for what he did to their mother. I've often thought that if Bump hadn't been there, and Livie and I had been walking down that road, that bear could have killed us. Mother Nature just plain doesn't care how young or how old you are, and her creatures don't always care to ask whether your intentions are good. Sometimes when you're not looking, she can jump right up and shake you hard.

"Anyway," Gramp had told him, "no one ever made fun of Bump for toting around that rifle again. Realizing that he'd probably saved our lives, he must have gotten a pie from every woman in town and came out of it with a bearskin rug to boot."

Not all his stories were as action-packed as the bear one. Gramp often told of raising chickens and pigs and growing corn, wheat, and potatoes in fields behind the house. He described the summer ritual of the whole family traipsing through the brush to the back side of the hill to pick blueberries, the kids' picking considerably less focused than the parents', blue streaks dribbling down the sides their mouths, betraying the fate of their efforts. Conner had often asked his grandfather if they could go up and visit the place, and the answer was always "sure, we'll have to do that someday," but someday had never come…until now, that is. Still, Conner found himself dreading it.

Part of the reason it never had, Conner supposed, was that Dad and Gramp had been waging a mostly silent war for years. Something between them had broken like an old car part. If it hadn't been for his always cheerful and peace-making grandmother, Conner doubted there would have been any contact between them at all. The visits were cordial and pleasant, cookies and snacks laid out on the table, but the tension between his dad and Gramp hung over every visit like a grim vulture. They rarely spoke and barely sat in the same room for more than a few minutes. Conner always wanted to ask his dad why they were like that, but he was scared to, and maybe he didn't want to know. His father certainly never seemed inclined to reveal any details.

It had been like that for as long as Conner could remember. A yearly visit, gifts, and sweets from Grammy, stories from Gramp, and then back to the airport for the flight back to Virginia. They never spent any real holidays like Christmas or birthdays together, and that was just the way it was, but maybe that was for the best. Last year, his friend Luke's family had a big New Year's Eve party across the street. The raucous gathering was topped off by his inebriated uncle backing over the family's Siamese cat, Sukie, during an ill-advised bid to go out for more beer. Luke's account of the chaos and screaming that ensued was morbidly entertaining. "Cat pizza," Luke had called it, who was never fond of the little brown-and-white beast that often passed the time chewing the power cord of his gaming console. The cat scratched and hissed at anyone who came near her, with the exception of Luke's little sister, Emily, the departed cat's unfortunate owner. Luke said his parents even went so far as getting Emily a few sessions with a therapist to cope with her grief. Eventually, a replacement cat, Minkie, finally seemed to quell her anguish.

Families can be hard things to deal with, Conner thought.

⁊

The stars were flickering in the sky above when Conner and his dad pulled off the highway. They took a left turn off the exit and swung into the first service station, where Conner spotted Gramp's weathered red pickup truck under a bright fluorescent light. Rust crept up the sides of the vehicle as if the earth itself was trying to drag it back into the ground. Marcus opened the door, setting off the interior lights and pausing to look at Conner. "It's going to be okay, Son. You'll be okay. I love you."

"I love you, too, Dad," Conner said with a hint of resignation in his voice about his situation. It was real now, and there was no getting out of it.

Marcus pressed a button on the door, and the trunk popped open with a muffled thump. Conner opened his door and walked around back, lifted the hatch, and took out the foliage-green backpack he had bought online three years ago. He hefted it onto his shoulder and walked with his dad over to his grandfather, who had stepped out of his truck and was leaning with one arm slung over the door.

"Marcus…Conner," his grandfather said, giving them each a solid look in their eyes.

"Dad," Marcus replied.

"Hi, Gramp," Conner said.

That was the extent of their exchange. Conner gave his Gramp a quick hug, then turned around and hugged his dad. Marcus ran his hand over his hair and told him to listen to his grandfather and stay out of trouble. Fifteen minutes later, Conner and Gramp were driving down the road, the bright headlights—apparently the only new parts on the truck—illuminating the trees ahead in a U shape.

"It'll be another hour and a half or so to the Farm, so get some sleep if you want. I've got the radio to keep me company," Gramp said.

The radio crackled out country music from another time. Conner had never understood country music, although he had heard some songs by Johnny Cash that sounded all right. The rest, the same, offering way too much information for his taste. Conner leaned his head back on the seat and closed his eyes, slowing drifting back into another dreamlike state, but still hearing the sounds of the road and the music faintly playing in the back of his mind.

When Conner first came to, he didn't know if his grandfather had said something or if he had just woken up on his own. The truck was approaching a stop sign at a T-junction, and his grandfather said they were coming into town. There were no streetlights, but the moon cast a dim blue light that made it easy to see, almost like a cloudy day. They turned left and headed across a small bridge with water off to the right. The pond had a small solitary island far in the back, black pines silhouetted by the moonlight sprouting from its center. They passed what looked like an old general store and a few ramshackle houses as they drove up a hill. The houses looked strange to Conner: They were mostly white and had board siding that was wider than typical house boards, almost as if a child had assembled them out of blocks.

They reached the top of the hill and turned right off the main street and immediately left onto the lawn of an ancient white two-story farmhouse with a dark roof and wraparound porch. The barns he remembered from the pictures extended right from the house, dark gray in color, the second almost twice as large as the first, dwarfing the main house. Across the main street was a cemetery with white and gray stones that extended back to a dark tree line of more pines. Directly across from the Farm on a small rise was a one-room schoolhouse with a small playground next to it. It had a long set of swings with four identical drooping seats, except for one on the far left that had a little blue toddler seat. There were two basketball hoops at the ends of a short court with weeds growing up out of the cracks, a set of monkey bars, a seesaw, and a merry-go-round in the center that was tilted up on its axis. A single fluorescent streetlight stood on the corner of the playground, illuminating the house and the schoolyard. The scene looked nothing like he had envisioned it, a lively bright farm with sheets hanging to dry on an outdoor clothesline, chickens clucking back and forth in the sun. This scene was more like something out of a horror movie. He could almost see himself trapped inside the house as ghostly figures dressed in eighteenth-century clothes and hats slowly walked out of the cemetery, arms stretched out in front of them, intent on dragging him underground to their dark graves.

Conner's grandfather put the truck in park and turned off the ignition.

"Well, welcome to Morgan Township, population two hundred and three up until today…now two hundred and four," Gramp said with a smile.

Conner stepped out of the truck and took a deep breath. The air was brisk, more biting than it was supposed to be in the middle of summer, and the wind rustled through a stand of reddish bamboo bushes that looked like round, fat porcupines. He followed his grandfather up onto the porch to a red screen door, which Gramp opened with a rusty-metal stretching sound. His grandfather fumbled for a specific gold key on his car keys, inserted it into the dead bolt, turned it with a scratch, and pushed the weathered white inner door open, holding the screen door open with his right hip.

They entered a kitchen and when his grandfather clicked on the ceiling light, the room came alive. A round kitchen table stood off to the right between another door and a stout white fridge with a curved top no taller than Conner. Across from the table was a yellow-enameled metal cookstove that looked like something Conner had seen in Colonial Williamsburg with his family a few years ago. On the back wall was a slate sink and a counter with a square, lace-curtained window above the sink.

"Follow me, my boy, and I'll take you straight up to your room so you can unload your gear."

Conner nodded and walked behind him into a small dining room with a dark wooden table in the center. A kerosene heater with a brown metal mesh front stood off to the right, and a double set of French doors closed off a formal living room straight ahead. There was a narrow staircase leading up to the right.

His grandfather headed up the stairs, each step creaking louder than the previous one. The staircase came to a small landing and turned sharply right. A little black window on the wall of the landing looked out behind the house. As he climbed the stairs, Conner noticed they all seemed to lean precariously to the left, and he briefly envisioned himself crashing through them into the darkness below. At the top of the stairs, there was a door to the immediate left and an open octagonal sitting area with four more doors. Each door jamb was crooked and off-angle, like the builder had thrown the whole house together in a maniacal hurry. His grandfather opened the second door leading into a tiny bedroom, the bottom of the door scraping on the floor, and pulled the chain on a hanging ceiling light, which swung back and forth.

"Well, here you are," his grandfather said.

The room was sparse, a twin bed with a blue comforter, a small full bookcase, and a squat dresser the total complement of furnishings. There was a single window with white see-through lace curtains and a green pull-down vinyl shade with a few tears in it. The walls were covered with battered wallpaper depicting old ships and bottles, and were accented by the occasional water stain that had crept through the cake-like plaster.

"Bathroom is the door by the head of the stairs; my room is the one across the hall. Other rooms haven't seen visitors in a while, I suppose, but you're welcome to explore," Gramp said.

Gramp turned to face Conner directly. "I know this isn't easy for you, Conner, but I'm glad you're here. We'll have fun, I promise." Conner nodded.

"Well, I'll let you get settled. Holler if you need anything. 'Night."

"'Night," Conner said.

Gramp walked out of the room and closed the door behind him.

Conner let his pack slide off his right shoulder and fall to the floor with a thump. The bedroom—and whole house, for that matter—seemed to have a dusty, musty old smell to it. He sat down on the bed, the metal springs creaking, and stared at the window. His parents had toyed with the idea of sending him to summer camp once, but he had complained and protested so strenuously they had finally relented and abandoned the idea. That was nothing compared to this, he thought. At least there you were surrounded by other kids and had other stuff to do. This house was dead. Dead rooms, dead furniture, and real honest-to-goodness dead people right across the street. Conner stood up and walked over to the window, pulling the lace curtains and the brittle shade to the side with a crackle. Yup. Right there in the dim light were the gray and white headstones extending back into the enveloping darkness, and the lone streetlight illuminating the sad playground across the road.

He didn't deserve any of this.

Chapter 2

Conner rolled over into beams of sunlight slicing past the edge of the shade on the window, and the realization quickly set in that it wasn't a bad dream; he was here. He shifted out of the covers and put his feet on the cool boards of the floor, which were painted light blue—probably sometime in the previous century, or the one before that. He reached over and dug through his pack next to the bed, pulling out a pair of gray cargo shorts and a black T-shirt with a faded American flag on it, and got dressed. He stood up, slipped on his white sneakers, leaving them untied, and headed downstairs.

"Gramp?" Conner said as he entered the dining room at the bottom of the stairs. No answer. He walked into the kitchen, the floor creaking all the way, and saw a cereal bowl and spoon on the table. A yellow box of generic bite-sized shredded wheat stood next to it, with a folded piece of paper tucked under the edge.

"Headed to Lakeside early to pick up supplies," the note read. "Be back sometime after 12. Gramp."

The hands on the clock above the table read 9:00. Conner filled the bowl half full with cereal and retrieved a glass milk jug from the fridge. The milk poured thick and creamy, not the fat-free white water he drank at home by any stretch. As he ate, he looked around at the mish-mash of items hanging on the walls. Above the fridge was a black-and-white picture of two guys, one who looked like Gramp in his younger years, and another man, each holding a respectable-looking fish in his hands. There was a calendar opened to July with a picture of a lake and a mountain in the background; a framed news clipping titled *Blanchard Gazette* with a photograph of a car on its side in a ditch with people standing all around it; and an odd line of seven rusted ice cream scoops hung neatly in order, largest to smallest. Gramp likes his ice cream, I guess, Conner thought to himself.

He took his empty bowl to the sink, spritzed a tiny bit of dish soap on it, rinsed it around, cleaned the spoon with a bit of the soapy water and his thumb, and put them both on a wire drying rack beside the sink. He opened the fridge and pulled out the milk again, pouring some into a small glass he found in the cupboard, stacked haphazardly with mismatched cups and dishes of various sizes. He gulped it down, rinsed out the glass, and set it upside down next to the bowl.

Conner walked into the dining room, taking in his surroundings as he went. This place was going to take some getting used to. Just like the musty smell, the room had an old look about it, frozen in time. He opened the French doors and stepped into the living room. He looked over the pale-green fabric couch, two padded chairs, and a dark-brown, almost black, upright piano. He lifted the piano lid and pressed down on a couple of the keys, which emitted hollow, out-of-tune, *ting* noises. On the walls were two shelves filled with various little trinkets: a brass ashtray in the shape of a fish, a line of small bells painted with different outdoor scenes, and assorted pine cones and dried horse chestnuts. There was a white door with a silver side-to-side latch next to the fireplace, which he opened with a snap, revealing a tiny room with a door leading to the outside, probably the main entrance to the house during some bygone era. He stepped through a second door into another bedroom with three windows, a high bed, a chair, and a vanity with a tarnished-looking silver mirror. Another brown kerosene heater, larger than the one in the dining room, had a bent pipe that disappeared into the wall. From this bedroom, an open doorway led into a room with a window and one chair, and a black iron sewing machine built into a table with a tilted lattice pedal near the floor. This room smelled as musty as the rest of the house, maybe even more so, and Conner wondered how anyone could have lived here. Then he remembered that *he* lived here now, at least for the next few months.

How depressing.

Conner walked back through the house into the kitchen and opened the door to the outside. The sun was bright, with no clouds or breeze. The air was crisp, almost like breathing a drink of cold water into your lungs, not at all like the mugginess of Virginia in July, where you started to sweat after walking ten feet from the house. Conner walked across to the playground, kicking up small puffs of dirt on the gravel road as he crossed. It was empty, and the swings he had seen last night hung motionless in the still air. He sat down in one of them, glancing over at the blue kiddie swing he had noticed last night. The cemetery across from the house didn't look nearly as creepy in the daylight, with little yellow flowers peppered among the graves. There were rows upon rows of stones in a variety of shapes, some small and unassuming, others built like miniature versions of the Washington Monument, seeming to declare to no one in particular that someone important was buried here.

Conner swung back and forth slowly in the swing, the tips of his sneakers scraping on the crumbling blacktop. Off in the distance, he heard the familiar sound of a bike chain turning, growing louder as it approached. A thin girl emerged on the road riding a red bike slightly too big for her, tricked out with pegs on the back wheel. Conner watched as she rode up to the intersection and then took a skidding turn to the right into the playground. She looked about his age, maybe a year younger, and wore blue denim shorts and a yellow short-sleeved shirt with a faded purple flower on it. Her hair was jet black, hanging straight on the sides just above her shoulders and pulled up into a short ponytail on top. She wore black low-cut basketball sneakers, and she had a purple bracelet around her right ankle.

"Hey," she said, just noticing that he was there, furrowing her brow like she was encountering a hobo in her backyard.

"Hi," Conner answered.

"Who are you?"

"My name's Conner."

"Did you just move here?" she asked, her expression relaxing a bit.

"Sort of, yeah…I guess. I'm here visiting my grandfather for the summer."

"Where do you live?" the girl asked.

"Right there," Conner answered, nodding his head toward the Farm.

"Yikes. Oh well, okay, I guess," she said with a startled look on her face. "I'm Raylee, Raylee Drew. My dad calls me Sun-ray."

"Do you live around here?"

"Yup," she said, looking down the road. "Right down the hill, my whole life."

Raylee stepped off her bike and let it fall to the ground with a clatter. Conner looked at the bike on the ground, definitely a hand-me-down. No one would allow their new bike to crash to the ground like that. She skipped with two steps over to the tilted merry-go-round and jumped between two of the rails onto the center, the metal giving off a deep echoing bang.

She's cute, Conner thought. One of those girls that on first sight made his stomach turn with a little twist and his hands go clammy, the kind of girl that usually walked the hallways of the school surrounded by a small entourage of friends, ignoring him entirely as he chanced glances at them. Conner had never had a girlfriend; the concept itself was enough to make him freeze up like a kid caught shoplifting. There had been one girl, Callie, that he had liked for almost a year, but he barely dared to speak with her, let alone ask her to hang out with him. She had bright big blue eyes and blond hair that she always wore in a French braid, and she liked to paint her nails with glitter polish. She gave off the impression of being too refined for bumbling boys her age, Conner included. Most of his guy friends were the same as he was, hanging out with each other and doing their best to pretend they were completely oblivious to the roving clusters of girls in the halls, and the girls pretty much did the same. It was as if the school was divided into two warring factions that had been forced to live in close quarters with each other, always on guard for an incursion by the enemy into their home territory.

"Want a ride?" Raylee asked, standing in the center of the merry-go-round, a bar grasped firmly in each of her hands.

"Sure, I guess," Conner answered, although he didn't quite understand what she meant. He stepped off the swing, walked over, and climbed onto the round metal plate, holding the warm metal of one of the bars with both of his hands.

He started to push off with one foot when Raylee said, "No, wait; just hold on tight."

Conner sensed he'd better listen to her and do what she said, and with that, she began walking in the center of the plate, uphill to the slant, and the merry-go-round started to move. Slowly at first, then faster and faster and faster, until she approached a fast trot. She increased her pace, and the steel plate spun even faster. Conner could feel gravity (or was it centrifugal force? He couldn't remember.) starting to drag him out toward the edge, and he had to sit down and wrap his feet around the support bar toward the center to stay in place. Faster and faster—Raylee was almost running now, her feet making hollow metal banging noises as she kept increasing her speed. She didn't appear to circle like him, but instead stayed in place in the center as she pumped her legs and arms as if she was on a tread-mill. The world around Conner kept spinning faster until all he saw was a blur of blue sky, brown ground, and flashes of white from the school-house. Blue, brown, white, blue, brown, white, faster and faster! Raylee was at full sprint now, and Conner became distinctly aware that a wave of nausea was building in his stomach. His hands gripped the bar as tightly as he could, but he felt as though he was going to be torn away at any second and flown skidding across the ground. He closed his eyes tight and tried to focus on his grip.

"Okay, okay!" he finally shouted. "I think that's good!"

He heard Raylee start laughing as she reluctantly began to slow the pace. The rotations continued as Raylee approached the walking speed she had started with, then she grabbed one of the bars and started revolving around on the opposite side to Conner. When the plate began to slow to a halt, she jumped off and yelled, "Jump!"

He stood up and jumped, promptly staggered to the left, and fell clum-sily on the blacktop.

"Oooh, sorry...are you okay?" Raylee said, concerned but giggling at the same time. "I should have warned you it might be hard to walk for a few seconds."

Conner felt a wave of embarrassment as he put his hands down on the ground in front of him and tried to stand. The world was still moving and undulating in jumpy starts and stops, but at least the nausea was going away. He had no desire to vomit shredded wheat chunks down his shirt in front of this girl.

"I'm fine, no problem," Conner said as he pulled himself upright but stayed seated. "Is that fun for you?"

She cupped her hands over her mouth.

"Yeah, sorry about that," a breaking giggle still in her voice. "We used to do that all the time at recess until this kid Davey flew off and skidded across the pavement on his face. The teachers banned it after that. We don't go to school here anymore, they closed it and bus us over to Lakeside now, but I still like to come by and take a spin now and then. I didn't mean to scare you. You did good hanging on, though."

"Thanks, I guess," Conner said, a small smile beginning as he rose to his feet. "I just didn't expect that."

"Well, anyway, welcome to Morgan, the end of the road."

"Looks like it," Conner said, motioning over toward the cemetery with his head.

"Oh, them," she said. "They're no problem. They pretty much keep quiet and to themselves. Every family in town has people buried there. My grandpa is in the back corner. You should see it in the spring when everyone brings their flowers to put on the graves. Looks kind of cheery."

What a weird girl, Conner thought. It was going to be a long summer if all the kids around here were like her.

"Why did you say 'yikes' when I said I was staying there?" Conner asked, gesturing to the Farm with his chin.

"Oh," Raylee answered. "No one used to live there when I was growing up. It was the haunted house in town, I suppose. We used to tell stories about seeing ghosts peeking out the windows at us when we were on the playground. Some kid would yell 'ghost!' and we'd all start screaming, running, and hiding, looking at the windows for it. On Halloween, when we went trick or treating, the older kids always dared the little kids to go up and knock on the door. I never did. I figured if there were ghosts there, they probably just wanted to be left alone, like everyone else. It's not their fault they're dead. If I were a ghost, I wouldn't want a bunch of stupid kids looking through the window of my house. I'd give them the scare of their life if they did, that's for sure."

"I guess there could be," Conner said. "It's just as creepy on the inside as it is from out here."

"Why are you here?"

"My parents sent me to stay with my grandfather for a few months."

"Mr. Williamson?"

"Yes."

"I met him when he first moved up here to stay. I'd seen him a few times before that. It always seemed like he was here for a day or two working in the yard, and then he would drive off, and I wouldn't see him again for a long time," Raylee said.

"Yeah, he used to live in Connecticut with my grandmother. I used to visit them there sometimes."

"Where's she?"

"She died a few years ago."

"Oh, sorry."

"That's okay," Conner replied. "After she died, my dad said Gramp didn't want to be in their house anymore; it reminded him too much of her, so he sold it and moved up here. I guess he grew up here or something, and he used to tell me stories about this place. It doesn't look like I thought it would."

"Why?" Raylee asked. "Too creepy and dreary?"

"No," Conner said. "It's just that Gramp always talked about it as 'the Farm.' I guess I expected a big red barn with horses, cows, and chickens walking around. It's nothing like that."

"I'll ask my dad; he's lived here, like, forever," Raylee said. "Well, it was nice to meet you; I have to get going." She walked over to her bike and picked it up. "I guess I'll be seeing you again. Sorry about the ride. I'll take it easier on you next time."

"I doubt there'll be a next time," Conner said.

"That's what they all say the first time I give them a spin, then they always come back for more, begging for another go. Well, see you later!" Raylee said as she pushed off with one foot and coasted out of the playground and back onto the road.

"See you later," Conner called after her.

Raylee waved a hand in the air as she picked up speed and cruised down the hill. Well, at least he wasn't totally by himself up here. He had thought he might be the only person here his age, and even though grown-ups were okay, it wasn't like having other kids around. Adults were always looking at you like you were a pupil of theirs, asking annoying questions about what subjects you were taking, who your favorite author was, and so on. He never really knew how to talk to adults other than his parents. It felt like they were testing you to see how much you knew, and he could always hear the tone of their voices change when they spoke to you—it was different from how they talked to other adults. Almost like you were a little kid, needing them to use small words and exaggerated inflections, with a big, phony smile to make you feel comfortable. It was annoying.

All the grown-ups he knew in Virginia used the "adult speaking to child" talk, except Mr. Phillips, who lived alone two houses down. He was always drinking beer and sitting in a fold-up beach chair in his front yard and would strike up a conversation anytime Conner or the other kids went by his house. He was friendly enough, but he made Conner uncomfortable for some reason, like he was trying a bit too hard, and his mother had told him to stay clear of him.

Conner walked across the road back to the house, taking a closer look as he went. There was a big green sliding door to the right of the kitchen, then the first barn, only slightly taller than the house, and next to the more massive barn that was twice as tall as the house. There was a weather vane in the shape of a running deer on its peak. Conner went into the kitchen and looked at the clock. He'd only been outside for about forty-five minutes, but it felt longer somehow. He opened the door in the kitchen leading out toward the barns, and it stuck partway with a scrape on the floor, but then opened when he gave it a push with his shoulder.

He walked into a room that seemed like an old shed of some sort. It smelled musty, kind of like the rest of the house, but also had the slight scent of cut wood and rusting metal. There was a red vinyl couch against the back wall with lumps of yellow foam spouting up through long slits and metal springs sticking out underneath, and he could see the inside of the sliding door he had seen from the outside. There were a few cabinets, a bench with a vise and hammers and other tools he couldn't identify, and three rows of shelves on the wall with glass jars that held an assortment of screws and nails of what must have been every size ever made. One of the walls had faded newsprint lining it, and he stopped for a moment to read one of the papers. The date on the top was 1942, and there were ads for all kinds of things for sale: wheelbarrows, washtubs, and other farming supplies. The prices were ridiculously low, like three dollars for a metal folding table. He turned and looked toward the back of the shed and saw a recessed floor with cut wood stacked neatly along its walls, filling in under a staircase that looked like it went up into the main house.

Conner walked through the woodshed and came to another door. This one swung open easily, and he stepped into a small barn open to the top with a loft above him and a second loft on the opposite side. There was a room to his left with benches on all three walls and cluttered with more tools, and a small window looking out toward the back of the house. The floorboards were about a foot wide and covered with dust and dirt, certainly a nightmare for anyone with allergies. Along the back wall of the barn was an old machine with a large curved comb on the top it, and a few harnesses lying on the floor. Right next to it was a galvanized steel tub with two rollers on top that he recognized as an old washing machine. Well, Gramp was all set for the end of electricity and civilization if that should ever come to pass, he thought.

Conner walked through the barn to a sliding wooden door on the far side and gripped the metal handle, which was smooth like a river stone from years of use. He tried pulling it to the side, but it wouldn't budge. He worked it two more times with more effort, then gave up, turning around and walking back through the barn into the shed to the kitchen.

He went back up the stairs to his room, lay down on the bed, and closed his eyes. He was still trying to accept the fact that he was here and half expecting to be back in his room in Virginia when he opened them. He opened them, but he was still here, on the edge of nowhere.

☙

Gramp returned just after noon, and the two of them unloaded the groceries and stocked them into the cupboards and shelves in the kitchen. His grandfather had a specific place for every item, dry goods in the bottom cabinet, cans stacked neatly in a line on three shelves. After they finished, Gramp went into the shed and came back with a bundled red rag in his hand.

"Every kid in the country needs a good knife to survive up here," Gramp said, and he proceeded to unwrap the rag and remove a dark leather sheath with a thin, four-inch yellowed handle sticking out. He pulled the knife from the sheath, revealing a gray blade six inches long, with a gleaming sharp edge running the length of the bottom and a matching edge running two inches from the tip along the top. Gramp said it had been his father's knife, and he had carried it with him all the years he had worked in the woods, sometimes as a logger, other times as a guide for out-of-state hunters.

"A knife needs a purpose, though," Gramp said, "and it's just been collecting dust."

He handed the knife to Conner handle first, and he felt the weight of it. In the center of the blade on one side was small print etched into the steel:

```
G. WOSTENHOLM & SON
WASHINGTON WORKS
SHEFFIELD, ENG
```

"Made in the late 1800s in England," Gramp said. He took the knife back, held it level, and balanced it on his finger where the blade emerged from the gun-metal gray hilt.

"See, perfectly balanced, good for throwing…although I wouldn't recommend it with a knife this old," Gramp said. He handed the knife back to Conner.

"Of course," Conner answered, smiling.

The only knife he had ever owned was a red pocketknife that came apart after only a year, although he could understand why this particular knife might be frowned upon by the parental community of suburban Virginia.

"Thanks, Gramp." Conner stood up and undid the nylon belt of his shorts, threading it through the two slits on the leather sheath. He seated the knife on his right side and refastened his belt.

"Next item on the list of necessities for living up here," Gramp said, reaching into his right pants pocket. He pulled out a small brass cylinder and handed it to Conner. Conner opened it to reveal a compass with a black needle that bobbed and swung around until it finally settled on a fixed point more or less in the direction of the kitchen door.

"The white tip of the needle points due north," Gramp said, although Conner knew that. "Whenever you go into the woods, you can use it to find your way back. All you have to do is line the needle up with the N. If you go up in the woods behind the fields and get turned around, follow the compass south or east and you're bound to hit a road that'll take you back to civilization eventually."

"What if you head north?" Conner asked.

"Well, over a hundred miles of nothing but woods, critters, and logging roads…then Canada and the North Pole," his grandfather replied with a grin.

Conner put the compass in his pocket and thanked his grandfather again.

Gramp said he had some bills to catch up on, so Conner decided to head back outside. He walked down the length of the house and barns until he came to an overgrown, narrow road cutting a curved line along the top of the fields and disappearing into the woods. Conner started to walk, small insects buzzing in front of his face. After fifty yards or so, he was in the trees, the house no longer visible behind him. The air felt refreshing in the woods, with the scent of fresh pine and soil floating in the air. As he continued, the road turned sharply to the left then straightened out. The woods opened up a bit, evidence of recent cutting, and he could see stumps and downed branches littering the ground around the remaining trees. At the end of the straightaway, the road turned right through a wet patch. Conner stepped carefully on the logs and branches sticking out of the mud, pushing under some low-hanging branches, careful to balance himself from one step to the next. He only faltered once, his foot squishing into the black mud and making a sucking noise as he pulled it out. His white sneaker was no longer white, and he made a mental note to wear his hiking sneakers the next time. The road was a long, gradual hill, and sweat was starting to bead on his forehead and run into the corners of his eyes with a stinging sensation. He dragged his arm across his face, pulled the compass from his pocket, and opened it. The needle swung back and forth as it had in the house, finally settling ahead and to the right of the road. He aligned the capital N on the compass with the needle, looked around, and put the compass back in his pocket.

Conner rested the palm of his hand on the knife handle and realized that it made him feel safe somehow. He doubted the knife would help in a bear encounter like the story his grandfather had told, but still, it was better than nothing. He went on up the hill toward the top with birds chirping and flitting around him in the trees, ignoring his presence. There was a steady buzzing sound of grasshoppers as they went about their business in the tall golden grass that reminded him of summer. Once he reached the top of the hill, he was sweating even harder, and he wiped his forearm across his eyebrows again to clear his eyes. He ran his hand along the back of his damp neck, feeling a few bits and pieces of pine needles that must have come down on him when he was navigating the wet patch.

The road veered left again, and Conner stopped to look back where he had walked. He could see over the tops of the trees from here and could make out the hazy ridgelines of mountains far to the south. He wondered for a moment how long it would take him to walk to them—probably a few days or so at least.

The woods started to close in around the top of the road about a hundred feet from where he stood, and just as he began to walk again, an uncomfortable feeling came over him—the sensation that someone, or something, was watching.

Goosebumps rose on his arms, and his legs felt momentarily weak and rubbery. He looked around but didn't see anything, and told himself he was just paranoid. The old story of the bear must have messed with his head more than he thought. It was easy not to be unnerved by a story like that sitting in the living room of your house sucking down a root beer. It was altogether different now that he was by himself in the woods. Not like the park near his home in Virginia or the stand of trees behind his friend Tommy's house. These woods were green and dense, and who knew what lay beyond what he was able to see. An image flashed in his mind of a bear watching him from the brush, a low guttural growl resonating in its thick, black chest.

No, that's stupid, he thought. A city kid afraid of a little walk in the woods. Still, the desire to explore further evaporated like a puff of smoke, and after glancing one last time down the road, he turned around and started walking back toward the house, willing himself not to break into a run. He reached the wet area a few minutes later and felt a wave of relief at seeing his footprints in the mud. He could make out his wet tracks on the logs where he had stepped before, and he followed them back with exactness, save for the one step that had resulted in a muddy sneaker. Ten minutes later, he reached the entrance to the field, and then he was back near the house. The light was brighter here in the open, and the fear deep in his stomach quickly started to dissolve.

Conner walked up to the front of the house and sat down on the porch. A breeze had kicked up since he'd left, and its coolness felt good against his skin, small salt crystals on his arms the only evidence of his perspiring on his walk.

The playground lay empty across the street, and he wondered whether that girl would be back tomorrow. He stood up and went back into the house.

Conner and Gramp sat down to lunch in the kitchen: ham sandwiches with tomato, lettuce, Swiss cheese, and mayo, and salty kettle chips.

"Well, what did you discover in your exploration of the homestead today?" Gramp asked.

"I looked around the shed and first barn," Conner said. "You have a lot of tools out there. Do you use them all?"

"When I need them, I suppose. There's a right tool for every job. If you don't have the right one, you won't get the job done right, and you'll just get frustrated."

"I tried the door to the big barn, but I couldn't open it."

"Oh, well, that one sticks a bit; maybe that's something you can help me fix this summer," Gramp said. "I'll take you out there later. The chickens and goats are out there, and I'll show you how to feed them and clean out their pens. I've thought about buying some pigs; it would make a nice home for them. They're lots of work, though, pigs. You have to always keep an eye on them. They like to dig and root and can make quite a mess of things. It'd be nice to have a couple, though, especially for the bacon. Tasty."

Conner laughed at the morbid idea of raising pigs just for the bacon.

"I walked the road up to the top of the hill but turned around there. Where does it go?"

"Up to the spring house."

"Spring house?" Conner said, a bit of leafy green lettuce hanging out one side of his mouth.

"Yeah," Gramp replied. "This house doesn't have a well. All the water comes from a spring on the top of the hill."

"But that's so far away," Conner said, puzzled.

"Yup, it is, but that's where the water is. It's a freshwater spring. There's a concrete foundation up there that collects the water, and then it flows down to the house, gravity fed. A three-inch pipe at first, then it goes to two and eventually to one until it reaches the back sill. By the time it gets down here, it has enough pressure to force it up into the house, and then we can use it. It's the best setup for a place like this. Wells sometimes go dry, and you need electricity to run the pump. This way, you don't need to rely on the power company. Not bad for lights and TV, but you don't want to be dependent on them. We could live up here without electricity forever if we needed to. We have the kitchen woodstove and the kerosene heaters. When we get those fired up, the heat goes up through the floors through the vents, and once the walls are all warmed up, the house can stay that way all winter if we need it to."

"Doesn't the water freeze in the winter?"

"Well, you're a sharpie, aren't you?" Gramp said with a smile. "Comes from me, I guess. You're right, gets downright frigid up here, cold enough to freeze your spit solid before it hits the ground some days. The pipes from the spring run underground deep enough not to freeze solid as long as we let the faucets drip a bit. The spring house goes six feet deep, and there's a little roof on top of it with insulation. My father told me it did almost freeze up completely one winter when the temperature rattled the mercury in the thermometer, but the out pipe is down close to the bottom, so barring another ice age, the water should keep coming. It's like a little lake: The ice forms up top, but the fish live down below just fine as long as it doesn't freeze solid to the bottom. If that happens, we won't just be worried about water, that's for sure. I'll take you up there so you can see it. The spring is the heart of that mountain, giving water and life to all the plants and livings things near it, including us."

Conner sat for a moment, hesitating because he didn't want to seem ridiculous with his next question.

"Um…are there any bears or things in the woods?" he asked.

"Sure, there are bears around. Deer, rabbits, foxes, coyotes, raccoons, all sorts of critters," Gramp said. "But you probably won't ever see a bear; they like to keep to themselves, and they don't like people. They smell you coming from a mile off and will hightail it away from you. They don't make a sound, and you won't hear them at all."

"What about the one that guy shot when you were a kid?"

"Oh, well that was scary, for sure, but we had old Bump to protect us, and that kind of thing doesn't happen too often. I only remember one other time a bear gave us trouble, when I was twelve or so. It was late one night when we heard a ruckus from the barn—woke the whole house up, and the pigs and chickens were going wild. My mother, sister, and I all came down to the kitchen, and my father was there thumbing shells into his rifle. He told us to stay put, and he went out to see what was happening. He wasn't afraid of anything, man or beast. I was shaking like a leaf. He came back a while later and said a bear had torn through the door in the back of the barn and made off with one of our pigs. It was Claudia, one of Livie's favorites. My sister liked to name all the pigs, but I never saw the point myself. When it was time for the…er…end, so to speak, I didn't want to think I was eating a friend. My father told us to stay in the kitchen, and he went down the road to the houses nearby. About twenty minutes later, he came back with Bump and two of his other friends, and they all had their rifles and lanterns. They said they were going to look for the pig and the bear, and I remember my mother telling them they were a bunch of fools. I was feeling braver by that point, and I asked them if I could go, but he told me to stay at the house."

"What happened?"

"Well, a couple of hours later they came back," Gramp said. "They all sat in the kitchen, and Mom poured them some coffee. My father told us they'd followed a trail through the brush up to the top of the hill past the spring, and they got to a stand of thick saplings where they could hear grunting and chewing noises. They debated about going in after the bear, but they knew if they did find it, the brush was so thick, it would be right on top of them when they did. No one wanted to find themselves in that situation, so they turned back. The next day, I went up there with my father and Bump. We found the trail leading into the brush and pushed our way through. Well, you've never seen such a sight. There, in the middle of a little clearing, was the front half of old Claudia. Her eyes were fixed wide-open showing the terror she must have been going through when that bear dragged her out of the barn. She must've weighed two hundred pounds."

"Did you ever find the bear?" Conner asked.

Gramp gave Conner a small smile. "No. He never came back, but he must have been a brute to carry away a pig that size in the dead of night. Hungry, too. I wouldn't go out at night alone for the rest of the year, and every time I heard the snap of a branch, my first thought was that it was that old bear coming back for seconds. You don't have anything to worry about, Son," Gramp said, seeing Conner's cheeks starting to tense up. "Most of the bears around here have moved far back into the mountains, benefits of an annual hunting season. Like I said, if you do run across one, he'll be more afraid of you than you are of him."

"I'm not so sure about that."

His grandfather let out a laugh and got up to clear the plates.

※

The next day Conner and Gramp got up early and loaded an old green canoe on top of the red pickup, a task much more complicated than it initially seemed it would be. Conner lifted one end of the canoe onto the tailgate. He clambered into the truck bed, and with some grunting and repositioning, managed to lift it and balance it precariously on his shoulder, straining his arms almost to the breaking point. They pushed the canoe forward toward the cab of the truck, and Conner, with all the effort he could manage, lifted it onto the top of the cab with his grandfather pushing up from behind. Once the bow of the canoe was past the windshield, they both stopped to breathe for a moment.

"Phew!" his grandfather exclaimed. "I love this old canoe, but I swear it weighs as much as a tank. Did you notice the wooden slats inside it?"

"Yes," Conner replied between deep breaths.

"Well, at one time this was a wooden canvas canoe, the way they used to make them. Over the years, the canvas started to crack and wear thin in places, so I had Harvey Jakes apply a coat of fiberglass to the outside of it.

It's not one of those featherweight canoes you can lift out of the water with one arm, but she's as solid and seaworthy as they get."

Once they had caught their breath, they secured the canoe in place with rope that Gramp had retrieved from one of the benches in his workshop. Conner stood on one side of the truck and his grandfather on the other, and after Gramp had tied the line to the small metal loops on the edge of the truck bed, he threw the line over the top of the canoe to Conner. He then came around and showed Conner how to tie a trucker's hitch, a knot he told him he would find useful his whole life. The rope felt rough in Conner's hands, burning his palms slightly as he finished tightening the knot. They did the same near the tailgate, then climbed into the cab, and Gramp fired up the truck.

They drove for about twenty minutes on the road leading west out of town until they reached a narrow wooden bridge with no rails on the sides. On the right was open water surrounded by tall reeds, with a few boulders poking up in the near center like hippos relaxing in the midday sun. To the left, the water ran under the bridge in a small stream, bubbling and flowing over bands of rocks.

"This is North Bog," Gramp told him with a wink, "one of my favorite secret spots." They parked in a shallow turnabout and untied the canoe from its perch on top of the truck. Getting it off was less painful than getting it on, with gravity pitching in to do its part, but Conner had a moment of dread when he realized they would have to repeat the arduous process of getting it back up there at the end of the trip. They carried the canoe to the water, Conner at the bow and his grandfather at the stern, holding it by the triangular blocks built in for that purpose. Conner slipped the canoe into the water, walking right in with his hiking sneakers, the coolness enveloping his feet and lower legs.

Conner felt the bow of the canoe begin to lift in the water, and soon it was easy to maneuver it around with just the tips of his fingers. He lifted his left leg into the bow, dripping water as it went. Grasping the gunnels with both hands, Conner lifted his other leg into the canoe, tipping left and right for an uncomfortable second or two as he plopped onto the front seat. He reached back to his right and grasped the wooden paddle Gramp had placed in the canoe after they got it off the truck, and he dipped it into the water, where it quickly hit the pebbly bottom with a crunching sound. Conner felt the canoe shift as his grandfather climbed in and pushed off with one leg, sending the canoe gliding forward into the flat waters of the bog.

Gramp let the canoe drift into the center of the open water. Conner looked back and noticed the two life jackets in the center. Not wearing them, he thought. A different world up here than the "don't go too fast on your bike and always wear your helmet" protective life in Virginia.

As they floated, Gramp demonstrated the basic paddle strokes; forward, back paddle, draw, and sweep to steer the bow. He told Conner he could do most of the steering from the rear by turning his paddle like a rudder close to the side of the stern, but that bow steering techniques could be useful, if not required, if they were on a fast-moving river or encountered any shallow rocks or downed trees they needed to maneuver quickly around. Conner paid close attention to Gramp's instructions, and soon they were gliding up the bog, the rhythm of paddling getting more natural for him as they went. Gramp told him to switch sides when his arms needed a change, and Conner marveled at the fact that he could create little whirlpools in the inky water next to the canoe as they went. Bright-green lily pads peppered the water, and Conner avoided them at first. It just didn't seem right to cut his paddle down right on top of them, ruining a perch for a small frog or a dragonfly.

They paddled along in silence for a half hour, the bog meandering right and left. Small birds flew about on the banks, perching on the branches of brush and small trees like little sentries of the woods. Now and then Gramp would identify them out loud: chickadee, white-breasted nuthatch, red-winged blackbird. Conner was impressed that Gramp could identify the different species without hesitation.

They continued up the bog for what seemed like miles, but probably wasn't more than one or two, the soft grass extending a few hundred yards on each side of the water, bounded on the far edges by thick pines. They came to a long straightaway, and Conner noticed the outcropping of a little island on the left with a scraggly pine tree on it.

"We'll eat lunch there," Gramp said, nodding in the direction of the island, and he used his paddle to direct the canoe straight toward it.

They pulled up close to the rocks with a scrape, and Gramp stuck his paddle in the mud below the shallow water to stabilize the canoe so that Conner could stand, hunched over, and put his foot out on the rock ledge. He half crawled out the rest of the way, taking the bow line attached to the canoe with him, as instructed. He looped the rope around a protruding rock, and Gramp again used his paddle to push the stern against the shore. He reached down and grasped the little cooler and his canvas backpack in one hand, then stood up and stepped off onto the rocks much more gracefully than Conner's undignified scramble out of the canoe.

"Well, it's a beautiful day, isn't it?" Gramp said.

"Yeah," Conner said, looking up at the blue sky and white clouds moving silently through the air. Conner could see a green, hazy mountain range in the distance. The island they stood on consisted of a rock-ledge base with smaller rocks dotting it here and there, and long cracks filled with thick sprouting grass covered the top. There was a shallow recess with a brown puddle in it, probably the remnants of rain that had fallen recently. Conner walked to the head of the island and sat down. Gramp, green cooler in hand, sat down beside him. Gramp opened the white lid and pulled out a paper bag with two tuna fish sandwiches he had prepared just before they left, made with small pieces of celery and onion on whole wheat bread. He reached into his pack and brought out a couple of root beers, along with a bag of potato chips. Conner unwrapped the wax paper on his sandwich, and they sat and chewed in silence for a time.

"How much further does the bog go up?" Conner asked.

"Oh, at least another five or six miles; it intersects with a river up there. That goes another sixty or seventy miles up to a big lake in the middle of nowhere. We won't be going very far today."

"Have you ever been to the lake?"

"No," Gramp said, chewing a mouthful of tuna fish sandwich off to one side of his mouth. "I've been up to the river a fair bit, though. I used to go spring fishing with my grandfather up that way. We usually camped overnight along the way. Nobody goes up there much, so the fishing is excellent. Easy to catch your limit."

"Does anyone live up there?" Conner said, looking off to the distant mountain range.

"Oh, I suppose. There are small hunting cabins up in the woods and maybe a hermit or two. Hard to get to, and even harder to get back from, but that's the way they like it, I guess. You see where those two mountains come together there, forming a kind of V to the east? There's a little pond up there with a few camps on it. The only way to get there is to take a little overgrown road to it—strictly four-wheel-drive territory. My grandfather had a camp in the woods there near the pond, though he never took me there. My father did once when I was a boy, after my grandfather had passed. We found the cabin, but it looked as old as the hills, with cobwebs in all the corners, and critters had made a mess of the place. Inside was an old oil-drum woodstove, everything covered in dirt and dust. The place gave me the spooks, and we didn't linger too long. We were staying with a friend of my father who had a camp right on the lake. I haven't been up there in many years, don't know if that old camp is still standing, but I suspect it probably collapsed under the weight of winter snow by now. Mother Nature has a way of taking back what's hers and erasing any sign we were here at all."

After they finished lunch, Gramp stuffed the sandwich wrappers into his pack and pulled out a baggie of chocolate chip cookies for dessert. Conner ate a few cookies with his root beer, the paddling and exertion of loading the canoe making his body crave sugar. When the cookies were gone, they sat quietly and listened to the silence of the bog, broken only by the wisps of the breeze tickling the tops of the marsh grass. Wordlessly, they decided it was time to head out, standing to stretch their backs, and then climbed back into the canoe.

On the way back, Gramp suddenly stopped paddling and pointed to the shoreline. There, standing as still as statues in a museum, were a cow moose and a yearling, both observing them intently, trying to decide whether they posed a threat. Conner was amazed at how large and muscular the cow moose looked, her long nose sniffing at the air. They drifted quietly by, the moose watching their every move until they rounded the next bend and the moose disappeared from sight.

"Well," Gramp said, "not a bad start to your wilderness adventure, I suppose. You've seen your first moose. Never understood why one mouse is a mouse, and more than one is mice, and more than one dog is dogs, but a moose is a moose, whether it's one or ten. Same for deer. Wonder why they got such special naming treatment."

Conner gave a small laugh in agreement, wishing for a moment that he had brought his phone along so he could have taken a picture. His phone, which was usually a fixture in his front pants pocket or his hand, seemed out of place up here, and it was resting quietly on top of his dresser back at the Farm. Maybe being connected and online twenty-four seven was overrated.

For some reason, that made him smile.

Chapter 3

A week went by with Conner spending most of his time poking around the house and barns. As promised, his grandfather had taken him into the big towering barn, sunlight shining through the boards and illuminating the dust from the bundles of yellow hay stored above. There were four empty stalls against one of the walls, with lonely harnesses and ropes hanging from hooks. There was a large open pen on one side with a boarded fence that came up to his waist. It was here they had kept the pigs, his grandfather told him, but now it served as home for six goats, four of which were lying down in the hay, making snuffing and snorting noises as they slumbered. They were tan-white and smaller than Conner had expected, about the size of collies except for two that approached the size of adult golden retrievers. Conner looked for signs of bear claw marks or broken boards but found none, the story of the rampage still fresh in his mind. The other two goats were wandering aimlessly around the pen, sniffing the ground for something to chew on as they went.

Against the opposite wall was a wire mesh enclosure where the chickens resided. There were ten of them, dark-brown, almost black, and like the goats, they were milling about, bobbing their heads almost in synchronization with each other. The same musty smell that permeated the house was stronger here in the barn, mixed in with the unmistakable pungent stench of barnyard animals.

Gramp took him over to a small door in the back corner and opened it to show him inside, a faint unpleasant odor immediately assaulting his nostrils. There was a bench in the back with two neatly cut-out circular holes. An old "two-gunny" outhouse, Gramp explained. No sense wasting time when tending to the animals by walking in to the house, although Gramp admitted he hadn't seen fit to use outhouse in recent years. Conner peered down one of the holes with a grimace. No way would he sit on one of those with who knew how many creepy-crawlies lurking beneath, waiting to scurry across your backside.

After they had explored the barn, they walked outside through a sliding door in the goat pen. There was another separate, smaller door leading from the chicken coop to the outside. Gramp explained that during the pleasant summer months, he usually opened both sets of doors and let the animals go in and out to the fenced-in barnyard as they pleased. He said you could often judge how hot it was outside by how many animals remained in the cooler air of the barn.

Next, Gramp took Conner on a walk up the hill he had explored the previous week. He smiled to himself as his grandfather, leading the way, negotiated the muddy patch in the same manner he had, stepping on almost the same submerged logs and branches. When they reached the top of the hill, Conner realized they were at the same spot where he had felt spooked and had turned around on his solo hike. No feeling of being watched this time, but just the same, he was glad he wasn't alone. They walked down the darkening road and around the corner, where it opened up into a small clearing surrounded by pine and oak trees. In the rear, there was a wet area filled with moss-covered rocks, and in the center was a low, gray-shingled roof on a concrete foundation; it reminded Conner of a two-person pup tent.

The spring house, Conner thought to himself.

Dark-green moss carpeted the lower edges of the roof, and moisture crept up the sides of the foundation.

Gramp negotiated the wet area by stepping carefully on the moss-covered rocks, warning Conner to take it slow because they were slippery. Conner followed, careful to step on the same stones his grandfather had used. There was a wire-mesh-covered opening under the short peak of the spring house. Conner peered into the darkness and was able to make out a pool of water filled up to ground level. His grandfather shone a flashlight inside the structure; the water looked clean and clear, and Conner immediately felt a dry thirst well up in his throat.

As if reading his mind, Gramp stepped over to a sapling next to the spring house and removed a small tin cup from a fork in one of the branches. A weathered gray string tied between the handle and the branch looped down to a point just above the ground. To the left of the tree was a clear pool of open water in a recess of the thick green moss. Gramp submerged the cup in the water, raised it, and took a drink. He handed the cup to Conner, who took a drink as well, the water cold and refreshing as it slid down his throat. He wondered vaguely about pathogens and bacteria, but if Gramp trusted it, it had to be okay. Conner was surprised the water was so cold, contrasting sharply with the warm, humid air that hung around their heads. Gramp explained that the spring bubbled the water from deep under the ground up into the forest floor.

"Best water you'll ever taste," he said. "Fools pay two dollars for a little bottle of this, soiled by the taste of the plastic."

The woods beyond the spring house grew thick with thin trees topped with bright-green leaves, and Conner asked if that was where the bear had taken its unfortunate pig victim.

"Yup, that's the place," Gramp said.

Conner could see why no one in their right mind would venture in there after a pig that had been taken by a bear.

"What's beyond those trees?" Conner asked.

"Trees, trees, and more trees, for miles and miles," Gramp answered.

He told Conner it was probably best if he didn't venture too far beyond the spring house by himself, that the woods could become confusing, and even the most experienced woodsman could get turned around and lost in there.

Not a problem, Conner thought, staring at the woods, which faded progressively darker as it went. Not a problem, at all.

❧

When they got back to the Farm, Gramp headed out on another errand in town. Conner was sitting in a black rocking chair with a cushioned pad next to the open kitchen window when he heard the whirring and crunching noises of an approaching bike. He peered through the lace window curtain; it was that girl who had almost made him throw up his breakfast a week earlier. He got up quickly, looked in a small mirror above the break-fast table, ran his hand through his brown hair, and went outside.

"Hey, you," Raylee said as she maneuvered her bike into the playground, skidding her right sneaker on the road as she turned. "Still here, I see," she said with a smile.

"Yeah," Conner answered. "Still here...I haven't seen you around the whole week," Conner said, attempting to be nonchalant and matter-of-fact in his tone. He didn't want to give the impression he was sitting up nights waiting for her.

"Yeah," she said, straddling her bike with her feet on the ground. "We had to go visit my grandmother for the week. She lives in New Hampshire on a lake. We go there two or three times during the summer."

Conner was trying to think of something witty to say when he heard the crunching sound of another bike approaching. A bone-thin boy with short spiky blond hair and wire-rimmed glasses appeared, riding a black bike, most likely another hand-me-down by the looks of it. He wore tan shorts and a short-sleeved shirt with thick yellow and black stripes.

"Hey, Sting-ray," the boy said with a grin to Raylee.

"Hey, Bumblebee," Raylee retorted.

"Conner, meet Dickie Chesterfield...Dickie, meet Conner," Raylee said with sarcastic formality in her voice, like they were two dignitaries at a meeting of world leaders.

"Who's he?" Dickie said, looking back to Raylee.

"He lives in the haunted house. The ghosts hired him to look after the place," she said, giggling.

Dickie looked Conner from feet to head with an air of contempt. "I'm Dickie."

"Conner."

"So I am led to believe. Jeepers creepers, you live in there?" he said, ges-turing to the house with his head.

"Yeah. I'm staying here for the summer with my grandfather."

"Mr. Williamson?" Dickie said. "Sorry to hear that."

"Why is that?" Conner said, growing annoyed.

"Oh, nothing. No offense to you, good sir. He's just a boring grown-up like all the rest. Can't expect much more in a town like this, though, I suppose."

Dickie hopped off his bike and headed over to the swings, plopping down on the swing closest to the road. "This is my swing. You are not to swing it, sit in it, or even look at it. It's mine, and I have claimed it for myself. There are to be no sitters in my swing without my express written permission."

"No problem," Conner said. This kid was odd.

Dickie looked at Conner with narrowed eyes. "Where are you from?"

"Virginia," Conner replied. "Right outside of Washington, D.C."

"Do you know George Washington?" Dickie said. "I read all about him in school. Likes to chop down trees and lie about it."

Conner knew the kid was making fun of him and he didn't like it, not in front of this girl. "No, haven't met him. Abe Lincoln and I are pals, though."

"That's good," Dickie said, his eyes narrowing. "Don't go to the movie theater with him. Bad things could happen. Bad things."

Conner was starting not to like this kid. He looked like the kids who got picked on by the bigger kids at school but for some reason never had the good sense to keep their mouths shut and blend into the scenery like he did. Those kids always had to be at center stage, challenging a system stacked against them. They disrupted the standard pecking order and only brought unwanted attention to the rest of the sheep that stayed in line.

"Shut up, Dickie," Raylee said. "You're such a dweeb."

"I prefer to be addressed as the king of all dweebs."

"You're that, too," Raylee said, smiling again.

"Want another merry-go-round ride?" Raylee asked Conner.

"No, thanks, I think I'll pass on that one."

"Wise decision, my good man," Dickie said, the obnoxious edge of his tone softening a bit. "She knocked one of my fillings out on that thing. I'll stick to my swing, thank you very much."

"Oh, well, surrounded by chickens, I guess," Raylee said, walking over and stepping up onto the plate. "I'll just have to entertain myself."

Raylee walked around the center of the plate, moving it at a slow pace, showing no inclination to increase her speed. Conner walked over to one of the other swings and sat down, his feet scraping back and forth on the ground.

"So, what do you guys do around here?" Conner asked.

"You're looking at it," Dickie responded. "You've got the apex of excitement right here."

"You're such a dork," Raylee said, turning her attention to Conner. "Morgan's not a bad place to live. School's worse. I'd rather be doing this than sitting in a classroom having a teacher bark at me all day long. We go swimming in the pond a lot, and sometimes we go looking for wild animals in the woods. My dad says he had a job when he was my age. He wanted me to work in the store, and I sometimes do, stocking the shelves with expired mac-and-cheese and maple syrup, and sweeping the floors. It's boring being inside, but I like getting money."

"I'd never hire you to work in my store," Dickie said.

"Well, you don't have a store, doofus."

"What do you do at home?" Dickie asked Conner.

"Not much," Conner answered. "We go swimming sometimes at the community center, but it's too hot to do anything else outside in the summer. Mostly I play games on my computer."

"You'd never catch me in one of those public pools, brimming with little floating and peeing kids. What games do you play on your computer?"

"Mostly war or fantasy games, that kind of thing."

"Sounds righteous," Dickie said. "Violent?"

"Yeah, some of them, I guess. I have a couple rated M."

"What does M stand for?"

"Mature. I mixed two in with some other games I bought with my birthday money once, and my mother didn't notice." He couldn't believe this kid didn't even know the basic lingo of computer games. What planet was he visiting?

"*Mature*, huh? That rules you out, Death-ray," Dickie said to Raylee.

"You too, doorknob," Raylee said with a flat tone, keeping her eyes and her slow, steady pace on the plate.

Dickie pushed off with his feet, holding both swing chains in his hands and starting a rocking motion back and forth to gain speed and altitude. "Do you have your games with you?" Dickie asked as he swung past Conner in an ever-increasing blur.

"No, my parents made me leave my laptop at home, and I don't think my grandfather even owns a TV," Conner said. "They said it would be good for me to get out and experience the real world instead of sitting inside all day looking at a screen."

"Well, they sure sent you to the wrong place to experience the real world," Dickie said. "You're currently located at half past nothing on your way to void."

"I'm starting to get that feeling," Conner said. He sneaked a glance over at Raylee on the merry-go-round, her firm, tan legs moving rhythmically, one step in front of the other, her eyes looking down as she went. Definitely cute, Conner thought. Things could be worse, he supposed. He could be all alone here, and in some way, Raylee and maybe even this weird kid made the place seem a bit more tolerable.

"Let's take him to meet Auntie!" Dickie blurted suddenly, now swinging back and forth so high he almost brushed the hanging branches and leaves of the tree behind the back fence of the playground.

"Ha...that's a plan," Raylee said.

"Auntie?" Conner asked.

"Auntie Wilamena," Raylee said. "She owns a little shop in town, sells all kinds of weird stuff. My mom thinks she might be a witch—or at least she said that once."

"What kind of stuff?" Conner asked.

"Oh, you'll see!" Dickie said.

Conner wasn't sure he liked the sound of that. Then again, it wasn't like he had other big plans for the day.

"Do you have a bike?" Dickie asked.

"No...not here."

"That's okay. We'll ride slow."

The three of them set off down the road, Dickie and Raylee coasting slowly on their bikes, Conner walking between them. They passed houses on the right and left as they went down the hill, and Conner could see the blue pond that bordered the center of town in the distance. Most of the houses looked well kept, but every so often they'd pass one with out-of-control weeds and debris strewn about the lawn. One had what must have been ten dirty blue coolers with white tops lying about the yard, some on their sides, all empty. Halfway down the hill, Dickie braked his bike to an abrupt stop.

"Uh-oh," Dickie said, motioning with his chin to the bottom of the hill, where the hood of a dark-blue pickup truck marked with a large gold badge and the word SHERIFF was poking out of a side road.

"What's the matter?" Conner asked.

"Oh, nothing," Raylee said. "It's just Sheriff Summers...he doesn't like Dickie."

"Great, well I don't like him, either," Dickie said, sounding exasperated. "Tell the story again...spread it around some more, why don't you... go ahead."

Raylee cheerfully obliged, explaining to Conner that last spring Dickie had found himself at home, alone and bored, and had decided to fill an old metal pail with kerosene, and started dipping strands of hay in it and lighting them with a Bic lighter he'd snatched from its usual place alongside his father's ashtray in the living room. He had become so fascinated with the flames that he didn't notice that the hay strands were starting to pile up in the spot where he was tossing them next to the garage, and without warning, the little pile ignited into a reasonable semblance of a campfire. Realizing the flames were licking up near the wood siding of the garage, Dickie leaped into action to stomp them out, promptly kicking over the pail of kerosene in the process. With a great *Whoosh!!!* what had previously been a minor problem became a major one, and Dickie looked on in abject horror as the flames quickly ascended to the roofline of the garage.

When the fire department finally arrived, Raylee went on, they were greeted by a frantic and crying Dickie, who was trying to extinguish the flames with the pitiful spray from a garden house. Sheriff Summers—first name Alvin (he and his two deputies, referred to by the kids in town as Alvin and the Chipmunks)—interrogated the clear suspect, obtaining a blubbering and barely coherent confession in record time. From then on, Sheriff Summers forever labeled Dickie a dangerous firebug who warranted close surveillance by law enforcement. Raylee herself tortured him for months by calling him "Bic'kie," a nickname he neither appreciated nor thought was very funny.

The three started down the hill at a slow pace, hoping to pass the sheriff without notice, but as soon as they were in front of his truck, he leaned his head out the window and ordered them to stop.

"What you up to today, Dickie?" Sheriff Summers said in a menacing tone.

"Nothing," Dickie replied, holding his bike between his legs. "Just minding my own business and staying out of trouble."

"Ha!" Sheriff Summers exclaimed. "I have a hard time believing that! Have a lighter or any other combustibles on you, by chance, Dickie?"

"No," Dickie replied softly, hanging his head and looking straight down at the ground.

"Well, I'd better not catch you with any—ever," the sheriff said, obviously enjoying the opportunity to torment Dickie in front of an audience. He paused and then focused his mirrored sunglasses on Conner. "And who do we have here?" he asked. "Another juvenile delinquent?"

"No, sir," Conner answered. "My name is Conner. I'm staying here for the summer with my grandfather."

"And who might that be?" Sheriff Summers asked, peering over the rim of his sunglasses.

"Granville Williamson," Conner answered. "Up at the top of the hill," Conner said as he gestured up toward the Farm.

"Okay, then," the Sheriff replied. "Mind yourself while you're visiting… we don't need any more troublemakers like young Master Dickie, here."

Dickie's cheeks flushed strawberry red, and the three started back on their way down the road. After they'd gone fifty yards or so, Dickie began to vent.

"I hate that jerk!" he said, his teeth gritting. "He's never going to leave me alone. I wish he'd get fired or something."

Raylee giggled. "It's not that bad. At least he didn't arrest you when you torched your parents' garage."

"I wish he had," Dickie said. "It'd be better than having to take his abuse all the time."

Conner, Raylee, and Dickie continued without speaking past the center of town where the general store stood, a sign hanging in the window informing the public that it also served as the authorized local post office. They crossed the short bridge with the pond on one side and an outlet stream on the other, which bubbled and frothed over rocks, then curved out of sight through the trees. The air was warm and muggy, accentuated by the buzzing noise of thousands of grasshoppers climbing about in the weeds.

Immediately after the bridge on the right stood a small blue house, set back from the road with a red brick walkway leading up to the entrance. There were various items strewn about on the porch—several chairs, all different in design, a string of wind chimes of all shapes and sizes, a small red table, and an assortment of dried hornet's nests nailed to the house wall and support beams. A big yellow lab with a whitish face lay on the porch, its front paws and nose hanging over the edge, wearing a look of "it's too hot, and I'm too old to bother getting up to say hello," although his tail did give a hairy thump as the three approached the house.

"Hey there, Little John!" Raylee exclaimed. She stopped, bent over, and scratched the top of the old dog's head. He rolled his eyes up to her, red underneath his lower lids, with an expression of gratitude for the scratch.

"That is one old dog," Conner said.

"Yeah," Raylee replied. "He's been around forever. He used to run around all over town, getting into trouble, chasing chickens and stealing food off people's porches. Everybody loves him, though, so they let him get away with a lot. The last couple years, he's slowed down, and he mostly likes to sit on the porch and watch the goings-on of the town. He's a wicked good boy, though, aren't you, boy?" She scratched his head more vigorously, and Little John responded by half rolling onto his side, raising a front and back leg to expose the white fur of his belly so it could get some attention, too. Raylee obliged by scratching his chest with both hands in a circular motion, little tufts of white hair floating up into the air. Little John let out a low, guttural groan of approval.

Raylee opened to the door leading into the house, a rusty bell at the top giving a sad jingle. Conner and Dickie followed her in, their eyes taking a moment to adjust to the dark room, red curtains on the four windows casting a deep rose hue. Two long tables, one on each side of the room, were cluttered with hundreds of glass and porcelain bottles and plates, and a big square dining room table in the center held two stuffed raccoons and an assortment of deer antlers. To Conner, the room looked like a chaotic mess, not like a going business concern, in any case.

The three of them walked to the back of the room to a door-less "doorway" with hanging strings of blue beads. Raylee pushed them aside with a clacking sound and walked through.

"Auntie?" she called. "Auntie, are you in here?"

"Land sakes!" a loud voice replied. "Of course I am…where else would I be?"

As Conner walked into the room through the bead barrier, he saw a stout woman washing potatoes in a metal strainer in the sink. She wore a blue frock and looked as wide as she was tall, which Conner estimated to be about four and a half feet. Auntie twisted off the tap with a squeak, dried her hands with a pink dishcloth, and turned to greet them.

"To what do I owe this great pleasure of a visit?" she asked.

"We just stopped in to say hello and introduce our newest Morgan resident, Conner," Raylee answered, looking back to Connor, still standing by the doorway. "He's Mr. Williamson's grandson, and he's staying with him for the summer."

"Is that so?" Auntie said, her eyes fixing on Conner. "What brings you to our fine town?"

"My parents sent me here for the summer," Conner replied.

"Well, aren't you the lucky one!"

Conner didn't consider himself lucky, particularly since he fully expected to return home to a split-up family. He looked around the kitchen and saw that it was just as cluttered as the front room, with photographs and paintings hanging haphazardly on the walls, and small vases and blue and red plates filling up every inch of available counter space.

"Everything's for sale here, except for the old dog on the porch," Auntie said. "Just name me a fair price, and it's yours to take home and treasure forever."

Conner couldn't imagine taking anything from this place for *free*, let alone paying money for it, but he nodded.

"You all just have a seat and tell me what the latest gossip is."

The kitchen chairs were arranged in a curve under a bay window looking out the back. They all took a seat, and Auntie plopped her considerable girth into a rocking chair by the sink, which creaked as she adjusted herself in it.

"Nothing new, really," Raylee said. "We've just been hanging out and waiting for something to happen. Oh, and Dickie had another run-in with Sheriff Summers a few minutes ago," she said with a grin.

Dickie grimaced. "Did not...he just won't leave me alone."

"Well, I suppose that's what a young boy gets for playing with fire, so to speak," Auntie said.

"Goodness sakes, where are my manners?" she said then, hoisting herself out of the chair. She proceeded to set them up with ice-cold orange sodas, returned to her seat, and gave them a rundown of all her latest activities—harvesting carrots and tomatoes in the back garden, fixing a broken hinge on her shed door, and so on. Auntie perked up and recounted a visit by paying customers the day before, who went home with a beautiful painting of the pond on a crosscut section from an oak tree. "Guess I might be able to retire early, after all," she said with a laugh.

"So, Conner," Auntie said, turning her attention to him, "what do you think of our small slice of paradise in the woods?"

"It's nice, I guess. Quiet."

"That it is," Auntie nodded. "Especially for people from away, like yourself. Sometimes I think they get the heebie-jeebies from how silent it can be around here, especially at night."

"Tell Conner about the weirdos that live in the woods," Raylee said with a slight smile.

"Weirdos?" Conner asked.

Auntie scowled at Raylee. "You trying to scare our young guest here? They're no weirder than anyone else. People around these parts like to keep to themselves, that's all."

"I mean the one about the little boy—you know," Raylee clarified.

"Land sakes almighty, you don't think he wants to hear about that!" Auntie said.

"*I* sure don't," Dickie said. "It gives me the creeps."

Conner's interest was piqued. "What about the little boy?"

Auntie explained that a few years back, there was a family that lived down in woods by the river that flowed out of the pond. They kept to themselves, a couple of the women only coming into town to sell vegetables and buy supplies from the general store every few months. They had just shown up one year and lived there quietly, but nobody really got to know them or even knew exactly how many of them there were. Then one day, a small boy of only three or four came wandering up the main street with no shoes and only wearing a pair of dirty blue overalls. He was thin, with dark-brown hair. He looked confused and lost, and Mrs. Johnston, who was sitting on her porch, asked him if he needed help. He didn't say a word, only shook his head a little and sat down on the dusty edge of a drainage ditch by the side of the road. He sat there for a good fifteen minutes until finally, concern mounting, the lady walked over to the store and asked if anyone had been looking for a small boy who was lost. Jeb, the owner of the store, came out and walked up to take a look at the boy. He and Mrs. Johnston asked him some questions—where he was from, who his folks were—but he refused to say anything and just sat there picking at the dirt and pebbles with his fingers.

By this point, the two of them thought something peculiar was going on and were about to call the sheriff when a lone man walked out of the woods, a good six feet tall, dressed in a loose-fitting coat that looked like it had been a fancy-dress coat in some previous century. The man walked over to the boy and said, "That's where you got off to," grabbed him by the arm, and pulled him along with him. Mrs. Johnston asked the man if the boy was his, and he just gave a curt nod and started walking away. She said they were worried about him, and they tried to follow along for a bit, but the man just kept heading back to the woods, the boy in tow.

They disappeared out of sight into the woods, and Mrs. Johnston didn't think much about it afterwards until a few months later when she was watching the news out of Bangor, and they were doing a story about a little boy who had disappeared while camping with his folks in the nearby state park. The parents had been setting up camp when the boy wandered to the edge of the woods chasing dragonflies, and then, just like that, he vanished. No scream or yell; he just up and disappeared. The news program showed a picture of a small boy with a red shirt and a beaming smile. To Mrs. Johnston, he looked a lot like the boy she had seen in town, only a little younger, and she reported it to the sheriff's office over in Daltry.

The next day, a couple of the sheriffs and a game warden walked down the river to see if they could locate the man and the boy, but all they found was a deserted little cabin. There were old barrels and broken furniture lying about the property. They looked inside the cabin, but all they found was a rusty spring and mattress, some pots and pans, and a toy fire truck lying on its side. No one knows what happened to the family that was living there, and they never came to town again to sell vegetables or buy supplies. The sheriff's office searched the area but never found anything.

"Some folks," Auntie said, "think the family had kidnapped the boy from that campground and took him as one of their own. They figure that once the boy was spotted, they just moved deeper into the woods where no one would find them. For years after, there would be reports of people seeing folks way back in the woods when they were hunting or fishing, but they would disappear like ghosts. Others claim to have caught glimpses of people peering into their windows late at night. Anytime an animal would go missing, or a basket of potatoes disappeared, they would blame it on the people in the woods."

"Do you think they're still out there?" Conner asked.

"Well," Auntie answered, "if they are, they must be hiding out, and if there was ever a place where you can just go off and disappear in the woods, this is the place."

Conner shifted in his seat uncomfortably. He was starting to agree with Dickie…this was a creepy story.

"Enough of that," Auntie said. "We'll be giving our young new resident nightmares. I have to get back to my potatoes. You kids run off now, and don't get yourselves into any mischief…you hear that, Dickie?"

Dickie groaned. "We won't. Why does everyone always look at me when they say things like that? This is bordering on harassment!"

Auntie just cackled, lifted herself out of her chair, and shuffled back over to the sink.

Back out on the porch, Dickie asked in a low voice, "Raylee, do you believe any of that?"

Raylee paused for a moment. "I don't know, but I'll tell you this: I swear a couple of times I've seen someone or something back in the woods, and I'll bet it's them, just watching us from a distance. For sure, I don't go into the woods at night, that's when they come out, I bet."

"Oh, baloney," Dickie scoffed. "There isn't any such thing as weirdos living in the woods, and they only tell kids that story to keep us from wandering too far. My parents used to tell me stories like that, and it scared me when I was little, but I don't believe a word of it."

They walked off the porch and headed back up the road toward the playground. Conner looked off into the distance at the wooded hill behind the Farm and thought that if they were living out there, he didn't want to meet them.

Chapter 4

A few days had passed since the visit to Auntie, and Conner found himself settling into his new temporary home in a way he hadn't expected. His grandfather took him out shooting with his old Winchester .30-30 lever-action a few times in the back field, something he had never done in his life, and he found a strange satisfaction in popping empty soda cans off the wooden fence that served as the target base.

Gramp had also taken him fishing on the river that led out from the pond in town. They walked for what seemed like hours down a grass-covered woods road, veering right and left at various forks. His grandfather told him that if he ever got lost to make sure he walked in the direction they merged, as that was almost always the way out. Conner thought about the story Auntie Wilamena had told about the people living down here, but he didn't say anything to Gramp, feeling safe in his presence.

They came to the river at midday. It was about forty feet across, its silky blue waters flowing over rocks and around bends, thick green brush on both sides. His grandfather taught him how to bait a hook with a worm, making sure to thread the point of the hook through the thick band on the night crawlers. The blackish-brown mush that came out of the worms as he hooked them made Conner feel a bit queasy, but he didn't let it show. They fished by wading in the river, as the brush on both sides was too thick to navigate, and he got the knack of balancing on and between the submerged rocks, only slipping a few times.

Shortly after they'd started fishing, Conner hooked a brook trout that put up quite a fight for its eight-inch length, and he ended up flinging it behind him into the branches of a tree. His grandfather had given a quick laugh, then retrieved the fish from the tree and whacked its head on a rock. The fish was dark-blue, almost black, with glimmering yellow and red spots, and its tail and gills still flicked with life even after the blow. Gramp slid the fish into the square opening of the wicker fishing creel on his shoulder. They caught seven fish, four for Gramp and three for him, and left the river to head home after they had reached a small waterfall. Conner couldn't imagine they would ever find their way out of the woods, which were thick and seemed almost impassable, but eventually, they came to another old woods road and followed it out back to the town.

Back at the Farm, Gramp cleaned the fish, rolled them in cornmeal, and fried them with butter in a black cast-iron frying pan on the kitchen wood-stove. They ate the fish with crisp white corn, baked potatoes, and thick homemade biscuits slathered with real butter. The trout was delicious, kind of like the salmon Conner's parents sometimes cooked up for dinner, but required more care in eating as he had to use his fork to strip the reddish meat away from the delicate, comb-like bones. His grandfather showed him that you could eat the crisp fins as well, which were crunchy and salty.

He hung out with Raylee and Dickie almost every day the next week and grew comfortable with them, almost as though they'd been his friends for years. Together they explored most of the areas in town, stopping off at the general store now and then to refresh themselves with penny candy and grape sodas. They took a few hikes farther back into the woods, finding small streams and even a shallow cave, breathing the fresh pine-scented air as they explored.

One day, they came across what looked like the broken foundation of what must have been an old cabin, and they picked through rusty discarded pails that were lying about in various stages of decay. Conner had asked if this was where the people in the woods with the little boy had lived, but Dickie said no, that was way down the river somewhere, though he had never actually seen it for himself.

Dickie and Raylee were always sparring with each other, calling each other goober or nerd, and seemed as comfortable with each other as siblings. Conner couldn't help but feel an ever-growing affection for Raylee, and he hated to admit to himself that it was developing into a big-time crush. She was athletic in the woods and sure of herself in a way Conner had never seen in a girl; she didn't mind getting muddy or dirty, hopping over logs like a young deer.

Although he didn't feel comfortable saying anything, he began to suspect that she was starting to feel the same about him, and every so often he would catch her looking at him and smiling with her thoughtful and whimsical smile. A few times when they were together, he had almost said something, but his inner anxiety and Dickie's ever-lurking presence led him to keep it to himself.

At least for now, he thought.

⁂

One night, Conner awoke suddenly, confused for a moment as to where he was, the moonlight casting a blue glow from the window, but quickly realized he was in his room at the Farm. He shook the sleep from his head and looked around the room. It was colder than it had been since he had been here, and he shifted in the bed and put his feet on the floor, in the process coughing phlegm from his lungs, the hollow noise startling him for a second. He couldn't help but think that it sounded a lot like his father's regular coughs. They both suffered from allergies to dust and pollen. It seemed to be a family curse, the need to clear his lungs continually. A few years back, he'd had to start using an inhaler to be able to sleep at night. It was an awful, tight feeling, like a huge iron hand gripping his chest, making him jerk awake from the edge of sleep and gasp for breath. The more he would think about it, the worse it would get, until a short puff from the inhaler would loosen his chest and allow him to fall back asleep. He still carried the inhaler with him, but in the last few years found he needed it less and less. He sometimes took an allergy tablet at night when he could feel it coming on, which had the secondary benefit of rendering him unconscious the moment his head hit the pillow.

Conner stood up from the bed and shuffled out the door and down the hall. He stood in the dimness of the bathroom, illuminated only by a small nightlight that shone weakly from the side of the mirror above the sink. Conner flushed and quickly washed his hands with water only, shaking them dry, and walked back into the hall. He headed down the staircase to retrieve his aluminum water bottle from the fridge, pausing at the land-

53

ing to look out the window facing the back of the house. He yawned as he looked out over the moonlit field, bordered by a thick stand of pine trees off in the distance.

He was just about to continue down the stairs when something in the tree line caught his eye and he stopped. It was faint, but there was a definite color change amongst the trees. He squinted his eyes to focus and saw what looked like the silhouette of a faceless person standing in the trees.

Numbness ran through Conner's body as the figure became sharper in his view. He would have called out to his grandfather but felt paralyzed. Whoever it was, they stood motionless. His eyes shifted involuntarily for a moment in the blue moonlight, and he lost sight of the figure, but when he looked slightly to the left of where he had seen it, it appeared again in the same place. Yes, someone standing in the trees, watching the house. Conner jerked back to life and ran down the last few stairs, his breath racing and hands shaking from the adrenaline dump to his body. In the dining room, he paused at the table and looked back up the short stairway to the window. After a few raspy breaths, he thought again about calling out to his grandfather, but he didn't want to wake him if it was only his imagination at work.

He crept back up the stairs and looked out the window again…to his horror, the figure was still there, and he saw a tiny, dim orange glow briefly flare from the figure's head.

Conner raced back up the stairs, down the hallway, and into his room, and jumped into his bed, pulling the covers over his head. In his panic, he had again forgotten to call out to his grandfather, and now he didn't know what he should do. He stayed in his bed, breath still racing, and reached his hand down to the bed frame, finding the hilt of the knife Gramp had given him. It gave him some comfort to know it was there, but there would be no sleep for him tonight.

The next morning, the sun was shining brightly through the shade on the window, and Conner rose and got dressed in a pair of khaki pants and a dark-blue T-shirt with a pocket on the left side. He walked out of his room and down the stairs, pausing to look out the window where he had been frozen by fright the night before. The scene looked pastoral and calm, a slight breeze causing the tall grass in the field to sway back and forth like seaweed in an undersea current. The woods were green and bright and didn't look anywhere near as foreboding as they had in the middle of the night. The spot where Conner thought he'd seen the figure stood empty, and he started to think that maybe his eyes had been playing tricks on him.

No. There *was* someone there—he was sure of it. The cigarette or cigar light, or whatever it was—it was there. Conner turned and headed down the stairs into the kitchen, where he could already hear Gramp moving about, getting a breakfast of scrambled eggs and bacon ready for the two of them.

❧

"Well, we're quiet this morning," Gramp said after a long silent pause during the meal.

"Didn't sleep too well last night," Conner replied.

"Bad dreams?"

Conner picked at his food, carefully considering what he would say next. "Gramp?"

"Yes?" his grandfather answered, shoveling a forkful of buttery eggs into his mouth.

"Is there anyone else living around here, like maybe off in the woods?"

His grandfather paused from taking another bite and smiled. "Why do you ask that?"

"I don't know; it's just that sometimes I get the feeling someone is watching us."

"Well," his grandfather said, wiping his hands with a cloth napkin, "this place is pretty remote. I suppose people are living out there. Some people like their privacy. It doesn't mean they are bad people. They probably want to keep to themselves and not be bothered by others, or by society in general, for that matter. I can understand how they feel sometimes. The news is depressing. War this, famine and protest that—it's no wonder some people don't want to be part of it. Sometimes I don't want to be part of it myself."

Conner resolved in an instant to come clean about his experience. "Last night, I came down to get my water bottle, and I think I saw someone standing off in the trees watching the house, watching us."

"Out the back?"

"Yes," Conner stammered, "it was hard to see, but there was someone standing in the trees watching the house."

"Well, I don't have the land posted. You know what that means, right?"

Conner shook his head.

"It means you honor the traditions of Maine rural life, and you let people come onto your land to hunt or fish or forage, as long as they respect the land by leaving it like they found it and don't take more than what they need. Some people move up here from away and immediately post no trespassing or no hunting signs all over their land, cutting people off from it who may have grown up going on that land. It's not a smart thing to do. If everyone did it, you wouldn't be able to go anywhere in the woods unless it was your property. The paper companies own most of the land up here, and they let anyone use it so long as they don't damage the roads or trees…it's decent of them, and as I said, it's the Maine way."

"So, people can come on your land anytime they want?" Conner asked.

"Well, yes, I guess, as long as they respect it, and me. I've let my land stay open and have rarely had any problems. One time, some people were four-wheeling and tearing up the road in the springtime, but I knew who they were and just asked them not to run on the trails during the mud season, and they agreed. They even went out and fixed the ruts they left. It's more like that than not. People up here generally respect what's yours, and more often than not will do the right thing. It's a beautiful thing, when you think about it. Although it's great to have land to call your own, it's nice to be able to go off and explore when you want. Remember the other week when we went fishing down the river? That waterfall we sat and ate lunch by is the same one I used to go to with my dad. It holds many memories for me, even if it's not on my property. I was glad to be able to bring you there and start creating some memories of our own, and maybe someday you'll come up here with your kids and start the whole process over again. That's the special thing about living up here."

Conner ate a piece of crispy, half-burnt bacon, the way his grandfather liked to cook it, and thought about what he had said. He couldn't even imagine having a wife, much less any kids, but he understood what Gramp was trying to say.

Gramp continued, "The person you think you saw was likely passing through, maybe scouting out a spot to hunt come fall. I wouldn't worry about it."

After breakfast, Conner and his grandfather washed the dishes by hand in the sink, drying them with a soft white dishcloth that must have been twenty or thirty years old, and it had that faint musty smell like the rest of the house. Once they finished putting the dishes away, Gramp said, "Let's head out into the barn; it's high time we repair the hole in the wall where the critters are getting in."

Out in the barn, Gramp used a hand saw and two sawhorses to cut up some planks that were measured to fit over the hole in the southwest corner. Conner loved to watch him work, although he could feel himself getting a little frustrated at the pace—meticulous with everything he did, carefully measuring and marking the wood and cutting it neatly on the pencil lines he had drawn to guide him. With all the boards cut, they went into the workshop, where Gramp carefully selected nails from several of the glass jars lining the shelves, and they carried everything around the outside the barn and began to repair the hole. As they worked, Conner could feel sweat forming on the back of his neck in the midmorning sun, the only reprieve coming from the fluffy clouds that moved steadily across the sky like a herd of white bison.

Conner held each of the four boards in place as his grandfather nailed them securely. It took about an hour and a half from start to finish, and once they finished, they stood back and surveyed their work. It wasn't exactly pretty—the repurposed boards they used were beaten and worn—but it would serve its purpose. Functional over fashionable, as Gramp termed it.

"Well, that should keep the critters out," Gramp said. "Why don't you get the big broom and sweep the floor of the barn, then feed the chickens? I have to head into town to pick up a new battery for the tractor. Let's say we meet back in the kitchen around noon for lunch?"

"Sounds good," Conner said.

Conner headed back into the barn. He liked the fact that his grandfather gave him a job to do and then left him alone to do it. Back home, whenever he was asked to clean out a room or bring out the trash, he felt like he was being watched by his parents to make sure he did it. Gramp wasn't like that, and it made him feel more grown-up somehow.

Conner retrieved the straw broom from the workshop and started to sweep the little bits of hay and clumps of dirt that littered the floor. Dust rose all around him, and the sunlight shining through the gaps in the barn boards became a yellowish sparkle, like tiny diamonds floating in the air. He organized the dirt in small piles about ten feet apart, then used the hand brush to push the debris into a dustpan and dump it into a white plastic barrel in the corner. In no time, the floor started to look reasonably clean, giving him a feeling of satisfaction.

Next, Conner went over to the chicken coop inside the north wall, opened the wire door, and went inside. The chickens were all out in the barnyard, so he didn't have to deal with rudely shuffling them around as he cleaned. He used a wooden-handled scoop shovel to scrape up the droppings and soiled hay, depositing it in another plastic barrel just outside the coop door, and threw down some fresh hay. After finishing up, he went into the house-like structure within the coop, a barn within a barn, he thought, a board against one wall with six little boxes, each holding a nest. A wooden plank served as a ramp for the chickens to access the nests. He peered into each of them but didn't see any eggs. Sleeping on the job, he guessed. There was a door in the coop enclosure that led out to behind the barn, allowing the chickens to go out into the fresh air as they pleased to pick and scratch at the ground, and he could see one of them just outside, going about its business.

When he finished with his chores, he looked down at his clothes, covered in dust from head to toe, and he banged on his chest and pants, releasing the dust back into the air.

Later that morning, sitting in the kitchen and sipping on an icy soda, Conner heard the familiar bike tires and verbal banter of Raylee and Dickie arriving at the playground. He opened the door and headed outside, shielding his eyes from the sun with his left hand as he looked across to it.

"Hey, Conner!" Raylee said. "Just getting up, city boy?"

Conner started across the grass to the playground. "No, been up since the crack of dawn working on cleaning up the barn. Hey, Dickie."

"Hey, Conner," Dickie said, not bothering to turn back to look at him as he dropped his bike next to the chain-link fence by the basketball court.

"What does Mr. Williamson have in the barn?" Raylee asked.

Conner approached the monkey bars next to the merry-go-round and grabbed onto the warm gray steel of a top bar. "Chickens, and a few goats."

"Chickens!" Raylee exclaimed. "We had chickens once. My dad thought it would be a good idea to have fresh eggs and the occasional chicken sacrifice for dinner. They were a huge pain. They kept getting out and wandering into the road, and one got smashed flat by a truck. She avoided being dinner, I guess. Dad built a better coop, but those things were nothing but trouble. I'd go to feed them, nice person that I am, and they'd peck at my ankles as I was spreading the seeds around. Ask your grandfather to get you a horse—that would be more fun. You could ride him around."

Conner smiled but thought to himself that he would be terrified to ride a horse. He had seen the westerns where people had been shot out of the saddle, hitting the ground with a smack and tumbling over and over, dirt flying. No, he had no desire to break his neck riding a horse and suspected they were probably a great deal harder to clean up after.

Dickie was over by the small court shooting baskets, missing almost every time. Raylee shouted, "Air ball, air ball!" at one of his more pathetic attempts. Conner thought it was doubtful Dickie was on the school basketball team. He didn't seem to have an athletic bone in his body.

"You know," Conner said to Raylee, "I saw something last night."

"What?" Raylee asked, immediately interested.

"In the middle of the night, I saw a person standing way back in the woods watching the house. It creeped me out. I think he probably must have seen me in the window looking back at him, but he didn't move. He just stood there and kept watching. I didn't sleep for the rest of the night."

"That's all he was doing?" Raylee asked. "Just standing there watching you and not doing anything?"

"Yeah, it was creepy."

"Where was he again?" Dickie asked, listening in and pausing in his free-throw attempts.

"Out back, in the tree line."

"Hey, let's go back there and take a look!" said Dickie. "Maybe he left something behind, like a clue as to who he was, or a dead body or something."

"Maybe he left a deuce in the grass, too," Raylee said, laughing.

"That would be something he left for you," Dickie said. "You could pick it up, dry it out, and add it to your collection."

Raylee stuck her tongue out at Dickie, flipping her black hair out of her face with a jerk of her head.

"Okay," Conner said, "let's go check it out. I think I know right where he was standing; it was by a couple of the big trees near the edge of the field."

"Adventure time!" Raylee chimed.

They left the playground, walked the road past the barns, and headed down the dirt road that led to the hayfield, then cut through the tall golden wheat to the tree line, Raylee leading the way.

When they reached the trees, Conner said he thought it was more to the right, so they moved off in that direction, each of them carefully scanning the ground as they went.

Conner stopped and looked around. "This is it...I think it was right here."

"I don't see anything," Dickie said. "Not even a deuce."

"Look closer, and smell around a bit," Raylee said, giggling.

"Wait a minute, what's this?" Dickie said. He reached down and plucked something out of the grass. He sniffed it quickly and grinned. "Yep, looks like a home-rolled cigarette. Probably a blunt."

"Blunt?" Conner said, although he quickly realized what he meant.

"You know—ganja, dope, weed...a blunt. Wacky weed. Like Mr. Clemson grows in his backyard but thinks nobody knows."

Raylee walked over and took a sniff from Dickie's hand. "No, it just smells like my dad's pipe tobacco. It looks like we have Conner's perp dead to rights."

"I did see a faint glow in the dark," Conner said. "He must've been standing here smoking and watching the house."

"Yeah, look, there are two more over there. What was this mystery person doing?" Dickie asked.

"You idiot," Raylee said. "Didn't you hear what Conner said? He was standing here watching. How many times do you have to be told something before it sinks into that melon-sized head of yours?"

"Three or four times, usually, at least according to the teachers at school," Dickie replied, but his tone was serious. "Maybe he was casing your house for a robbery." Dickie looked back at the trees behind them. "He'll wait until you're all asleep, and then he'll slip in the back door and steal all your valuables, and maybe stand over your bed in the night with a big knife and grin down at you while you're all comfy and cozy asleep."

"You are such a little freak," Raylee said.

Raylee was right. He *was* a little freak, Conner thought. Still, it was unnerving to have physical evidence that there was indeed someone standing back here last night. Even though he knew Dickie was making a joke, it made a shiver run up his back to think there was someone there, watching…maybe watching them right now.

Dickie tossed the butt to the ground. "Let's get out of here; I don't like this. Don't like it one bit," he said as if his former joke scenario was now starting to work on his mind.

They all agreed on that point without saying another word, and they headed back across the field and the road leading to the house. Inside, Conner pulled three soda cans from the fridge, and as they sat and sipped on the cold sodas, they talked about what they'd found.

"Maybe I was wrong…maybe hillbillies *are* living out in the woods all by themselves," Dickie said. "They probably need food and supplies, and they're checking out the houses to see what they can steal."

"Doubt it," Raylee said. "Even if they are out there, they wouldn't be creeping around this close to town. Somebody might see them."

Conner wasn't sure. The story about the little boy had unnerved him, though he wasn't going to admit it to Raylee and Dickie. Still, if a family *was* living back in the woods, they'd have to come out now and then to get supplies as Dickie said, wouldn't they? He was thinking on this when his grandfather's shape filled the screen door, and he heard the familiar sound of the rusty spring pulling back.

"Well," Gramp said, "what do we have here? Company in this neck of the woods?"

"Hey, Mr. Williamson," Raylee and Dickie said in unison.

"Hello there, you two. Come to visit Conner? Mighty neighborly of you," Gramp said as he carried in a brown paper bag and set it on the counter. "What are you three up to today—besides drinking all my cold soda?"

"Oh, nothing," Raylee said. "We were investigating the mysterious visitor who's watching your house late at night. We went back into the woods where Conner saw him, and we found some cigarette butts. I guess he was real, and not something the city boy here just imagined in the dark."

"That a fact?" Gramp said as he removed items from the bag and placed them on the shelves. "Well, I wouldn't worry about it too much. Like I told Conner, here, probably just someone scoping out a place to hunt in the fall. Lots of people looking for good places to hunt hereabouts. Nothing to worry about."

"Yeah," Dickie said. "But what was he doing just staring at your house?'

"Like I said, no worries. As long as they don't make a habit of it, I have no objection. Why don't you three just run along and find something to do, but stay out of trouble—no shenanigans, you got that?" Gramp said, grinning.

"Sure, Mr. Williamson," Raylee said. "We know not to get into any trouble. Sheriff's got it in for Dickie as it is."

"Oh brother, here we go again," Dickie groaned.

"I'm just teasing you," Raylee said. "Don't be so sensitive, twerp."

"Yeah, but I wish you'd stop. I wish everybody would stop talking about my little mishap."

Gramp gave a short laugh as the three of them shuffled out of the house through the front door.

Conner suggested they go check out the barn and chicken coop, so they walked around the side of the house to the barn door. When they went in, Conner was momentarily pleased with himself about how orderly and clean the place looked. They inspected the coop, and Raylee reiterated her chicken concerns. Conner dismissed them, though. He thought it was perfect to hear the sound of the chickens clucking and milling about—the barn would seem lonely without them. They went out through the back door, and Conner showed them where he and his grandfather had repaired the hole.

"What was getting in?" Dickie asked.

"Not sure, but Gramp said it was probably raccoons, although he also said a couple of summers ago, foxes set up a den under the porch, and he came home once to see the mother fox sitting on the porch with two babies—kits, he called them—acting like they owned the place. They didn't make a nuisance of themselves, he said, so he left them be. He said maybe one of the kits grew up and came back to start its own family in the barn."

"I don't mind foxes," Dickie said, "but coyotes are scary."

"You're scary," Raylee said.

"You can hear them some nights howling and barking back up in the mountains," Dickie said, ignoring the dig. "They run in packs, and my dad says sometimes they chase down baby deer and eat them. He said that's why he shoots them whenever he sees them."

"That's mean," Raylee said.

"Is not. Besides, coyotes would probably eat you, too, if they had half a chance."

"Nope, not me," Raylee said. "I'm too fast."

Conner thought she was probably right. He had seen her run a few times, and she *was* fast. He had avoided ever getting into a running match with her because he was sure she would have beaten him handily. Once she got going, she seemed to float across the ground, feet barely touching the dirt. Very different indeed from the awkward clumping motion he made whenever he ran. He could run pretty well when he was younger, but after a growth spurt, everything kind of went out whack, and he could no longer coordinate his arms and legs like he used to. They were like four alien appendages stuck to his body, growing long and out of proportion to the rest of him. No way he was going to embarrass himself by challenging her to a race he would surely lose.

Still, Conner thought, as they began to walk down the road, heading no place in particular, there was something strange going on around here. He was sure of it. Back home, he'd never felt scared like last night. Oh sure, there had been times after he had binge-watched horror movies when he had trouble sleeping afterward. There was a scene in one of those movies where a ghoul with a breathing mask had been tormenting a girl in her bed—that had completely freaked him out. He checked his closet and under his bed a couple of times before he was finally able to get to sleep that night. However, that was just a movie. It wasn't real, like this, and he knew he was never going downstairs in the middle of the night to get a drink again.

Ever.

Chapter 5

A couple of weeks passed, and one day Conner realized he was more than halfway through his planned stay with Gramp. Although it had only been a month and change, it felt longer. Sometimes it felt like he had always been here, growing up and playing in this small town that was becoming his adopted home. His grandfather took him fishing a few more times, once in an aluminum boat with a little motor they had borrowed from one of his friends. They motored out to three small islands in a nearby pond and hung their baited lines in what his Gramp said were the deeper holes. They caught a bucketful of white perch, his grandfather saying that they were an invasive species and there was no limit on how many you could keep. They took the perch home, and his grandfather expertly filleted the white meat off the tiny bones. Gramp fried them up in the cast-iron pan, and they ate them along with some collard greens they picked from the fields. They topped off the meal with blueberries they had gathered in the thick brush up near the spring house, drenched in heavy, thick cream. Conner felt like he was hungrier at the end of every day up here than he ever was at home, and he told Gramp as much. His grandfather said that was because of two things—hard work and fresh mountain air.

During the last few weeks, Conner had worked hard. They had finished whipping the barn into shape, and one morning they climbed into Gramp's truck and drove half an hour to a farm along one of the main roads to buy chickens. They picked up six Rhode Island Whites to add to the brood of dark Black Rocks. Gramp paid the farmer, a hulking mass in dirty blue overalls with arms that looked like tree trunks, and they returned to the

Farm. After a brief acclimation phase, the chickens made themselves at home, as if they had always lived there.

Conner continued his daily task of feeding the goats and chickens. The chickens would cause a ruckus every time, fine dust and feathers flying as he approached the coop. Chickens might not be the smartest animals, but they knew the source of their food. On sunny days, they were free to go outside, where they would peck furiously at little bugs and forgotten seeds in the dirt. The outdoor enclosure was protected by a chicken-wire fence to prevent them from wandering off on an adventure and maybe getting attacked by a stray dog or a fox, or squished flat in the road like Raylee's.

The vegetables in the field required constant attention as well, and he put in long hours pulling out sticky weeds that threatened to steal nutrients from the soil. Gramp explained that it would soon be time to dig out the potatoes he had planted early in the spring, which would make an excellent addition to the carrots, tomatoes, and greens they were already harvesting. They also tended to and collected beets and cucumbers, as well as zucchini, which seemed to grow in crazy abundance, although it was one of Conner's least favorite vegetables.

Over the next week, Conner took some time to explore the house further, going into the closed-off bedrooms and looking through the closets and drawers lined with old newsprint. Sometimes he felt like he shouldn't be snooping, but he couldn't help peeking to see what mysterious items might be resting within, undisturbed by the passage of time. In one drawer, he found a dish with ancient pennies in it, as well as a couple of hardbound journals written in faded blue cursive that was almost impossible to read. He had asked his grandfather about them, and Gramp said they were written long ago by *his* grandfather, who used to keep a record of the daily events on the Farm. Gramp had shown him an entry from April 1912 that read, "Heard news of the steamship *Titanic* sinking in the Atlantic, many lives lost." How strange it must have been, Conner thought, to have heard about it through the slow newswires and papers, not like the twenty-four-hour, nonstop, minute-by-minute news coverage of today.

In one of the back bedrooms, Conner found a small entryway leading into an attic space under one of the eaves filled with wooden crates covered in yellow-white tablecloths. In one of them, he found a dark-green wool jacket that looked like an army jacket, and he brought it down to show his grandfather. Gramp said it was the Eisenhower jacket from his youth. Conner had tried it on, unleashing a musty scent when he put his arms down the sleeves, but it was way too short for his arms. Too bad, as it was kind of sharp-looking. He returned the jacket to its box, where it would probably stay for another fifty years, waiting patiently for some other kid—maybe *his* kid someday—to find it.

He spent time with Raylee and Dickie every day, taking hikes, skipping rocks in the pond, goofing around on the playground, their routine broken up by the occasional visit to Auntie's. During their most recent visit, Auntie had removed a tarnished silver chain necklace from a drawer with a piece of quartz crystal fastened to a little metal holder and gave it to Conner. A "sacred amulet to keep you safe and protected," or so she had said. Conner accepted the necklace and thanked her, although it was not something he was ever going to wear. Still, given the weird events of the last few weeks, he decided to carry it in his pocket, to be on the safe side. He could use any protection he could get.

His feelings for Raylee continued to grow, and one day when they were walking along the main road in town, Dickie notably and uncharacteristically absent, Raylee had started to skip, jumping from one step to the next. She told Conner to follow her lead, but he had begrudgingly just sped up his pace to keep up with her. She had laughed and egged him on, and then done an extraordinary thing: She clasped his hand in hers and more or less forced him to start skipping. Conner did his best to match her skips, impeded by his lack of coordination, but a warm and at the same time terrifying feeling swept through his whole body like a wave reaching up onto the sand, his hand in hers.

They stopped when they reached the bottom of the hill, Raylee gently letting go of his hand. They continued, and from what he could see, Raylee didn't indicate that anything out of the ordinary had just happened. Conner, on the other hand, felt that his face had gone flush, and he even felt a slight tremble in his arms—out of fear or happiness, he couldn't tell; the two things just mashed together in his head in a swirl of emotions.

He liked her, more than just as a friend. He was tempted to say something but held back for fear that she might laugh at him and tell him he was being silly. He noticed, though, that they were becoming more and more comfortable and affectionate with each other, and every so often, like a small red squirrel clinging to the side of a tree, she would sneak a quick look at him, and smile.

The two of them kept on that way, never verbally acknowledging their evolving new world together as an inseparable couple. A world they both knew was due to be disrupted one day when he would have to go home, back to his other life.

He didn't want to think about it.

❧

What set this particular day apart from others was none other than Dickie. Although it had not occurred to Raylee and Conner, Dickie had noticed that they were hanging out with him less and less. A couple of times, he had biked over to the playground and checked around the barn, not seeing either of them, only to find out later that they had been together in town, in the woods, or down by the pond. It was hurtful, especially since she had been his friend first. Who was this kid to come into his town and steal her? A few times when they were all together, he had taken verbal shots at Conner instead of his usual target, Raylee, and it had caused a growing feeling of tension among the trio.

Finally, he had just broken down and confronted Conner, asking him directly if he liked her. They were on the playground, Raylee not yet with them early that morning.

"Yeah, of course…I mean, I guess so," said Conner, quickly assessing that this was not an innocent question—there were signs of tears welling up in the corners of Dickie's eyes.

"You know, she liked me best before you got here."

Yeah, that's because you were the only other kid around, Conner thought to himself, but quickly dismissed it from his head; that type of remark was not going to help the situation. "It's not like that. We're just good friends."

"Liar! I see the way you two look at each other. A regular Romeo and Juliet, you two are. And in case you hadn't noticed, you've been ditching me the last few weeks and going off on your own, without me, doing who knows what." A small tear managed to escape the corner of his eye and streak down his cheek.

"I'm sorry, Dickie," Conner said, really meaning it, but inwardly more than thrilled at the description of his relationship with Raylee. Romeo and Juliet? "I didn't mean to make you feel that way…really."

"Sorry? Sorry, nothing. You two don't want me around; you want to be by yourselves, holding hands and stuff. I hate you both!"

Conner noticed a deep red flush creeping its way up Dickie's neck almost up to his ears, tendons standing out on this thin neck, and he started to wonder if Dickie was gearing up to take a swing at him. Reflexively, he braced himself for anything. But before he had an answer to that question, Dickie turned and ran, jumped on his bike, and pedaled furiously down the road away from the playground.

A little while later, Raylee came up and knocked on the door. Conner answered and let her in. She had on pea-green knee-length shorts adorned with utility pockets and a blue short-sleeved shirt with a red stripe running down one shoulder. They sat at the kitchen table snacking on crackers and drinking milk, and Raylee told a story of how Dickie had come by her house and accused her of liking Conner better than him. As she was speaking, Conner blushed, and he secretly hoped that it was true.

"I don't know what gets into him," Raylee said. "It's not like I'm his girlfriend or anything. We've known each other all our lives. He's like my kid brother, for gosh sakes."

"I didn't mean to make him feel like we were excluding him," Conner said. Although maybe he didn't care all that much if he had. In truth, he was just happy to spend time with Raylee without Dickie hanging around them.

"You didn't. I didn't. Just Dickie being Dickie. But I guess I do feel a little bad. Maybe we could make it up to him."

"How?"

"Well, I have a new backpack I got for Christmas that I haven't used. Maybe the three of us could take a hike up the mountain and have a picnic. We could show him everything is okay."

"That sounds good," Conner said. "When do you want to go?"

"Why, you got something on your busy schedule today?" Raylee asked, smiling.

"No, of course not," Conner said with a scowl, "maybe we could meet back here around noon?"

"Sounds good; I'll bring Dickie. Don't worry. I'll straighten him out before we come and it'll all be fine. I've never seen this side of him before. He's so sensitive. I guess I never knew," she said, raising her brown eyebrows.

"Okay. See you then," Conner said, and Raylee headed out the door to her waiting bike.

Later that morning, Conner told his grandfather the plan, and he said that it sounded all right to him, and that Conner could take whatever he wanted out of the kitchen or the pantry to add to the lunch.

At the appointed time, Connor sat out on the porch of the Farm waiting for Raylee and Dickie. The sun was beating down with midday heat, alleviated only slightly by a northeasterly breeze that made the leafy green bamboo brush sway back and forth slowly at the tops. He noticed that his palms were moist and he had a tenseness in his stomach, like when he had to give an oral presentation in his Environmental Sciences class last year. He didn't need this stress. It just seemed so unnecessary. Freaking Dickie.

Conner saw Raylee and Dickie come riding up the hill on their bikes, Raylee wearing a red pack on her back. They both glided onto the grass, skidding their sneakers in unison until they came to a stop and laid their bikes down. Conner immediately noticed that Dickie avoided looking directly at him, choosing instead to scrape the edge of his sneaker on the lawn to dislodge a small dirt clump that clung to it.

"Dickie," Raylee said, turning to look at him. "Don't you have something to say to Conner?"

"Sorry," Dickie mumbled, still looking down at his sneaker.

"Nothing to be sorry about," Conner said, hopping up from the porch. "Let's get going."

Dickie accepted this quick change of subject with noticeable relief, and the three of them headed out past the barns and onto the woods road. As they walked along, grasshoppers buzzing in the grass, Conner surveyed the trees behind the Farm.

"You know, it just occurred to me: What about the guy, the watcher?" Conner said, realizing that in the heat of the "love triangle" dispute, he had forgotten all about the unnerving incident of a few weeks before.

"Nothing to worry about, my good lad," Dickie said. "I came prepared."

He pulled a sleek pearl pocketknife out of his blue shorts front pocket and opened the blade.

"I see you came prepared as well," Dickie said, his eyes locking onto the knife on Conner's belt. "Between the two of us, I think we can sufficiently intimidate and scare off any unseemly characters we might encounter in yonder woods."

"Wow, I feel safe now," Raylee said, obvious sarcasm in her voice.

Conner smiled.

They walked along the woods road and up the hill Conner had previously explored on his own and again with Gramp, eventually coming to the spring house at the end. Conner suggested they eat lunch there, but Dickie argued against it, saying they were barely out of the backyard. Raylee didn't object to extending the hike, and Conner begrudgingly agreed, but he still kept thinking about the watcher in the woods and Gramp's warning about venturing too far past the spring house. But after thinking about how Raylee had arranged the day as a sort of "peace offering" with Dickie, it didn't seem right to refuse the request, no matter how uneasy it made him. It was one thing to be out in these woods with Gramp at his side; he just felt safe with him, like Gramp could handle anything they might encounter with calmness and confidence. Dickie, on the other hand, left a lot to be desired in that regard.

It was a good day for hiking—clear sky, and the thick green trees keeping the temperature at bay. As they walked, the sunlight cut through the leaves, casting a golden lattice pattern on the ground. They followed a narrow game trail that led away north from the spring house, although it soon started to deteriorate to the point it felt to Conner like they were walking in the raw woods. The usual cadre of small birds flitted about in the brush, and tiny flies jiggled about in the sunlight, occasionally bumping into their faces. A quick brush of the hand sent them on their way. Conner patted his top pocket and felt the compass he had placed there, remembering what Gramp had said about how to find his way out of the woods should he ever get lost. He pulled it out and took a sneak bearing with it as they went. They were heading northwest. It was slight comfort, but comfort nonetheless.

A half hour later, the brush started to close in around them even more, tightening its grip on the small hiking party, and Conner was becoming more and more concerned about finding their way back. Just when he was about to say something, they came into a small clearing.

Conner felt a wave of relief when Dickie declared that yes, this was the spot to set up camp, even though they weren't camping but just having lunch. Conner and Raylee both nodded in approval. They gathered around a large flat rock that would serve as a picnic table, and Raylee fished around in the top of her pack, bringing out a brown paper bag. Wax paper–wrapped sandwiches and a yellow bag of potato chips appeared, and it dawned on Conner that he'd forgotten about Gramp's offer and had brought nothing to contribute. However, it seemed that Raylee, most likely sizing up the attention span and forethought of teenage boys, had brought everything they needed. She even had three water bottles and a Ziploc bag with brownies in it, and she carefully arranged everything on the rock.

"How far away from town do you think we are?" Dickie asked.

"Maybe a few miles," Raylee answered.

"Maybe not far enough, I think," Dickie stated.

"Far enough for me, especially with Conner's creeper hanging around," Raylee said, smiling. "Besides, you picked the spot, Dickie."

"Great, now I'm thinking about that again," Conner groaned.

"Do not worry, my young ward…remember, I have defenses," Dickie said, reaching into his pocket and pulling out his pocketknife again.

"Yeah, sure," Raylee said. "I'll bet you could give him a nasty paper cut that might require some ointment and a pink Band-Aid."

"Won't have to worry about that…just the sight of me being armed will scare him off!" Dickie replied, waving the small blade around in swirling circles above his head. Conner winced.

"Put that thing away before you give yourself a haircut," Raylee scolded. Dickie begrudgingly complied.

They talked and laughed as they ate their sandwiches and chips. They sat and talked for almost an hour, telling stories and the occasional off-color joke. Then they noticed, all at once, that black clouds were beginning to form on the horizon, and the woods, as if a light switch snapped, took on a menacing dark hue.

Conner ran his hand across the front of his neck and looked around. "I think we probably better get headed back."

"Aww…the boogeyman coming to get us, is he?" Dickie said.

"Yeah, sure…whatever. Let's get going. It looks like it's going to rain."

"All right, fine. Let's get moving, troops!" Dickie commanded.

They stuffed the crumpled wax paper, the baggie, and the lonely remaining brownie into the brown paper bag, and Raylee put it in her pack and zipped it shut. They headed off in the general direction they had come from, pushing their way through the thick brush and eventually landing on the same narrow trail. The clouds were thickening, blocking out what remaining sunlight there was and turning the sky to the blue-black of tar.

By the time they arrived at the spring house, the clouds were bubbling and churning, reaching down at them like giant hands. Thunderstorms in the area were notorious for coming on quick and leaving quick, but getting trapped and bouncing back and forth among the mountains like a caged lion waiting to be fed at the zoo, hitting the same spots over and over again with waves of biting wind and torrential rain. As the three finally approached the Farm, they could hear deep rumbles in the distance, and a stiff breeze began to swirl Raylee's black hair.

"Phew…I think we dodged a bullet there," Raylee said.

Conner nodded in earnest agreement. Being up on the mountain during a thunder and lightning storm was the last place he wanted to be. When he was nine, his family had taken a day hike along a river in central Virginia, and a predator thunderstorm had ambushed them. The flashes of brilliant strobe lightning and heavy crashes of thunder, topped off with wild winds and drenching waves of rain in a nightmarish cacophony, were etched in Conner's memory. They had resorted to huddling together in a ditch just off the trail, the trees above swaying and thrashing under the onslaught. From then on, every time he heard a rumble in the distant sky, his insides seemed to seize up involuntarily. His father, in contrast, seemed to enjoy and welcome the storms and would set up a lawn chair in the garage with the door open and watch them barrel through as he sipped on a beer. Conner did not join him in watching these spectacles. He was more comfortable hiding out in his bedroom, shades pulled and headphones on to drown out the sensory experience to the maximum degree possible.

"My knife!" Dickie suddenly cried out, startling Raylee and Conner. He frantically grasped the pockets of his shorts as if he was trying to extinguish some unseen flame. "It's gone!"

"What did you do, dummy, drop it in the woods?" Raylee asked.

"I don't know; I just had it, it was in my pocket, no…no, no, no!"

"Well, that's one knife that didn't last long," Raylee said, which struck Conner as being somewhat unsympathetic to Dickie's apparent anguish.

"We have to go back!"

"Are you crazy?" Raylee said. "There's a storm coming. There is no way we're walking back there for a stupid knife. You'll never find it anyway."

"She's right," Conner said. "It's too far…and you could have lost it anywhere."

"It's probably right there by that stupid rock. Come on, guys, let's go back," Dickie said, a tear glittering in the corner of his right eye.

"No way," Raylee said. "Maybe we could go back tomorrow and look for it."

Dickie groaned. "Someone could steal it!"

"Don't be stupid," Raylee said. "No one is going to steal it. Who's going to steal it up there? There's nobody up there. It's probably lying right there on the ground as you said. It will still be there tomorrow."

Dickie was still pawing around his pocket as if doing so would magically make the knife reappear.

"Look, I have to get going," Raylee said, picking up her bike and straddling it. "I'll catch up with you guys tomorrow. Don't worry, Dickie. We'll go looking for it tomorrow; I'm sure we'll find it," she said as she pushed off. Dickie remained silent as she picked up speed, accelerated past the playground, and disappeared down the hill.

Conner stood there with Dickie for a moment, feeling a little bit sorry for him. He reached down impulsively to check his knife, which was still there securely on his hip. "It's okay, Dickie, we'll go back there with you tomorrow and help you look for it."

Dickie just hung his head down and didn't say anything. After a minute of silence, and starting to feel awkward, Conner headed up to the porch. As he opened the screen door and started in, he paused and glanced back at Dickie, who was still standing there, now looking off into the woods.

Conner went inside the house, hearing the first drops of rain pinging the wire mesh of the door as it closed.

᠙

The next morning, Conner awoke early and got dressed in a pair of blue shorts and a red T-shirt. He went down for breakfast and saw that the house was quiet. There was yet another note on the kitchen table, held in place by the napkin holder. "Gone to town to pick up chicken feed and groceries, back around 3. Gramp." Conner set the note down and went to the cupboard to retrieve some cereal, more shredded wheat today, and pulled a bowl from the shelf. As he ate, he looked at the note again, marveling at the fact that, unlike his parents, Gramp did leave him to his own devices sometimes. He finished up his breakfast, washing his bowl and spoon and placing them in the wire drying rack beside the sink.

He sat in the chair next to the kitchen woodstove and pulled on his sneakers. He wasn't sure what to do next—one of those moments when you just sort of end up staring off into space, not knowing if you should stay in or go out, read or watch TV, get some work or chores done, or forget it all and go back to bed. He felt tired. The storms last night had shaken the house and lashed it with rain, lightning flashing brilliant white in his window, making it hard for him to fall completely asleep. He peeked out the kitchen window; it looked dark outside, the line of thunderstorms still lingering in the vicinity, he supposed. It was over now, but it looked like cannon mist hanging over a battlefield out there.

After a few minutes, he went outside. There was still a faint ozone smell, a telltale sign that a storm had recently passed. He started to think about his promise to Dickie, and he hoped that maybe he had forgotten about it. It certainly didn't look like the kind of day to go traipsing around in the woods looking for a pocketknife. He was just about to go into the barn and check on the chickens when he saw Raylee pedaling fast up the hill toward the house. She didn't bother to slow down when she reached the lawn, and just sort of let the bike hit the ground in a barely controlled crash, springing off it at the last moment.

"He didn't come home!" Raylee shouted.

"What? Who?"

"Dickie," she said, gasping for breath. "He didn't come home last night. His mother came over to our house this morning and said he never came home and did I know where he was. I told her about where we hiked to and that he had lost his knife, but that we had all made it back to your house and, and…" Tears ran down her red cheeks.

"Wait, you mean he never got home?"

"Yes. Didn't you hear what I just said? Dickie never came home last night."

Conner felt his head go numb, and his heart started to pound. Could he have tried to go back up the mountain last evening in search of his knife? It didn't seem probable. That would have been too crazy, even for Dickie.

"My dad, Dickie's dad, and Mr. Jenkins just left to go up and look for him," Raylee said.

"No one stopped by here."

"No, they said they were going to drive up North Road to the top of the mountain and walk into where we were from there, it's closer. I can't believe it. I can't believe that idiot would do something like this!" More tears slid down, creating a crisscross pattern on her face.

Conner turned and looked toward the tree line. "I'm sure he's fine. Maybe he just got turned around in the woods and got lost. I'm sure they'll find him."

"Maybe," Raylee said, sounding very unsure of herself, sniffing.

They sat down on the porch, still damp from the rain, and watched the clouds skitter across the sky. Raylee was starting to sob now, and Conner didn't know what to do. He put his arm around shoulders, and she immediately leaned hard onto his chest. "It's okay. I'm sure they'll find him," was all he could think to say again.

⅌

But they didn't find Dickie that day. Soon after the men had gone looking for him, Dickie's mother called the sheriff's office and reported him missing. A search party of game wardens and some of the town's residents had gone off looking for him, dividing up the mountain into grids and starting to search them, one by one. A rescue helicopter flew in from the south and was assisting in the search, arriving in the early afternoon. The deep drumbeat of its blades could be heard in the distance, getting louder and then quieter as it spanned the search area.

When Conner's grandfather arrived home from his errands, Conner told him what was going on, and Gramp quickly threw together a pack and headed up the mountain, joining the search. Conner asked to go with him, but Gramp told him to stay at the house in case Dickie came back. Dickie's father and his companions linked up with the game wardens at the spot where the three of them had had lunch, but there was no sign of Dickie or his knife. By the time the sun was starting to fade behind the mountains, there were no less than twenty-five volunteers and at least six wardens involved in the search.

Conner and Raylee sat on the weathered wood planks of the porch, watching what light remained in the sky grow dimmer and dimmer. They were worried about their friend and feeling slightly guilty. They had not considered the possibility that he might go off on his own to find his missing knife. A fat, silver-brown groundhog stuck its head up from under the decking and examined Conner and Raylee, unfazed and unaware of the drama unfolding, only curious why two people were sitting there disturbing its peace. There was nothing they could do now. Everyone, it seemed, was looking for Dickie. Conner told himself it would only be a matter of time before they found him. Lost, dirty with pine needles, green moss, and mud, hungry, but safe. They had to.

"I can't believe this is happening, it doesn't seem real," Raylee said.

"I'm sure they'll find him," Conner said, realizing he sounded like a broken record. He looked up at the sky, which was turning blue-black again. "I'm *sure* they will. Gramp is up there looking, and he knows every part of the woods."

"Dickie's such a freaking idiot. I can't believe he would go back up for a stupid knife," Raylee said, familiar tears forming again in the corners of her glowing brown eyes.

"It's okay…it will be okay," Conner said, but not convincing himself it was that certain.

Conner thought for a moment about where he was. Not six months ago, he was in school in Virginia, worried about his algebra grade and playing video games at night. Now, here he was at the edge of the world, concerned that his friend was lost alone in the woods, maybe even dead. It was surreal. He had been unnerved by the quiet and dark woods when he had first come up here, but over time, he had become more comfortable in his surroundings. Except for the mysterious stranger in the dark, he was becoming fond of the woods. The quiet, the pine needle smell, the chirps of small birds, and the rustling of the leaves high up in the trees. It was like he had always been here.

Now, as he looked off to the dark tree line standing like a black fortress wall, the feelings of fear and apprehension he had felt in the first few weeks were creeping back. To be lost in the woods—it was a terrifying thought. Turned around, confused, thinking every branch break or tree creak was a threat to your life. He especially couldn't imagine it at night, alone, and without the glow of a fire to bring comfort and warmth and ward off the creatures that hunt in the night. He suddenly felt alone, and for the first time, he allowed his mind to drift into dark spaces that made his spine go cold.

Maybe they wouldn't find him. Perhaps he was gone forever, swallowed up by the woods, never to be seen again. Conner felt his jaw clenching tight and heard the faint sound of his teeth grinding together. The only comfort: Raylee's warm shoulder was resting against his.

Chapter 6

The dream had been the same for as far back as he could remember. Conner saw himself as a little boy, four or five at most, and he was with his father in a huge department store picking out a birthday present for his mother. He walked down the long aisles, people zooming past with purpose wearing heavy thick coats to fend off the January cold in Virginia. His father brought him over to a big display case, where he rested his small hands on the glass, warm from the glowing lights within. His eyes immediately seized upon a pair of large, ornate diamond earrings set in thick gold, and he pointed to them and said, "Those."

His father spoke with the woman behind the counter, a towering woman with bright-red hair and cheeks to match, and she removed the earrings, discreetly brushing a thin film of dust off them and setting them on the counter. He nodded, yes, those, and the woman gave him a small smile. His father looked down at him and asked if he was sure. He said yes, he was. They were sparkling and beautiful, like pirate treasure from one of his books at home. His father paid the woman, and she placed them in a blue velvet box, wrapped it with purple string and a bow, and they turned and walked back through the aisles they had come through to get there.

His father told him that he needed to pick out something for her, as well, and they stopped in a department with bags and scarves hanging from hooks on the shelves. Across from the shelves were large circles of coats, and as his father looked over various items, Conner gravitated over to the coats. As he reached them, he realized that if he pushed them gently apart and slid in between them, the fur would softly brush past his cheeks as he went. He reached the center and grasped the cold metal pole that served as the primary support for the rack, suddenly aware that the jumbled symphony of voices and clacking of different shoes on the tile floor that echoed through the store was muted. In this semi-quiet, he imagined himself in a fort, protected from the Indians and wild animals that lurked just past the protective walls. Conner became lost in his fantasy, only realizing after a bit the need to get back to his father. When he pushed back through the barrier, the sounds and lights of the store seemed harsh and offensive. His father was not there. A cold chill came over him, and he began to panic, walking around trying to find him. Suddenly his father loomed before him, coming out of nowhere, his face red with distress and dragging in tow a skinny male clerk wearing a red vest. His father clasped his arms around him, at the same time scolding him for wandering off.

Later that evening, he gave the earrings to his mother after she had blown out the candles on her fluffy white birthday cake, and she made a big show of fawning over them, saying how beautiful they were, and thanking him for such a lovely gift.

She never wore them, however. Not once. Only when Conner was older did it dawn on him that they were nothing more than cheap gaudy glass earrings, and the appreciation his mother had shown him was nothing but a ruse—the act of a mother who loved him, but didn't like what he had carefully selected for her.

He usually woke up right then.

It was not the case this time. This night, the dream took a new turn from the moment when he hid in the coat rack. The light above him darkened, sending a jolt of fear through him, and the muffled voices he heard became more muddled, shifting down in tenor and tone, sounding more and more like animals grunting than people talking. Panicked, he crawled on his hands and knees to the outer edge of the rack, poked his head out, and looked around.

The store was empty and dark, no people in sight, and illuminated only by the dim yellow glow of the jewelry cases randomly scattered around. The animal sounds continued to grow and seemed to come from all sides, but whatever was making them remained unseen. He pushed himself out into the aisle and stood up, his breathing fast and irregular. He started to walk fast as he looked for the safety of his dad, but the edges of his view dimmed, the sounds grew louder, and soon Conner could barely see a few feet in front of him as he broke out into a full-on run. As he ran through a labyrinth of aisles, calling out to his dad, the racks around him began to pulsate, and black branches and vines began to unfurl and reach out and lick the edges of his pant legs as he ran. They started to hook around his ankles and arms, cracking and snapping and slowing him down as he struggled to keep going, but soon he was dragged to a complete standstill. As the roar of the animals reached a deafening pitch, the branches and vines rose up to cover his face. He couldn't breathe or see, and a scream rose in his throat like a black rubber plug he couldn't dislodge.

Conner awoke with a yelp, still trying to brush the branches off his face and chest, but all that was there was his T-shirt, soaked with sweat. He sat up in his bed, breathing fast, shaking, but quickly realizing that he was out of the dream and back in his room at the Farm, dimly lit by the light from the bathroom down the hall.

He struggled to catch his breath, and his thoughts turned back to Dickie. Still missing Dickie. He lay back down on his damp pillow, but sleep was over for this night.

❧

Gramp had made scrambled eggs with sour cream, making them light and fluffy, and strips of crispy, maple-smoked bacon that he smoked himself in a little smokehouse out behind the barns. They ate in silence, as they had the last few mornings. There wasn't much to say. Over a week had gone by, and Dickie was still missing. There was simply no sign of him at all. Conner suspected that his grandfather felt personally responsible for the failed search. He did, after all, know the woods in the area better than anyone else in town, and he could track and stalk animals like a Micmac Indian brave, or so he liked to say. Gramp didn't say it anymore. He couldn't find any sign or tracks that led to the lost boy, and it obviously weighed heavily on his mind. Dickie's parents had sunk into despair over the last few days, knowing that good outcomes for people lost in the woods generally happened within forty-eight hours of their going missing. That time had come and gone, and people were beginning to whisper that he was probably injured, or worse.

Conner finished up his breakfast and washed his plate, fork, and glass, setting them in the drying tray. Without a word to Gramp, he headed out the kitchen door, through the small barn to the big barn, to do his morning chores. The chickens were lively this morning, having become accustomed to Conner's presence in their little world. Conner opened the top of an old oak barrel and scooped out some feed with a cut-off half of a milk jug, and then opened the wire door leading into the coop. He sprinkled some food on the ground, which the chickens immediately clustered around, and then he opened the door leading out into the back pen. The sky was dull again today, threatening more dreary rain and cold. Conner sprinkled more feed in the back pen, three of the new, younger chickens immediately following him out, picking at the ground with their small beaks as they went.

Conner opened the second barn door to the interior goat pen and walked inside, two of the five goats standing at attention when he did, and left the door open so they could venture outside. He glanced back to make sure the outside gate was closed, having learned from experience that goats led a relatively dull existence, and an opportunity to explore beyond the confines of their pen was immediately seized upon.

Walking over to the wooden ladder leading up into the loft where the hay was stored, he climbed the wooden rungs. At the top, he swung himself around and went over to the neatly stacked hay. He reached down and grabbed a few armloads, dust and small flecks clouding around him. He carried it over to the edge of the loft and dropped it down to the goats, a big clump landing directly on the head of a brown-and-white one, and it bleated at the indignity. The goat gave a shake, and the hay fell to the floor of the pen, the other goats eagerly starting to chomp away. Conner didn't always feed the goats hay—vegetable scraps were always on the menu, and fresh grass still replenished itself regularly in the outdoor pen in spite of their constant munching. Sometimes, Gramp let the goats out into the field, where they chewed on weeds and grass and the occasional lettuce leaf if it proved too tempting. Gramp had told him that goats were the best natural weed munchers known to man if you kept them in line and away from the growing vegetables, and they had the added benefit of converting and depositing their food in the form of rich fertilizer for the crops.

Conner climbed down the ladder and went out into the pen, the goats and chickens wandering around, seeming to ignore each other. It was a perfect system, Gramp had said, each animal doing its job to keep the Farm running and in good shape. Symbiotic nature at its best. Every few weeks, they scraped up the chicken and goat manure and added it to a pile outside the barn. His grandfather had said you had to let it sit and "brew" for a time before you could lay it on the fields. If you used it too early on the crops, it could kill them. The manure pile was right next to a wooden compost bin that reminded Conner of a pauper's coffin, where each night they deposited their scrap vegetables, egg shells, and coffee grounds, providing further future sustenance for the growing rows of crops. No meat scraps were allowed. "Green manure," Gramp had called it. Conner gave a quick turn of the compost with a pitchfork, which had to be done to keep the decomposition process working uniformly. The first turn of the fork revealed a patch of eight or ten earthworms that they sometimes gathered for fishing excursions on the river and bog.

So far this summer, they had already harvested cucumbers, tomatoes, and kale, which Conner never ate when his mother served it, but it tasted just like fresh spinach to him. They also dug red beets and picked corn, snap peas, and a few other vegetables. They worked in the fields almost every day, weeding, watering, tending, and harvesting, and never seemed even close to the point of having everything "done." Blackberry and raspberry bushes were growing on a trellis near the barn, along with seven Duchess apple trees peppered with small red-and-green-striped apples. Conner had picked one once and bit off a little piece, but the strong sour taste made him spit out the chunk with a glob of drool.

All of their salads and vegetables came from the fields, and Gramp would barter some of it with neighbors in exchange for samples of their particular crops. The rest went to one of his friends who, for a small percentage, sold it at farmers' markets in the area. Gramp had told him that small farms and homesteads relied on each other, helping each other as best they could. It was a community, wholly removed from the commercial businesses that sought to destroy their competition any way they could.

Gramp canned some of the vegetables on the cooktop stove using a steel box he said had been made by an Amish-owned business nearer the coast. Conner was surprised to learn there were flourishing Amish communities in Maine, associating them more with Pennsylvania and Midwestern states. He and his grandfather sterilized the jars in boiling water, filled them with whatever they were doing that day, sealed them, and placed them back in the boiling water. Gramp also had a stout steel pressure canner—which looked like a robot—that he used to can other items, something to do with acidity, but Conner didn't quite grasp the concept. Gramp told Conner it was a meticulous process you had to do with the utmost precision, lest the results end up spoiling or worse, create toxins like botulism that could make you super-sick or even die. Conner wished his grandfather hadn't shared that particular information, and he looked at the mounting jars of canned goods in the pantry with a degree of trepidation from that point forward.

As the summer drifted by and surrendered its warmth and sun to the creeping chill of fall, Gramp explained they would shift to harvesting squash and pumpkins from the fields, adhering to the cyclical process that governed all farms. Control was only a perception, and a lousy one at that. He said you could no more dictate nature than you could lift off the ground and fly like a bird. You had to continually adjust to deal with what Mother Nature was serving up if you wanted to survive. Sometimes there was plentiful rain and ideal sunny conditions, and sometimes there was drought. It was all part of working on a farm. Some farms liked to hedge their bets by using chemicals to stimulate the crops and kill pests, but Gramp explained that all those things you put in the earth don't just go away, they become part of the food you eat, and part of the very ground itself. "You wouldn't sprinkle pesticides on your cornflakes in the morning, would you?" Gramp had said. "'Course not," Conner had replied. "Correct, so why would you put it in the earth where you grow your food?" It made sense. Gramp said the so-called "new" ideas of organic farming had been well known and practiced without a name by generations of small farmers, although he was supportive of the trend. In his opinion, many of the ailments that plagued people these days, like unhealthy weight and even asthma came from the poisons used to grow the food everyone gulped down from the supermarket without a second thought. "The sooner we get back to doing things the way we used to, the better off we will all be," he had said. Yes, it all made sense.

After he finished his animal feeding chores, Conner swept and straightened out the rest of the barn. In spite of everything that was going on, it felt good to see the space looking clean and orderly, and it gave him the early-morning satisfaction of having accomplished something worthwhile. He headed out the door to the road and walked across to the playground to think.

Conner sat on a swing, thinking about Dickie, and what, if anything, he could do. He came up blank. The search was continuing, and the thumping of the helicopter had been replaced by the buzz of a low-flying prop plane during the nights, searching for any sign of him. If Dickie had some matches or a lighter with him, he could start a fire, then put green boughs down on it to make it smoke. However, Conner didn't think Dickie would have any matches, in any event, especially given his sketchy history with fire. It seemed completely hopeless.

After a half hour of frustrating contemplation, Conner stood up and started down to the town center, thinking more as he walked. When he reached the bridge over the outlet, he noticed Raylee's bike up against the porch rail at Auntie's place, so he wandered over and climbed the steps.

He opened the screen door and peered inside, but no one was visible. He walked through the shop and into the kitchen, empty as well. Then he heard the sound of muffled voices coming from beyond the back door, so he went out. Raylee was sitting on the tattered remains of a cut tree stump in the yard, and Auntie was on her knees in the garden, wearing a bright-purple dress and a weathered hat that reminded him of the one the scarecrow wore in *The Wizard of Oz*. Raylee looked sullen and depressed, but Auntie was whistling a tune he didn't recognize and pulling up weeds with both hands.

She noticed Conner in the doorway and said, "Hello there, young Conner."

Raylee looked at him and said, "Hey."

"What brings you here today?" Auntie said. "Worry and fretting, I suppose."

She sounded way too cheerful, given the circumstances. Conner went over to the split-rail fence that ran alongside Auntie's garden and leaned against the top rail. The rail had thick splinters protruding in various places, and he shifted his elbow off a sharp shard. The fence had probably served some utilitarian purpose at one time, like keeping the roving deer out of Auntie's garden, but in its current condition, it couldn't keep out anything, he thought. There was a small red barn on the north edge of her property that looked like it might have been the home to animals at one time, but now it was silent and lonely. A rusting piece of farm equipment Conner could not identify rested along the wall on one side.

"Yeah, I suppose," he answered finally. "Heard anything today?"

"Nothing," Raylee said, studying her sneakers and kicking small dirt clods with her toe. Her sneakers were battered and worn, the rubber lips on the toes coming up on the sides, evidence of a summer of hard use.

"Well, they're still looking," Auntie said, focusing back on the weeds. "It will only be a matter of time. They'll find him. Tired and dirty and a bit skinnier, if that's even possible with that boy, but okay."

"How can you be so sure?" Conner said.

"Easy. Dickie is a good lad. A bit full of himself and prone to skullduggery, but a good lad nonetheless. I can't imagine the good Lord would think he needed to go quite yet. I'm sure they will find him soon, and he'll be back to his good old annoying self in no time."

"It's been a week and a half. How can Dickie be okay with nothing to eat?" Conner asked.

"Well, you can go a month without eating, and besides, blueberries are still around up on the mountain, and I expect he would have found some by now. As long as he found some water, he'll be just fine, and there's plenty of water up there. Like I said, skinnier, but fine. It's fortunate he didn't get himself lost in the middle of winter; then I'd be worried. He would have frozen up like a Popsicle. It's been warm these past nights. As I said, I suspect he'll be just fine."

"I wish I could be as confident as you," Raylee said, Conner silently agreeing. "He grew up here, and he's been up on that mountain a hundred times. There is no way he could have gotten lost."

"Oh, he could've got lost all right," Auntie said. "I've been here all my life, and there have been times I've gotten myself turned around in those woods. One time, I went up tipping balsam boughs to make wreaths with, and it started to get dark, so I made my way toward North Road. I started to get that nervous feeling when I didn't pop out when I thought I should have. The shadows started to fall across the trees, and it was getting darker. I felt like panicking, but I know that doesn't do any good, it'll just make you even more lost. Besides, I'm in no shape to be bounding over downed trees and crashing off rock piles in a panic. I just kept going for a spell, and wouldn't you know, I popped out on West Road, near two miles from where I thought I was. I have no idea how that happened, and if you had asked me, I could have sworn I was where I thought I was, but I wasn't."

The conversation wasn't making Conner feel any better. Worse, in fact. Surely this meant that Dickie could be lost just as quickly, and he could be wandering entirely in the wrong direction, away from the search parties and the plane.

"I don't know," Conner said. "I just have this weird feeling that something else happened, something more than him just getting lost."

Auntie stopped midway in pulling a small clump of yellow dandelions and studied Conner carefully. "You do, do you?"

"Yes…I guess so. It's just that I'm still thinking about the night I saw someone in Gramp's back field out the window—it just didn't seem right."

Auntie pulled a long weed out with her fingers, a clump of dirt hanging from the roots. "Well, I'm not telling you you're wrong. I learned long ago that the feelings I used to get were true more often than not. When I used to get them, I'd always be worried that others might judge me or think I was crazy, so I'd take those feelings, ball them up, and stow them away deep inside. As I got on in years, I stopped caring much what others thought of me, and I just let fly with whatever I'm thinking. Have you told your grandfather what you're feeling?"

"No," Conner said, looking at the ground. "I guess I felt the same way. I don't want him to think I'm just some paranoid kid from the city."

"He won't think that. Not in any case. You have to trust those feelings. Own them. Let them be part of you. Think of it this way: God gave you those eyes, and you believe what you see, don't you? He gave you those ears—and what nice ears they are, by the way—and you believe what you hear. God gave you taste buds, and you believe what you taste. He also gave you those feelings, and you should believe them, just the same as hearing and seeing and tasting. That's the way I look at it, anyhow. I think it would be best if you talked to him. Right soon, too."

"Okay," Conner said. "I will."

⁂

At dinner that evening, Conner told Gramp what he was feeling. Although he was understanding, Gramp still did not share the same concerns about the stranger. He said that Dickie was just lost, plain and simple, and hopefully, they would be able to locate him in the next day or two. It didn't give Conner much comfort. After dinner, he went to his room and lay on the bed, staring at the cracks in the ceiling that twisted, turned, and ran like little rivers on a topographical map around the yellow-brown water stains.

He glanced at the little bookcase filled with dog-eared children's books from bygone eras. Conner had thumbed through a few of them over the weeks, turning the yellowed, brittle pages and smelling the earthy smell that only old books can conjure. They had been abandoned for decades, longing for a child to read the words and look at the colorful pictures and smile with joy. One of the books was by Dr. Seuss, who he remembered from his younger years, *The Cat in the Hat* and all that, but not this one: *Bartholomew and the Oobleck*. It was about a king who was unhappy with the standard weather choices—rain, snow, sunshine, and the like—and wished for something new. His reward was a thick green muck called oobleck that eventually coated the unsuspecting kingdom and trapped all of its inhabitants in its gooey grasp. Sunshine saved the day, melting it away, the lesson presumably to be happy with what you have, because what you wish for might not turn out to be so great. That's how he felt—trapped in oobleck, unable to free himself.

There was more to this; he was sure of it. Moreover, he could not get past the image of the lonely figure smoking a cigarette off in the tree line. It would almost have been better if the person had come running to the window, screaming and yelling. At least then he would know who he was dealing with. It was the silence, the lack of movement, the quiet observing. It just wasn't right, and every time the image came back into his head, he felt cold and shaky. This person had to know something, just had to be responsible in some way. Conner was sure of it.

88

He sat up quickly and put his feet on the floor, thoughts crystallizing in his mind. If no one was going to do anything about it, he was going to have to do it himself. The very idea terrified him. Just months ago, he had been a city boy, as green as a Granny Smith apple. Now he was thinking of launching a rescue mission into the woods? It was absurd, stupid. But he couldn't shake the conviction that he needed to do something, *would* do something, and it became more real and tangible as the minutes passed. He knew he needed to tell someone about his plan. Not his grandfather— he would never agree to let him go. He wouldn't even let him go searching with him that first night. *Raylee.* They had grown close over the summer, so much so that she would sometimes complete his thoughts before he had a chance to say them out loud—like his father used to say *he* was (or used to be, that is) with his mother. Raylee would have to agree, and deep down, he hoped maybe she would come with him. They would have to find Dickie themselves. They had to *try*, at least.

⁊

The next morning, Conner gathered the items he would bring with him and put them in his backpack. A water storage bladder that fit into the pack, filled with spring water, weatherproof matches, a light-blue plastic survival straw for drinking water straight out of a stream, water purification tablets, three survival space blankets, a poncho, and a map of the county he had found in the glove compartment of his grandfather's truck. He also packed six granola bars from a box in the pantry, three apples, two bananas, an extra shirt and pair of socks, and, of course, his knife, his compass, and his cell phone, just in case. His father had bought the survival supplies for him before they had left for the trip. Can't be too careful, he'd said.

At the time, the thought of survival gear had seemed absurd; all his life they had lived in or near a city, and although the family sometimes took hikes in state parks, they had never gone off into the wild like this place. Conner tried to imagine his father as a small boy with his sister and Gramp coming up here to visit. He couldn't see it, but he concluded maybe there were things about his father he didn't know. The peace he felt up here was like nothing he had ever experienced, and he wondered how his life might have been different if his family had forgone the internet, the restaurants, and the buzz of the city to live simply in the country. Maybe they wouldn't be getting divorced. The idea was uplifting, but the reality was depressing.

He finished stuffing in the last of his items and zipped the pack closed. He wanted everything ready to go before he spoke to Raylee; if she said no, he would have to leave right away. She might decide to warn his grandfather of his plan. He didn't think she would do that, but he was not going to take the chance. Gramp had told him he was headed out early tomorrow to pick up some feed supplies and groceries, asking Conner if he wanted to come—which he politely declined, saying he just wanted to hang around the Farm and take care of the animals. Gramp didn't question his decision, understanding that maybe he just needed some time to himself. One time when he had asked his grandfather if he ever got lonely, he had told him no, "being alone is underrated." Gramp had said that people spend so much time trying to impress others with how much they know and filling any uncomfortable void in conversation with inane chit-chat, it sometimes did a person right to spend time alone with his thoughts. "Only when you are with just yourself can you be entirely yourself."

Conner looked through his drawers and picked out the clothes he would wear: his dark-green pants, a blue short-sleeved undershirt, and his jacket, and heavy socks to go with his hiking sneakers. He dug out his camo boonie hat and tucked a red handkerchief inside the band to make it fit more tightly on his head. He stashed his bulging pack at the foot of the bed and headed downstairs to do his chores. As he was finishing up, he heard the familiar sound of his grandfather's truck starting and driving out of the yard.

❧

Conner sat on the monkey bars in the playground waiting for Raylee. He had called her house on his cell phone, the first time he ever had, and told her he needed to talk to her about Dickie. She said sure; she would be right there. He wondered if she suspected what he was planning, but thought no, that was impossible. He couldn't even believe it himself.

A short ten minutes later, Raylee appeared coming up over the hill on her bike, crunching the gravel with her tires. "Hey," she said as she skidded to a stop and dropped her bike on the ground. "What's up?"

"Hey, Raylee. I need to ask you something, but before I do, I need you to promise you won't say a word to anyone about anything we talk about."

"How can I promise that if I don't know what you're going to ask? I hope you're not planning on robbing any banks."

"Just promise."

"Okay, okay, settle down, kiddo."

Conner told her his plan.

Raylee stared at him with eyes of disbelief. "It's not our fault. We didn't do anything wrong. We just went on a hike. How were we supposed to know he'd go back up there without us looking for a stupid knife?" Her hands were clasped on her thin hips like a displeased schoolteacher.

"Just the same, he wouldn't have gotten lost if it wasn't for us suggesting we go up there in the first place," Conner replied.

"Okay, so it's all our fault, but let me ask you something...are you completely nuts?"

"We can find him. You and me."

"How do you suppose we do that, dummy? If all the wardens and search parties couldn't find him, how the heck are we going to find him? They had a plane, a helicopter, and everything. We've got nothing."

"It doesn't matter," Conner said. "The fact is they haven't found him, and it seems like they're starting to give up, so we have to do it. Have you heard the plane today?"

"What are you saying?" Raylee said, sitting down on the edge of the merry-go-round. "You want to go up there and look for him?"

"Yes, exactly."

"That's insane. We'll never find Dickie. We'll probably get lost ourselves, and then they'll be looking for three lost kids instead of one. What does your Gramp think about all this? Did you tell him? Did you tell him what Auntie told you to tell him?"

"Yes, I told him how I was feeling. He listened, but I don't think he believed me. I didn't tell him about us going to look for him."

"*Us?* You assume a lot, kiddo. You didn't tell him because you know he'd tie you to a fence before he would let you do something that stupid. He knows a lot more than you do. You just got here, after all. You grew up in the city, and now you're talking about running off into the woods when you have no chance of finding Dickie, and you even want me to nod, hold your hand, and run off with you."

"I didn't just get here," Conner said, hurt and anger in his voice. "I've been here all summer."

"Oh-h…sorry; I didn't realize you were so sensitive about your level of outdoors experience," Raylee said, tipping her head to the side.

"It doesn't matter. I'm going. If you don't want to go, that's fine, leave me to it and don't say anything about it to anyone until after I'm gone. I'm going to leave my grandfather a note telling him I'll be back in a couple of days at most, with Dickie."

"You have completely lost your mind. You know that, don't you?"

"Maybe, but I'm going to do this, with or without you."

Raylee sat quietly for a moment and studied the mountains off in the distance. Conner could tell she was thinking about what she should do. It was all spinning in her mind. After a long couple of minutes, Conner stood up.

"Okay," Raylee said.

"Okay, what?"

"I'll go with you."

"You mean that?"

"Yes, stupid, I just said it, didn't I? I can't let you do something this insane by yourself. When are you going?"

"You mean *we*?"

"Yes, *we*. I meant… Jeez, you are a pain!"

"Right now. Go home and grab your backpack and some food and water, and we'll leave right now. I'll write the note and we can get started. You're not going to wimp out and tell, are you?"

"No," Raylee said, her eyes cold. "When I say I'm going to do something, I do it. You should know that by now."

Conner did know that. Raylee did what she said she was going to do, every time, without much concern for what others thought. It was the part of her nature that he admired most. Raylee stood up, picked up her bike, and straddled it. "I'll be back in twenty minutes." Then she left, pedaling fast around the corner and down the hill.

Conner walked back to the farmhouse and went into the kitchen. He found a notepad and worn-down yellow No. 2 pencil his grandfather kept on top of the fridge and started to write.

Chapter 7

True to her word, Raylee was back nineteen minutes later, backpack on her back. She wore a pair of tan hiking sneakers with blue laces, summer-worn blue canvas pants, and a dark-green windbreaker. Conner had finished up the note and tucked it under the candle on the kitchen table. He had kept it short, saying it seemed to him the search for Dickie was losing steam, and he and Raylee were going to do some looking on their own, and not to worry, they would be back in a couple of days. For a moment, Conner pictured Gramp reading the note through his reading glasses, and tried to imagine what his reaction might be. It wasn't good.

Conner walked out onto the porch, closed the kitchen door, and he and Raylee headed silently along the path by the barns and turned onto the road leading up the mountain.

The air was crisp, the first sign of summer's demise and fall creeping into the region. Two chipmunks and a red squirrel scurried about among the trees, collecting acorns and seeds for the impending onslaught of winter. Conner and Raylee walked side by side at first, then in single file, Conner in the lead, as they rounded the wet area on the road. Conner paused for a moment and surveyed the woods, Raylee stopping short and almost bumping into him. The breeze was light, so the woods were quiet except for the occasional rustling of the leaves in the trees.

At the top of the hill, they veered left, walking side by side again as the road widened and turned toward the dark area that housed the spring house. They stopped at the spring house and drank from the tin cup to conserve the water they were carrying.

"Okay, Chief, where to now?" Raylee asked, wiping her arm across her mouth.

"Back to where we had lunch; that's where we should start looking."

"Copy that."

"'Copy that'?"

"Yeah, with that hat on, you look like a soldier, so I thought maybe we should throw around some military jargon. My cousin David was in the army for six years. He talks like that all the time now."

"Well, okay, I guess," Conner said, not sure if she was making fun of him or not.

Seeming to sense this, Raylee said, "Relax, kid, the hat looks nice. I'm just joking with you. You look quite capable in it."

"Affirmative," Conner said, smiling, and they started to walk again.

They continued up the narrow path in the woods that led to the clearing. Conner examined the trail as they went, looking for any signs that Dickie might have come this way. Before they left Virginia, his father had given him a book on outdoor skills and survival that included a section on tracking game, and Conner had read portions of it on the ride and later in his room at the Farm. He looked for any broken branches or turned-over dirt or leaves, specifically for any recently made footprints that showed moisture. He saw nothing. The book contained images of the tracks all sorts of animals left behind, from raccoons to skunks to deer and moose. Conveniently pictured next to the tracks were images of their scat, and the detail in the drawings made him feel a little queasy. He sincerely hoped he wouldn't find any Dickie scat.

Finally, the woods started to open up into the clearing where they'd had lunch. They found the rock that had served as their dining table that day and stopped to look around once again.

"Dickie!" Raylee shouted, startling Conner, who reacted with a jerk.

"Shhh!" he hissed.

"Why? We want to find him, don't we?"

"I don't know…just don't yell like that."

"Yessir, Captain," Raylee said, rolling her eyes.

Conner scanned the edges of the clearing, seeing nothing but dark trees and brush. He examined the ground surrounding the rock, trying to spot any sign that Dickie had been back to this spot, but again saw nothing. They spent the better part of an hour poking around the clearing, looking at the ground, mostly in silence. Then, on the north end of the area, Conner noticed a small opening in the trees. The branches curved in around the top, giving it a cave-like appearance. It became progressively darker as it went in, finally turning to black. The size of the opening made Conner think it was an animal trail of some sort, probably for foraging deer and moose, or, God forbid, a bear, to pass through.

"Let's go through there," Conner said, gesturing to the opening.

"Why?" Raylee said. "If he did come back up here, he wouldn't have gone that way. He'd have gone back down the mountain the way he came."

"If he had, he wouldn't be lost."

Raylee thought about it for a minute but Conner knew she couldn't argue with the logic. "Maybe he got turned around or something," he said, "and headed that way by accident."

"I don't know…"

"Let's go that way for a while…look," Conner said, producing a small roll of flame-orange plastic tape from his jacket pocket. "I found it in Gramp's tool drawer. We can cut off little pieces and tie it to the trees as we go. That way, we can find our way back."

"Okay, Hansel," Raylee said, "you're the boss."

⚘

In silence, Conner and Raylee walked single file along this new path. The woods were quiet, the breeze too weak to penetrate the dense green roof of branches above their heads.

Maybe this is crazy, Conner thought to himself. All those searchers hadn't been able to locate Dickie, what made him think that he and Raylee could? Any way you looked it at, it didn't make sense for them to be doing this. He had a feeling deep inside that was urging him on, almost pulling him forward from the center of his gut, to keep searching. It was one of those feelings Auntie had told him to trust, and he would, at least for a while.

They came to a rise of ledge covered with thick tree roots that snarled across to the top. Conner stepped on each one like stairs, making his way up with Raylee close behind. At the top, Conner could see the path they were on starting to dissipate. It branched off in three different directions down the back side of the rise. Figuring that the most straightforward solution was always the best, he followed the middle trail, which led them down into a gully. At the bottom, the path turned to the right, and through the trees, Conner could see another clearing. At the edge of the tree line, he saw that the trail led into an open area of tall grass and dead trees, standing like gray ghost soldiers guarding the entrance to their territory. As they followed it, the path meandered right and left, seeming to avoid the wetter, muddier patches of ground. Despite nagging doubts, Conner thought they were on the right trail. There was design to the route, indicating a presence of thought, although he couldn't entirely dismiss the idea that it could be just animals choosing the path of least resistance.

Just as they were about to reach the woods on the far side of the clearing, he caught something out of the corner of his eye. It was a small, dark shape, starkly out of place in the yellow-brown grass. He walked over to it, looked down, and realized it was a black sneaker—dirty and covered with twigs, but a sneaker for sure. He saw immediately it was the same brand Dickie wore like a part of his anatomy all summer long. His heart skipped a quick beat, and he bent down to pick it up.

"Look!" he said, pulling the sneaker free from the mud with a slurp and holding it out in front of him like found treasure.

"Whoa!" Raylee said, her eyes widening. "That's Dickie's sneaker!"

"I think it is," Conner said, cradling the sneaker in his hands and looking around the clearing for any sign of the owner.

"Dickie!" Raylee shouted. "Dickie!"

Nothing; just the raspy sound of the breeze blowing over the grass.

"What should we do?" Raylee said, still in shock. "Should we go back and tell everyone what we found?"

"No. We keep going," Conner answered, hoisting his backpack off his shoulder, opening the top zipper, and placing the sneaker in the pack. He looked around on the ground and found a piece of broken branch from one of the trees. Using both hands, he pushed one end of the stick into the earth, twisting right and left until it squished down into the mucky ground. He removed the roll of orange tape from the front pocket of his backpack and unfurled a twelve-inch length. Reaching around to his right side, he pulled his knife from its sheath and neatly cut the tape. He took the strip and tied it securely around the top of the branch about three feet above the ground.

"Why?" Raylee asked. "Why don't we go back? They'll want to know what we found."

"He's been out here for days," Conner replied. "He could be just ahead. If we go back now, by the time they get out here, it will be way past dark. We have to keep looking now."

"How did he lose his sneaker—did you think about that? He didn't just walk out of it and not notice."

"I don't know, and I don't care. We need to find Dickie as soon as possible. We can't wait for anyone else to do it. There's no time."

Raylee didn't argue. She just glanced around the clearing as if Dickie would pop up from the grass at any moment, yelling, "Here I am!"

He didn't.

They continued on the path, and Conner could see that directly ahead it went back into the woods. There's no turning back, he thought—cliché, but the truth. His instinct was telling him they needed to keep going. It was the only way to find Dickie; he was sure of it. Wasn't he? Yes, he thought, ignoring the argument going on in his head. Yes, he was sure. Raylee followed behind him without a word.

As they went on along the trail, Raylee sipped from her canteen and Conner from the hydro straw in his backpack. They stopped in a shallow gully for granola bars and some chocolate candies Raylee had brought, dark shadows creeping across the forest floor as the afternoon sun slid slowly down through the trees.

"We're getting pretty far in," Raylee said, pushing a sweaty patch of black hair off her forehead.

"I guess so," Conner replied. Her remark reminded Conner to tie off another orange tape strip to a branch along the path, which he had been doing about every fifteen minutes of the hike.

"Even if we turn around now, we're not going to make it out before dark."

"That's okay, I brought a headlamp, and I have an extra flashlight in my pack."

"I don't think it's a good idea to be stumbling through the woods in the dark, even with a light. We should find someplace to make camp and start a fire. We're going to need more water, too."

Conner was impressed with Raylee's practical, no-nonsense survival instincts. He supposed that growing up in a remote area had something to do with that. They had already crossed a few small streams and brooks and decided that they would stop as soon as they found the next one. It didn't take long—a short half mile away, they came upon a thin brook burbling a channel through the moss-covered ground.

"That looks good over there," Raylee said, pointing to an open, level area surrounded by trees about twenty feet from the brook.

"Okay, sounds good."

They scrambled up a short rise, dropped their packs on the ground, and stood for a second, each waiting for the other to say something. Raylee finally broke the silence. "Well, I suppose you don't want a big fire in case a search party spots it and comes swooping down on us?"

"I guess. What should we do?"

"Dakota fire hole," Raylee said. "My dad taught me to build one."

"What the heck is that?"

"You'll see. Just go gather up some dry wood."

Conner spotted a downed tree some yards away and walked over to it. It had fallen some time ago by the looks of it, stripped of bark and dull gray in appearance. Conner started to snap off some of the branches and throw them in a pile, placing his foot where they grew out from the trunk to gain leverage. When he had enough for an armload, he gathered them up and walked back to the clearing. Raylee was digging a small hole with her hands, occasionally using a stick to break up the soil. Conner dropped the wood and sat down, asking if he could help. She said no, it was a one-person job. She kept digging until her shoulder reached ground level, then started to rotate her arm and bring out clumps of dirt.

"What are you doing?" Conner asked.

"Widening the base."

"What for?"

"Just wait, you'll see."

Raylee continued to pull dirt up from the hole, then finally stopped and said, "One last thing to do." She walked over to a stand of tall grass and plucked a wispy blade, holding it up to see which way it moved in the wind. Conner restrained himself from asking what she was doing this time; he didn't want to be admonished for his impatience yet again. Raylee walked back to the hole, moved to the side from which the breeze was blowing, and started to dig another, smaller hole at an angle about a foot from the first hole. Conner could see that it would eventually intersect the bigger hole. Her arm reached into the hole, the black dirt clinging to her arm like a dark sleeve more and more with each scoop she dragged out. Finally, with a little jerk of her shoulder, Conner could tell she had broken through, and she pulled out her arm.

"There, your basic Dakota fire hole," she said.

"Okayyy…How does it work?"

Raylee crossed her arms in an overdramatic fashion. "Simple, dummy. We put some twigs and a few of the sticks into the hole and light it up, then once it gets burning, we add in more wood. The chimney here is on the side the wind is coming from; the wind goes over the chimney and creates a draft that pulls air into the bigger hole, letting the fire breathe. The fact that it's mostly underground means no one can see the flames, and there won't be much smoke, either, if the wood is good and dry."

Conner shook his head in disbelief. There were no girls from his class back home who would know how to build a Dakota fire hole, or even know what one was—not that they would care.

Raylee placed dry twigs and grass in the hole, and Conner lit one of his waterproof matches, reached his hand down into the hole, and ignited them. It burned slowly at first, sending up a weak puff of gray smoke, but soon a solid orange glow began emanating from the hole. Raylee carefully fed in a few more sticks, saying they should wait a bit to get it going before adding any more. In the meantime, they walked over to the stream, and Raylee filled her canteen and Conner his backpack water bladder with stream water. Conner produced the small, greenish-brown water purification tablets that looked like baby aspirin from his backpack and plopped one of the pills into each. They shook the containers and let them sit, per the instructions on the bottle. Conner showed her his survival straw, which she had never seen before, explaining that you could drink straight from a stream if you had to. "That's great—we can drink out of mud puddles if we get desperate enough," she said, smiling.

The light from the sky turned deep orange behind the trees, the sun only peeking through occasionally, and the darkness began to crawl in around them like black fingers. The glow and crackle of the fire was a comfort, though, and they both positioned themselves on the side of the hole away from the air vent, slowly feeding in small sticks as the time passed. They ate a granola bar and an apple each from Conner's pack, pitching the cores off into the blackness that now enveloped them on all sides.

"I'm sure we'll find him tomorrow," Raylee said, surprising Conner with the sound of optimism in her voice. "I'm positive."

"We will," Conner replied, but the sound of his voice gave away his inner doubts.

They spread one of the Mylar survival blankets on the ground, looking like a large piece of crinkly tinfoil, and at Raylee's suggestion opened a second one and pulled it around their shoulders as they watched the warm glow from the pit. Conner couldn't help but immediately fixate on her shoulder leaning warmly against his. His insides felt nervous and twisted, but comforting and secure, all at the same time. Despite all of this—Dickie lost, their going off without permission on their own to find him in the woods, now enveloped by pitch darkness on all sides—there was no place Conner wanted to be more than right there. Sitting next to Raylee under a foil blanket.

❧

Conner awoke with a start, shifting awkwardly into a half-sitting-up position, breathing fast and his heart racing. There was a dim flickering glow coming from the fire hole, gasping its last embers. He glanced left in a panic, thinking for a brief moment that Raylee was gone. No, there she was, on her side wrapped in the Mylar, and he could hear her soft breaths. He rubbed his face, feeling tiny grains of sand in the tear ducts of his eyes, and he dug them out with his fingernail and dragged them down his cheeks, flicking them away. His breathing started to slow to a rhythmic pace, and he looked around at the dark trees. His eyes were adjusting to the darkness, and he could see an area of deep, black-blue sky through the treetops.

What woke him up? He couldn't remember dreaming anything, just the uncomfortable in-and-out sleep that comes with being on the forest ground. The breeze had dropped down to an almost imperceptible level, and he couldn't hear anything in the woods. Still, he was very uneasy, like hearing a nighttime knock at the front door right before you turn on the porch light.

Suddenly, he noticed something about twenty feet out beyond the clearing, a white patch almost hovering in the air. It was motionless, about six feet off the ground, just floating there. He squinted a bit to make it out, and to his horror, he saw eyes and a nose forming on what was without a doubt someone's, or something's, pale face in the blackness. The face was looking directly at him, black recesses where the eyes should have been. His insides froze violently, numbness swept over him, sharp needle sticks of pain in his face, and he felt a cry rising, pushing to burst out of his mouth. Before he could release it, the crash of boot steps came from behind him, then a hard thud to the back of his head that he heard before he felt, his teeth slammed together, and the lights snapped off.

Chapter 8

Granville sat at the kitchen table next to the two game wardens, Jim, as solid as a potbelly stove, and Harry, tall, lean, and hard as a red maple tree, reviewing a spread-out creased map. The wardens were both wearing forest-green uniforms with thick vests, radios and pistols secured purposefully on their hips. Granville had arrived home late in the afternoon, not finding Conner, as he had expected, but finding the note—the note that threatened to irrevocably and forever darken his world. He had called the warden service and Raylee's parents as soon as he read it, dropping it on the floor the second he reached Conner's signature, and it didn't take long for the news to spread through the town like the flu. His phone had started ringing shortly after, and he answered it religiously with the hope that there was good news on the other end. But it was only friends and neighbors expressing their concern and asking how they could help. Granville politely, but quickly, ended each call with a "thanks, I'll let you know" to free up the line.

"We're going to search the same grids we've been searching," Jim said. "You're sure you think they went up this road to the top?"

"Yes," Granville replied, quiet, sullen. "To the place they had a picnic."

He looked down at the map, still in a state of disbelief that Conner had done something so stupid, so foolish. And Raylee had gone along with it, that was the kicker. He thought her to be a more practical thinker than that. Her mother had looked at him like he was a criminal when she came to the house after finding out what had happened—her daughter dragged into danger by some reckless delinquent kid from away. It would be a long time before everything was right again in this town, he thought, and if anything happened to them…then never.

The only real honest-to-goodness tragedy he could recall before Dickie disappearing was when he was a boy and one of the homes near the pond had caught fire and a small girl, barely six years old, perished. She had actually been one of the cutest kids the town had ever managed to produce, light red hair, always in pigtails, a slightly turned-up nose, sand-colored freckles, and green emerald eyes that seemed to light up a path in the fading evening light wherever she walked. For more than a year after the tragedy, sadness hung over the town like a black fog. People who typically greeted each other cheerfully in the town center, chatting about the weather or what mischief their kids or animals had been up to, were curt and stern. The girl's family had left after the fire, choosing not to rebuild, never looking back. Too many memories, he supposed, memories that would be skinned raw at the mere sight of the rope swing dangling from the tree in the yard where she used to play, not a care in the world.

And now, one child was missing, possibly dead, and two others were missing. How much sorrow could a small town take before it reached its critical mass? Tragically, towns often seemed to become synonymous with the bad things that happened in their midst, those things becoming part of their forever identities. Newtown. Columbine. Waco. You didn't even need to say what happened there, everyone immediately knew, and it seemed impossible to erase the association. In Maine, this could be the fate for Morgan Township: the small town where children disappear, never to be seen again.

"Okay," Harry said, "they couldn't have gotten too far. We'll find them." He sounded so sure of himself, but Granville knew better. It was the warden's job to appear confident in his and his agency's abilities, but it was just an illusion. A made-up line that he had probably perfected over years of comforting the families of lost souls. Most of the time, it all worked out and the person was found unharmed. Other times it didn't, and that statement would hang in the minds of the inconsolable families forever, helpless to change the outcome. They just had to turn to whatever faith they believed in, clinging to it like a child with a favorite blanket or stuffed animal, forever wishing they could have done more.

Not this time, he thought.

"I'm going to start at first light," Granville said.

The wardens looked at each other, then back to him. "I'm not so sure that's a good idea," Jim said. "You're too emotional right now. Better you leave it to us. We'll have the chopper and plane flying over the area. If there is any sign of them, or smoke or something, they'll be able to spot it first. We're already contacting the people that participated in the last search. There's nothing you can do. It's better you wait here in case they come back."

"I'm going," Granville said, standing and looking Harry straight in the eyes, unflinching. "You're welcome to try and stop me if you want, but I wouldn't advise it."

Harry flashed a resigned look at Jim. "Well…okay, I'm not going to try and stop you, but you have to be smart about this. We have a radio and GPS in the truck you can take with you. Just check in at the top of every hour and give us your position and status."

"Okay," Granville answered. He wasn't going to argue, and it seemed a reasonable request. He got up from the table and headed toward the dining room and his den, stopping to look back at the wardens from the doorway. "I'll leave the place unlocked; use it for your search party base if you like. There are drinks in the fridge and food in the pantry—help yourselves. I'm going to ask a friend down the road to tend to the animals." He couldn't believe he was thinking about chores, but the animals needed to be fed, watered, and tended to, and none of this was their fault. They were blissfully going on with their daily routines, eating, drinking, pooping, and occasionally scrapping with each other. He envied them.

He had left a message for his son but hadn't been able to speak with him yet, but he hoped he'd be able to before he left. He wasn't sure what he was going to say. It wasn't going to be a good conversation, that much was certain.

❧

Conner opened his eyes briefly, seeing nothing but feeling a scratchy cloth on his face, tied tightly around his neck. He was lying on what felt like a net with hardwood on either side, his arms bound at the wrists in front of him, and his feet tied together at the ankles. He struggled to get a clean breath, hindered by the material around his face. He could sense movement, as though someone was dragging him, bumping up and down over roots and rocks as they went. For a moment, there was a pause, and he heard the muffled voices of two people talking, but could not make out any words. He started feeling lightheaded with an aching pain in the back of his head that pulsated and throbbed with each beat of his heart. The fear and horror he began to feel were quickly replaced by a thick fog as he drifted in and out of consciousness.

When he next awoke, Conner felt that he was stationary, lying down, cold air tumbling over his exposed hands and the steady droning of a small engine filling his ears, like the hum of the generator his neighbors in Virginia used during power outages after strong thunderstorms. His face was still covered, and breathing was a challenge, the air compressed around his nose and mouth. During a moment of semi-clarity, he thought of Raylee. Where was she? What was happening to her? Was she okay? There were no answers to the questions he was asking silently to himself. He couldn't muster the strength to move or fight. He felt paralyzed, though aware of the awful thing that was happening to him, but it was like a sweaty nightmare. Then he started to fade out again, feeling like he was falling into a black hole in the earth. What was happening to him? Then darkness took hold once more.

⁊

He was lying face down in the dirt, pitch black all around. His hands and feet were unrestrained, and he lay there for a moment grabbing at the earth with his fingers. Conner pulled his face up and looked around, but couldn't see anything. Lifting his head caused a sharp pain to shoot from his forehead down his spine, and he put his face back down onto the ground. Spit lingered in the corner of his mouth, and he sucked it back, only to immediately taste bitter dirt in his mouth. He spat it out, repulsed.

"Who's there?" An alarmed voice pierced the darkness. "Who is it?"

The voice startled Conner, and he immediately lifted his head back up with another jolt of pain, his body still flat on the ground. Recognition dawned.

"Dickie?" Silence. "Dickie? Is that you?"

108

"Conner?"

"Yeah, it's me."

"Is that really you?" Dickie blurted from somewhere out in the black.

"Yes," Conner replied, hearing the quick thuds of footsteps coming his way.

"I can't believe it's you!"

Conner felt the kick of a sneaker straight into the bridge of his nose. "Ow!"

"Sorry; I didn't mean to!" Dickie blurted. "I can't believe you're here!"

"Where's here?" Conner replied, a little surprised at how calm his voice sounded, a slight trickle of warm blood coming out of his left nostril. He had always been prone to bloody noses as a child, something he had inherited from his mother. One time, in a park with his mother, a gusher of blood had squirted out of his nose without warning, cascading down his shirt like a red lava flow. As his mother held a rag to his face, he had gotten glimpses of the terrified faces of the children around him. He figured it probably looked to them like his whole head had exploded.

Conner pushed himself up onto his elbows and wiped the blood on his sleeve. He was still dazed and foggy in his mind, even before the unexpected blow to the face, courtesy of Dickie's sneaker. He felt a pair of hands grasp at his shoulders, and he could make out the shape of a head right in front of his face as he rose up into a sitting position with Dickie's help.

Dickie was panting. "I don't know. I don't. I've been in this room for days. I never thought I'd see anyone I knew ever again. I can't believe you're here! I heard the door open a little while ago, but I just kept my eyes shut. I can't believe you're here!"

"Where is *here*, Dickie?" Conner asked a second time.

"I don't know. Really. I went up looking for my knife, and can you believe it?—I found it, right by the stump!"

Conner thought this tidbit and Dickie's apparent happiness over it seemed oddly inconsequential given the current situation.

Dickie sat directly in front of him, his breathing slowing slightly. "I started back down the mountain just as the rain was getting worse, and I tripped over a stick or something, and the next thing I knew, I woke up here, in this room. That was days and days ago. I yelled at first, but a voice shouted at me to shut up or he'd gut me like a pig. I don't know, I was scared to say anything after that. I've just been quiet. I cried for two days, but finally ran out of tears, and I've just been in this room ever since. I can't get out. The door's locked, I've tried it. During the day, the sun shines through the walls—it looks like a barn or shed or something. I hear voices and animals making noises, but nothing else. There's a little door over there next to the big door, kind of like a dog door or something. Whoever it is outside has been sticking trays of old food and a jug of water through it every day. They tell me to send the tray and jug back out, and I have. I can't believe you're here! I'm so happy!'

"What are you happy for?" Conner said. "I'm stuck in here too now."

"You don't understand; I've been alone this whole time. I've never been so scared. I didn't think I'd ever see anyone ever again. But now you're here!"

"That's great," Conner said, "I'm very happy for you."

Suddenly Conner's mind began to click again, and he realized he had forgotten Raylee. "Is Raylee here? Have you seen her?"

"Raylee's here with you?" Dickie blurted.

"I don't know. What I mean is that we were together, we came looking for you on our own, and then someone came into our camp last night and hit me on the back of the head."

"You mean you're not with a rescue party?" Dickie sounded immediately deflated.

"No. They've been looking for you for days, but they weren't able to find you. It seemed like they were slowing down and might stop, so we decided to come looking for you on our own."

"That was freaking stupid!"

Conner wasn't quite sure how to respond to that. "I guess you're right."

They sat in the dark, and Dickie described to Conner what his imprisonment was like. Voices during the day, silence at night. And the ritual of the tray and plastic milk jug filled with nasty-tasting water passed through the little door. He said there was a small wooden pail in one corner of the room where he'd been going to the bathroom. He had managed to hold his number two for three days, but it finally got the best of him, and he went, defeated. He sounded disgusted with himself, as if he had degraded himself to the level of an animal. Conner described in more detail how he and

Raylee had devised the plan to find him, then how they had walked along the trail and eventually found his shoe. Dickie said when he woke up in the barn, he was only wearing one sneaker. He didn't know what had happened to the other one. Fleetingly, Conner thought it was too bad the foot without the sneaker hadn't been the one to slam into his face. He described how they had made a fire and camped near a stream, and then he described the terrible moment in the night when he'd seen the face. Just repeating the story made a chill run down his back again and straight through his front into his stomach.

"We have to find Raylee," Conner said.

"How do you expect to do that?" Dickie said, his voice starting to ramp up in frustration and fear again.

"I don't know. But we have to make sure Raylee's okay. I got her into this. Or, more accurately, *you* got me into this, and then I got her into this."

"Hey, it's not my fault!" Dickie protested, whining. "These people are crazy. I only wanted to find my knife. I didn't ask to be kidnapped and thrown into a dungeon."

Conner took a deep breath. "I'm sorry. I know you didn't mean for any of this to happen… I'm just worried, that's all. She has to be here. She has to."

The two of them kept talking, going back over the events, until they found themselves repeating what they had already said. Wherever they were, and whoever was holding them here, it wasn't right, they agreed on that point. They eventually settled into an uncomfortable, tired silence, waiting for daylight to break.

❧

Granville paused in a clearing, looking carefully at the ground for any signs of the kids. The morning light was starting to creep over the tops of the trees, still casting shadows throughout the clearing. It was cooler this morning, dropping into the low sixties. Not cold by Maine standards at all, but cool enough to make him worry about two—no, make that three—kids spending the nights alone in the woods.

A crow squawked from a nearby tree, gazing at him with a wary eye, this unwelcome intruder into his realm. A chipmunk sprang from a nearby stump, hesitated, then scurried under a rotting log. Granville usually would not have paid much attention to the little creatures of the woods; they were such familiar companions. But today he noticed everything, the adrenaline of the hunt flowing through his veins making everything—the sky, the trees, the ground he walked on—look incredibly sharp and clear to his aging eyes. Eyes that had once required heavy prescription glasses were now almost 20/20 after the cataract surgery of a few years back. He had worn glasses since he was eight years old, and it was strange to adjust to a life without them, the familiar pinch and weight no longer on his nose. Glasses, when he was child, were not the sleek, lightweight models the kids sported today, or more often than not, contact lenses. He had no difficulty understanding the origin of the derogatory term "Coke-bottle" glasses, the thick chunks of glass leaving indents on his nose every day. Funny how things like that can work out, he had thought after the surgery. A disease that at one time in history had meant the eventual loss of vision now provided a path to freedom from a life of prescription lenses.

Granville stared at the ground for what he sought and quickly found it: bent-over grass, sneaker imprints in the mud. The tracks were easy to find; they went all the way up the hill from the Farm, and he had followed them as easily as following rabbit tracks in fresh snow. Granville shifted the weight of his pack on his back and moved his .30-30 rifle from hand to hand, every so often scanning the ground, more from a nervous tic than from arm fatigue. He followed the footprints until they led to the back of the clearing, where he saw the tracks led into the opening of a small game trail. Granville stepped into the threshold of the path and immediately noticed the orange tape tied to the branch of a pine. Smart kid, he thought, smiling. Conner was marking the trail.

Granville suppressed the urge to charge down the trail. Now more than ever was the time to be cautious and deliberate, watching for any sign of a change in direction. There would be no time to backtrack if he made a wrong assumption of where the next marker might be. He would be putting his years of woodsman skills to the test, a test he did not intend to fail.

He took his first deliberate steps along the trail, pausing every ten steps to look around at the ground and the surrounding trees. It was a skill his father had taught him for stalking deer. Aside from knowing the wind direction and keeping any game upwind of your position, careful steps and pauses were the best way to find quarry. Walk too fast, and you'll probably end up going right past them, his father had said. Deer were not stupid, and if they thought you didn't see them, they tended to freeze in place and let you drift right on by, completely unaware of their presence. Stopping and looking around might be all you need to make them nervous and get them to reveal their position. The technique worked well, as was evident by the collection of deer antlers on his barn wall. Hunting deer up here was not about antlers, though; it was about meat, pure and simple. Every year his family had counted on a deer harvest to supplement the protein the family needed during winter, and his father managed to get one every year without fail. Granville was unsuccessful his first few times out, but by the time he was twelve, he was able to harvest one each season with his father's help, albeit smaller and younger ones, more prone to making mistakes. The adult bucks his father tracked and shot were older and more experienced, wise to the tactics hunters employed. Only a skilled hunter with extreme patience and a second sense for stalking prey would be successful in the pursuit of them. Over the years, he had perfected his technique, to the point that, while hunting, the rest of the outside world ceased to exist, and he was one with the woods. He needed to put all of that knowledge and experience to the most critical tracking task he had ever faced, finding these kids...alive.

He pulled the collar edges of his red wool coat up around his neck to fend off the chill in the air and headed down the path to find his grandson and his friends.

Chapter 9

Conner sat in the darkness, Dickie asleep in the corner wrapped in a moldy old burlap sack. There had been no sleep for him: It was impossible without knowing if Raylee was okay. The ceiling was high, with rotten-looking boards, and the floor was littered with strands of dusty yellow straw—definitely a barn. A wooden barrel with rusted metal rings holding its decaying slats together sat in one corner with a hoe, handle snapped in half, leaning against it, and a few lengths of old rope and a decrepit harness hung on the wall. A barrel, a broken garden tool, an old harness, and some weathered rope—nothing that could serve as a weapon, Conner thought, except maybe the hoe. One of the walls did not show the sunlight that was creeping up through the boards, casting thin glowing lines on the floor. There was something beyond it, probably another room. The whole place reeked of the familiar smells of the barn at the Farm—hay, earth, rust, a faint hint of manure—but more decayed. More dead.

There was a large wooden door on one side with a pull handle that Conner had tried after the sunlight had first started to appear. Locked solid, no give to it all. There was also the smaller access door that Dickie had described to the left of the big door, but it was too little to squeeze through, only about a foot wide. Conner tested it to see if it was open, but it also was locked from the outside.

There was a workbench along one of the outer walls, cleared of tools or anything else that could be used to escape. There were some old boxes of nails and some mostly cracked glass canning jars filled with screws and washers. Conner also noticed the bucket in the corner that Dickie had described, but he didn't go over to look at it; the mere thought of it made him nauseous. Two beams ran across the ceiling, and the darkness from above made Conner think there was probably another space up there, as well.

What the heck? The situation was surreal, and it made Conner question in his mind whether this was happening. The dull pain in the back of his head convinced him it was. Who were these people, and what did they want? He took slight comfort with the notion that if they wanted him dead—or Dickie, for that matter—they could have done it already. He was helpless as they brought him here, and it would have been easy enough to finish him off and bury him someplace deep in the woods. Slight comfort, but it was something. He was a prisoner. They both were, and the people holding them were in control.

He had seen some prison movies, but for the first time, he got a real sense of involuntary confinement, entirely at the mercy and whims of others. There had to be a way out of this. He needed to think. He kept finding himself drifting into denial, thinking that this wasn't real, it was a bad dream, a fiction that he had created in his mind, but then he would snap back into the reality of the very room around him. It was real; there was no denying it.

"Top-top, don't stop!" a shrill voice rang out from outside the barn.

Conner's body jerked at the shout. Then he froze again like he had the night before, the same needle-like sticks piercing his body.

"Dinner time, boys!"

This time the voice was closer, and soon he heard the crunching of steps, heavy boots walking, then scratching to a halt. A snap, the sound of a metal bolt moving through its catch, and the small door lifted. Conner leaned left and peered through the door, seeing the ragged cuffs of jeans and a beat-up pair of dark-brown boots with no laces. A tray slid in through the opening, followed almost immediately by a plastic milk jug tossed in on its side, the yellow lid popping off as it landed, water spilling from its spout and turning the brown dirt black. Conner watched the water bubble and drain from the jug, unable to move out of pure fear. There was a pause, then unceremoniously Dickie's lost sneaker came bouncing and tumbling through the door, resting almost next to him. The door slammed shut with a bang, dust exploding into the air. He heard the same screeching sound as the bolt on the outside was fastened back in place. The noise caused Dickie to finally start stirring from his slumber. How could he even sleep? Dickie had been here for days; this was the routine. Institutionalized, Conner thought grimly, back to the prison motif.

Conner pushed himself to his feet and walked toward the metal tray, hearing the footsteps walking away from the barn. He could also hear whistling, a familiar tune, but he couldn't immediately identify it. He stood over the tray and examined its contents: half a loaf of bread with flecks of green mold on the crust edges, a glop of something that he assumed to be oatmeal or a semblance thereof, and two eggs, cracked from boiling. Breakfast in bed.

Dickie sat up. "What's going on?" he said, stretching his back.

"Breakfast, I suppose," Conner answered.

"Let me take a wild guess: moldy bread, some barfed-up oatmeal, and an egg, right?"

"Two eggs."

"I guess they've modified the menu for the new arrival, the new arrival being you," Dickie said, an attempt at humor that fell flat. "They've given me the same thing every day. More oatmeal at night, and a few blueberries or an apple if I'm lucky. I didn't touch any of it for two days, but then my hunger got the best of me, and I ate it. I found a mealworm in the oatmeal and puked it up that day, but it's food, I guess."

"You got another present, too," Conner said, gesturing his chin at the sneaker resting on its side.

"Hey!" Dickie exclaimed. "My shoe! How did that get here?"

"Remember? I told you Raylee and I found it in a clearing, and I put it in my backpack. I guess they went through my stuff."

Dickie clambered up and took three quick steps to the prize. Conner noticed the sock on his left foot was almost entirely black with dirt, matching the color of the sneaker he was still wearing. Dickie plopped down on his rear with a thud and pulled the sneaker onto his foot, not bothering to tie it.

"I should have probably taken the other one off too, but I don't know, it just made me feel like I would be accepting the fact that I'm stuck here, so I just left it on."

"I guess that weirdly makes sense," Conner said.

"Hey, what happened to the water?" Dickie barked, pointing his skinny, pale index finger at the quarter-filled jug resting on its side on top of a dark stain on the ground.

"It popped open when he threw it in."

"Well, go pick it up—that's all we've got for the day."

Conner stood up and walked over to the jug, bent down and picked it up along with the plastic cap, and snapped it back on top. He hated to admit it, but Dickie was right. No matter how crazy this whole situation was, they had to think about survival.

"Did he say anything when he dropped it off?"

"Just 'top-top,' whatever that means…oh, and he said, 'Dinner, boys.'"

"He's one of the brothers. There's at least two; he's the oldest I think, but I'm not sure. There's a girl, too, I think."

"You didn't say anything about that last night," Conner said with accusation in his voice. "You said you didn't know anything about them."

"Well sue me, Torquemada. I was just so surprised to be talking to you. I couldn't think of everything right away, now could I?"

"Torque-who?"

"Never mind," Dickie said, crossing his legs and rolling his eyes. "There are two boys, brothers, I think. One of them is older. The other one is just a kid by the sound of his voice. I've heard the older one yelling at him. The younger one whines a lot. There's a girl, too. I don't know how old. Did you ever notice that it's harder to tell how old a girl is by the sound of her voice? It's like that. She doesn't come out here much, though. I think there's a mom and a dad, I've heard other voices in the distance, but they never come close. That 'top-top' guy brings the food and water most of the time, I think. He likes to say that a lot. I've gotten a glimpse of him through the knothole in the wall over there, but I haven't seen the others. He's tall, with long dirty-blond hair, and I mean *dirty*. He was wearing overalls with no shirt when I saw him. Disgusting. When I was at the hole, he turned and looked straight at me. It freaked me out so bad I fell backward onto the ground, and I haven't gone back.

"You can't see where they're living through the hole or between the boards, but I've heard another door open and shut. I'm guessing the house is over there," he said, pointing beyond the wall with the workbench on it. "No one ever calls anyone by name. It's weird."

"They've never said who they are or what they want with you?"

"No, nothing like that. The only one that ever speaks to me is the older one. I don't want to converse, as you can imagine."

Connor walked over to the hole in the wall Dickie had indicated.

"I wouldn't do that," Dickie said.

Conner ignored him, walked up to it, and pressed his eye against it. He could see a small open area and then the tree line about thirty feet away. There was an old pail lying sideways on the ground, and a mound of dirt that had grass and weeds sprouting out of it. He strained his eye to the left and the right, but just as Dickie had said, he couldn't see any other buildings.

Dickie clambered up onto his feet, shuffled over to the tray, and reached down, picking up the bread. He ripped off a plum-sized portion and squished it into the oatmeal, scooping up a brown glob of it, and started to eat.

"Dig in," Dickie said, a mouthful of food garbling the words.

"No, thanks," Conner said.

"You say that now, but wait. This slop will seem like a gourmet meal in a few days."

"I'll wait until then, I suppose," Conner said, looking back out through the hole.

As Dickie munched away on his jailhouse slop, Conner walked around the perimeter of the room. The boards didn't seem like standard ones. He had noticed, looking through the hole, that they were two inches thick, too thick to punch or kick through, as if milled with their current confining purpose in mind. As soon as he'd made a complete loop, he went to the garden hoe and picked it up. The half handle was almost rotted, the rusting blade wiggling in its setting, and Conner suspected it would probably break off with even a modest amount of pressure.

"What are you going to do with that, start a garden?" Dickie said, pausing in his chewing, an unsightly clump of brown oatmeal clinging to his chin.

"Just seeing what we have, what we might use as a weapon."

"I'll tell you what we have...nothing; nothing at all. I spent the first days looking over everything in this room. There's nothing here. I even tried to dig my way out in the middle of the night, but that hoe just started to break apart when I tried, and the ground turns hard as rock a couple of inches down. Right over there," Dickie said, pointing his finger at a dug-up portion of ground, darker than the rest of the dirt floor. "There's no way out. I've tried it."

"Well, I'm going to keep trying," Conner said, feeling anger rise at Dickie's defeatist tone.

Dickie picked up one of the eggs, cracked it on the bottom of the pan, peeled it, and stuck the whole thing in his mouth, chewing it up as bits of yellow and white dropped to the ground in front of him. Once he had taken a few hard swallows, he reached over and picked up the milk jug, popped off the lid, and took a long swig, washing down the egg. He set the jug down on the ground. "Just face it, we're stuck here, you and me," he said through a burp.

"And Raylee."

"You don't see her here, do you? She could be anywhere. These hillbillies could have a whole colony of freaks hiding out in the woods."

"She's here. I'm sure of it."

"I'm not. I want to go home."

"Me too," Conner conceded. He sat back down on the ground, putting his arms on his knees and staring at the tips of his hiking sneakers, his mind drifting into a distant place of thought, trying to work out the problem that lay before him.

⁂

The day passed much as Dickie had said it would. Some muffled voices outside, but no direct contact. Conner checked the hole every so often, but the only thing he saw was a mangy brown-and-white dog sniffing around the edge of the woods. He had also tested the dirt floor where it met the walls. Dickie was right again. The ground was hard and unforgiving. Maybe he could pull the blade head off the hoe handle and use it to chip a hole out under or through the wall, he thought. It was worth a try, at least, maybe tonight after dark when it was less likely someone would hear him. However, the idea that he could scratch a hole big enough for them to crawl through seemed unlikely even in his most generous estimation.

Conner had managed to take a few drinks out of the communal water jug, lousy-tasting and warm, just as Dickie had warned. Still, it was better than nothing, and he knew he would need to keep his strength up by eating if he hoped to get out of here. He ate the remaining egg, overcooked and gummy, but couldn't bring himself to touch the foul-looking oatmeal. He finished off the egg with a chunk of bread.

They talked and talked because there wasn't much else to do. Dickie told Conner his life story, from kindergarten on up. His story was depressing, one of a solitary, socially awkward boy who didn't fit in with any of the little groups that had formed at his school, but he seemed oddly unbothered by it. Conner was mildly intrigued that the groups he described bore a resemblance to those at his own school. Dickie described the smart/popular kids, the athletic kids, the kids prone to getting into trouble and bucking the authority of the schoolteachers—probable future criminals, as Dickie described them. He also talked about the quiet and otherwise misfit, uncategorized kids, who kept to themselves, hoping to avoid the notice of bullies. Like Conner himself, they looked with longing to the kids who had found their rightful place in the world.

Dickie, on the other hand, viewed himself as being in a category of one: wickedly smart, and too worldly for the hicks of Morgan, resulting in his mother having to throw family-only birthday parties when he was a child with none of the other kids except Raylee ever in attendance.

Raylee. Conner was intrigued by her persona most of all, and he eagerly listened to Dickie talk about his life growing up with her as his only friend. She was outgoing, but not part of any particular group, like him, he said, not because she lacked the appearance, athletic ability, or intellect required for admittance, but rather by her own choice. As Dickie described it, it was like she had a bright glow around her that protected her from the judgments and stereotypes that were rampant in the schoolyard. A genuine individual, in every sense of the word. She hung out with whom she wanted to hang out with, avoided unnecessary gossip or confrontation, but never backed away from a challenge when faced with one.

Dickie relayed one vivid instance where a girl named Kelly, who had become a target of the popular kids, was at lunch when this boy named David spiked her milk with salt. When she took a drink of it, she immediately spat it out down the front of her blue shirt, instantly mortified, laughter erupting around her. Dickie said Raylee looked over from their table and saw David laughing and pointing at Kelly, accepting high-fives from the scraggly boys who followed him around and supported his every dumb move like mindless little soldiers. Raylee picked up the sloppy joe from her tray, removed the top bun, and walked over to the boy, smacking it right into his face before he knew what hit him. He fell backward off the table bench and landed on his back on the floor, the entire cafeteria going dead silent as though someone had turned off a switch. He quickly scrambled to his feet, arm cocked, ready to throw a fist at Raylee, but she just stood there, Dickie said, not saying a word and staring at him with a steely glare that said, *Go ahead, take your best shot.* David looked around for support from his friends, but they just sat there, stunned. Embarrassed, he fled the lunchroom, drips of seasoned meat and bun falling in pieces off his face as he went. Raylee calmly went back to her tray, sat down, and started to eat her carrot sticks. She was suspended for two days for the incident, never revealing to the principal why she had done what she did. It didn't matter to her whether he believed she was justified in her actions or not; she did what she felt was the right thing, instant justice, and that was that. That was Raylee.

Raylee. Powerful, independent, and beautiful. The story made Conner smile.

⚘

Granville carefully made his way along the trail, noting the bends in the grass and occasionally finding full or partial footprints on the forest floor. He had to keep adjusting direction to follow the prints, which were, not surprisingly, taking the path of least resistance through the thin birch and alders. He was just about to stop and take a drink from his canteen when he caught a faint whiff of something in the air. His heart quickened.

"Smoke!" he said out loud, startling himself with the sound of his voice.

He increased his pace and saw that the trail opened into a clearing near a tiny brook. There were footprints all around, moving in circles, disturbing the dull orange pine needles on the forest floor, and he saw it—a dark patch in the ground, a hole, blackened around the edges. He quickly walked over to it and peered down at the ashes. They had been here, all right, probably spent the night here. A fire pit dug in the ground by hand, no doubt about it. He allowed a small smile to form on his mouth. Smart kids, he thought. Must be Raylee's doing; he couldn't remember having shown Conner how to make a mountain man's fire, as he knew it from his grandfather.

He reached his hand into the hole and felt the ashes, which were still warm. They had been here last night. He pulled out his ashy hand holding a clump of the burned wood. He sniffed it and broke the blackened wood apart with the tips his fingers.

"Conner!" he shouted. "Conner!"

He listened quietly…only the sound of a soft breeze rustling the leaves on the trees, and the persistent babble of the water in the brook. He walked over to the stream and noted a few deeper footprints on the bank leading down to it.

"Conner! Raylee!"

Nothing. Not a thing.

Granville walked back over to the fire pit and began looking for the continuation of the trail from the clearing. He noticed an area that had been jostled up a bit, probably where they had slept, and he suddenly froze in place. A footprint. Not the print of the hiking sneakers he had been following, but of a boot. It was a big boot print, with a thick tread.

"Oh, no."

As he walked beyond the spot, he saw another boot print, this one with a more vertical tread and slightly smaller than the first one. They circled a few times, then headed off into the brush on the north side of the clearing, along with two parallel drag marks made by thick sticks or something of that type. At that moment, he felt utterly helpless, more helpless than he had ever felt in his life. Even more helpless than he had felt sitting in the hospital when his wife was dying, the clicking and beeping of machines in the hospital room, the sterile smell of bleach cleaner filling his nostrils, hearing his wife's ragged breaths as she struggled to breathe her last. The last two weeks of her life, she was unconscious, her eyes fused tightly shut. There was nothing he could do but sit by her side, hold her hand, and read her stories from the *Reader's Digest* he had purchased in the hospital gift shop. It was the worst time of his life. Until now, that is. The sadness and grief he had felt then were replaced by fear and anger now. However, unlike then, there was something he could do about this.

He didn't know what had happened here, but it wasn't right. They had been taken by whoever had made these prints, and the very thought of it made him want to fire off his rifle at the trees around him. He cursed himself for not having headed out last night in the dark after them, but he knew he could have easily missed the signs of their passing if he had. He pushed his feelings back down deep inside and turned back to the trail.

Focus, he told himself. He needed to focus, now more than ever. He walked into the brush, eyes in a hard squint, carefully following the trail left behind.

⁂

As the sun began to set behind the boards of the walls, Conner and Dickie found themselves running out of stories and things to talk about, and they both sat quietly, picking at the dirt floor with their fingernails.

"Top-top!" the yell came from outside the door. "Dinner time!"

Dickie, having adapted to the routine, had placed the tray and jug by the small door. When it opened, a filthy pale arm, ropey with blue veins and muscles, reached in and pulled them out one at a time, and a new tray and jug of water slid through. More oatmeal and bread as Dickie had predicted, this time with a couple of mealy apples. Dickie walked over and picked up the meal, such as it was, and brought it to the center of the room. He unceremoniously started eating.

"What are you thinking about?" Dickie said. "You've been quiet."

"I'm just thinking. Thinking about how we're going to get out of here."

"Well, let me know when you have it all figured out, Houdini."

"There has to be a reason they're holding us here. It just doesn't make any sense."

"Maybe they're going to fatten us, fry us up, and eat us," Dickie said. "But not with this food, they're not. I could go for a nice, juicy cheeseburger right about now."

Conner ignored the comment. "They must want something. I can't figure out for the life of me what it could be. It just doesn't make any sense."

"It doesn't have to make any sense. The freaks are out *there*, we are in *here*, and that's all there is to it."

Conner heard a faint noise come from the darkened side of the room. A creak and a scrape. "That sounded like a door opening," he whispered.

"Maybe," Dickie mumbled through a mouthful of old apple and oatmeal.

Conner stood up and walked over to the wall, placing the side of his face and ear against it. It felt rough and cold. He heard the scrape again, followed by the clink of a door handle. Soon they heard the heavy steps of someone walking away from the barn.

"What do you think?" Dickie said, taking another bite of the apple.

"I'm not sure, but it sounded like another door."

Conner thought about what to do next. He didn't want to yell out; that would attract attention. He reached down to the bottom of the wall and knocked on it with his knuckles three times. Nothing. He waited for a moment and tapped three times again. Still nothing. The time seemed to tick by in slow motion. He was starting to walk away from the wall when faintly, almost imperceptibly, a single knock came.

Conner turned his head swiftly to Dickie. "Did you hear that?"

"Yes," Dickie replied, turning toward the wall and staring at it, almost as if he thought he could see through it if he stared hard enough. Conner knocked twice in the same spot. Again faintly, two knocks back.

"It's her!" Conner exclaimed. "It must be."

Dickie's nose scrunched up a bit. "It could be anything. One of them, maybe."

"Why would they knock back? Why wouldn't they just come over to the door and tell us to cut it out?"

"I don't know. I don't think this is a good idea."

Conner ignored him and knocked four times. Four faint taps back.

"It's her! It has to be." A wave of relief passed through his body. She was here, and she was okay, at least for now. He was just about to call out Raylee's name when he heard muffled voices outside the barn and swallowed the words before any sound came out. He scanned frantically around the walls and ceiling with a newly invigorated desire to get out of here, to find Raylee, and get to safety.

He stared at the wall, unblinking for so long that his eyes began to burn and prickle. The wall just stared back at him, unrelenting.

Granville continued to follow the trail through the woods. It was not difficult. Whoever they were, they were not worried about covering their tracks. The path came into a small clearing, veered sharply to the right, and continued into the woods beyond. The footprints were the same—two sets of boot prints, and whoever was making them was dragging something across the ground.

He stopped for a minute to take a warm, metallic swig from the aluminum canteen he had owned since he was a boy. He had tried a few new ones over the years, but to him, the faint taste of plastic was even more off-putting than the metal. Moreover, his metal canteen could survive a battle and *had*, as evidenced by the dents and scratches on its surface. It had the added benefit of being able to withstand fire, a handy trick for purifying water. Try that with a plastic canteen, and you get a lump of goo.

He wiped the sweat off his brow with his left arm, then threaded the cap back on, which was attached to the canteen by a square-link chain. He shifted his rifle in his hands, instinctively and without thought creeping the lever action down a half inch and eyeing from above the chambered round within. He knew well enough that it was loaded, but after discovering the scene by the brook, he was taking no chances.

The sky was darkening, clouds racing across, and a brisk wind was blowing stiff in his face. His pace was starting to slow down after the initial rush of adrenaline began to subside. He could feel the individual thumps of his heart deep within his chest; no time to rest, however. Although the tracks he was following were at least a day old, he kept thinking he might come across his "quarry" at any moment.

He followed the trail until it came to a densely packed blowdown. Broken limbs were sprouting off downed trees like spikes, and he carefully lifted his legs, one after the other, over the branches, snagging his pant leg briefly as he went. When he stepped over the last log, his foot squished down into the mud. The ground was wet and littered with moss-covered, basketball-sized rocks half buried in the earth. The trail was still visible, heading off almost directly to the north, making a long S shape through the wet ground. Then he heard it: a faint gurgling sound, water up ahead. As Granville pushed on, he eventually saw the source, a stream gliding effortlessly along a three-foot-wide streambed, and he noticed brighter light through the trees ahead. He was coming to an opening in the forest canopy.

Sure enough, a hundred yards farther on, he found himself walking out of the tree cover and to the edge of a wide river that meandered in a southerly direction. He felt the sharp stab of realization in his gut when he saw that the tracks led directly to the water's edge at a ninety-degree angle.

No.

He kept going until the mud and water enveloped his boots and was almost up to his knees. The yellow reeds on the bank of the river were parted left and right, and the boot prints and drag marks ended at the water's edge.

It was at least thirty yards across. Too deep to ford, for him or for them, he thought. The only inescapable conclusion was too hard for him to acknowledge at first. They had gotten into a boat right here. He could see the deep groove of what must have been its hull in the mud. Reality smacked him in the face harder than a steel shovel.

He'd lost them.

He stood in the mud, letting the gravity of this development sink in, even though he looked to the right and left for any sign of a trail. There was none.

A springing wave of absolute resolve quickly replaced the moment of crushing defeat. Whoever these people were, they would have to land somewhere. It didn't stand to reason that they would follow the river south. All the streams and rivers in this area headed in a generally southerly direction, leading to civilization. They would be much more likely to run across people and even a search party if they went that way. It would not make sense, not if what he suspected was right, that they had taken Conner and Raylee against their will.

It had to be north. Granville quickly detached the radio the wardens had given him, clicked it on, and adjusted the squelch to quiet the static. He pressed the transmit button and spoke:

"Williamson here, over."

Nothing.

"Williamson here, calling out to the Maine Warden Service, searching for Conner Williamson and Raylee Drew. Anyone copy, over?"

No reply. Granville checked the GPS feature on the radio display and only saw a twirl of a little earth, indicating it was searching for satellites. Piece of junk. He tried to judge the distance he had traveled based on his walking speed. He pressed the button again.

"Found foot trail believed to be that of Conner and Raylee, and an encampment roughly eight miles from Morgan Township center, on a northwest heading from last known location. Encountered the tracks of two other unknown persons proceeding from the encampment leading to the edge of a river, possible the feeder river to North Bog. The trail ends there. Assume all parties boarded a boat and headed north. Unable to receive communications. Pursuing. Out."

He was sure they had headed north, for all the logical reasons he had considered, but also that was where his gut instinct was telling him they had gone. He had learned to trust those little instincts as he had grown older; more often than not, they proved to be right. He sometimes wished he could have figured that out much earlier in his life. It probably would have saved him some bumbling missteps along the way. Such is life. By the time you start to figure it out, you are closer to the end than the beginning.

Granville backtracked up out of the muck and started north along the riverbank. He would have to keep a sharp eye out on both sides to look for signs of a boat or portage, but the light of the day was fading fast, and he couldn't afford to make a mistake. He resigned himself to making camp, suppressing his urge to continue the pursuit in the dark. It was going to be an unbearable night, and the looming rain wasn't going to make it any more pleasant.

✧

Conner looked around in his dream, seeing the long, white-sand beach of the Outer Banks in North Carolina where his family sometimes vacationed. The surf was slowly curling onto the sand, like paper tearing in reverse. The infinite expanse of the blue ocean, dune grass standing guard against the waves that approached and retreated each day. The air had the clean smell of dry sand and ocean spray, but with a hint of desiccated crustaceans and seaweed. It was dusk, and the sun was an orange crimson as it settled in the west behind the dunes. He saw small whitish crabs scurry in and out of the little shelter holes they dug in the shore, looking to pinch their next meal and drag it down beneath the sand. He reached down and grasped a handful of sand, still warm from the sun's rays. He felt safe.

In his dream, he flashed back to the open truck tour they had taken to the northern part of the island the week before. The vehicle looked like it would have been more at home in Afghanistan than in North Carolina—a huge faded blue SUV with its top chopped off and a couple of black metal roll bars installed along its chassis like thick croquet wickets. It was hot and noisy, jostling up and down and side to side in the SUV as they passed through the last gate where the paved road ended. The tour guide/driver was a young man, not much older than Conner himself, with a shock of brown curly hair that sprouted downward from his red baseball cap, and a deep chestnut tan that screamed of skin exposed to the sun and the elements for work, not recreation. He was talking into a crackling microphone as he pointed out the sights, looking for the advertised main event, the wild ponies that inhabited and freely roamed the north end of the island. They managed to catch a few grazing lazily on the sparse yellow grass patches along the dunes. The heat was oppressive, stubbornly defiant against the air that blew around them in the open vehicle.

The guide had proved himself to be somewhat of an amateur comedian, his southern drawl adding to the effect. Conner wondered if it was real or a put-on for the tourists. He had gotten the lucky passenger seat next to him and pushed his body forward as far as the seat belt would allow, taking advantage of the weak stream of air-conditioning ineffectively burping out of the vents. His parents, and another couple and their daughter, were less fortunate, tucked away in the back two rows and receiving the full brunt of the bumps and jolts as they made their way over the sandy roads.

"These-here ponies up on the left are females. Every year, the rangers dart them with birth control so they can control the population. I know a few girls myself that could use that dart," the guide said. Conner looked back to his mother, who, as expected, had a disapproving grimace on her face.

Conner shifted back to the beach in his dream now, the sun fading deeper below the dunes and the sky turning a deep orange, a string of pelicans gliding silently along, the tips of their wings softly brushing the water.

Diamonds sparkled on the sea, and a warm breeze blew through his hair.

It was beautiful. Conner didn't want to leave.

Chapter 10

When Conner awoke, he thought it was still night, but no, he saw dim gray light peering in through the wall boards. How long had he been out? An hour? Ten? He couldn't tell. Being trapped in here was throwing his internal time clock off. He turned onto his side on the hay pile he had nested into a bed and glanced over at Dickie, snoring in the corner of the room. Well, at least *he* wasn't having any trouble sleeping. Conner pushed up into a sitting position and crossed his legs the way he'd seen people on TV practicing meditation. He couldn't quite understand why they thought it was such a great thing, keeping your eyes closed, humming all the time. He had tried it once, but couldn't keep his mind still as they suggested no matter how hard he worked at it. In fact, the harder he tried, the more jumbled his thoughts became. Oh, well, so much for meditation.

He was about to get up and give Dickie a shake when he heard a scratching sound outside the barn. Thinking maybe it was a chicken or goat, like at the Farm, he got up and walked over to the wall closest to the sound. The scratching got furious, and then he heard a muffled voice—a child's voice.

"There, gotcha surrounded!" the voice exclaimed. "Don't move or we'll shoot! Please don't shoot! We're coming out. Please don't! If you aren't out in three seconds, we're going to burn the place down, Roscoe!"

Conner took a step closer to the wall and accidentally bumped it with the tip of his sneaker. There was a quick scurrying sound of feet on dirt, and the voice ceased.

"Hello?" Conner said. "Hello? Can you hear me?"

Nothing. Silence.

"Hello? I can hear you breathing out there," Conner said, not sure that was the best move, but he figured what the heck, take a chance. Just as he finished the sentence, he heard a quick inhalation of breath and the fast patter of footsteps leaving the area.

"Shoot," he said aloud.

Conner moved over toward Dickie, thinking about the voice he'd heard. It was a young boy, and he was playing some game, not aware—or perhaps not caring—about people trapped in this building against their will. It made him angry, and his face started to flush, but Conner told himself that maybe the boy didn't know what the circumstances were. Even if he did know, it's not like he could do anything about it.

Dickie was lying on his right side with his hand up by his mouth, his thumb extended as if he'd been sucking on it at some time during the night. Well, I guess everyone occasionally resorts to what comforted them when they were little, Conner thought.

"Hey, wake up," Conner said, giving Dickie a light kick to the bottom of his sneaker.

"What? Huh, what? What's going on? Oh, it's just you," Dickie said, his half-closed, bleary eyes peering up at Conner in a desperate attempt to deny the reality that he was still here, trapped in this place.

"Nice to see you, too. There was someone outside just now. It was a boy—he was playing or something," Conner said.

"What do you mean 'playing'?"

"I don't know, like with some toys or something. It sounded like a little kid."

Dickie drew himself up into a sitting position, his eyes still sleepy-looking. "Well, what did he say?"

"Nothing, I guess. I called out, and the kid just ran off."

"Hallelujah, we're saved."

"Knock it off. I don't need you being sarcastic right now," Conner said, exasperated.

"Sorry; I didn't mean anything by it, I mean…well, what are we supposed to do?"

"I'm not sure, maybe try to talk to him if he comes back. Maybe he could get us out of here."

"If he's just a kid, I kind of doubt it," Dickie replied, his tone more measured.

"I don't know. It's something, at least."

"If you say so."

Dickie rolled back down to the ground onto his side, his breath leaving his body with a long, defeated *whoosh*. "I think we're going to be stuck here forever. If no one has found us by now, they're never going to find us."

"Someone will find us, and we are going to get out this. All three of us." Conner looked up to the rays of the sun cutting through the wall boards, illuminating fine particles of hay dust floating aimlessly in the air.

⁊

Night had fallen in the prison barn once again, and nothing but the same uncomfortable routine had occurred during the day: the crazy guy bringing two food deliveries, and nothing else. Conner lay awake in the darkened room, Dickie fast asleep again in the corner. How could he sleep so much? As Conner lay there, he heard the first deep rumblings of a thunderstorm in the distance, followed almost immediately by rhythmic plops of raindrops on the roof. The wind had picked up and found its way into the thin spaces between the wall boards, like being on an old wooden ship at sea. It came in gusts every few minutes, and the sound of the rain steadily increased.

Conner was exhausted. The adrenaline that had rushed his system during the first few days of his captivity in this dungeon had begun to wane, taking with it his physical energy and ability to concentrate. Maybe that was how Dickie was able to rest so blissfully at night. He had been here longer, of course. Conner struggled to keep his mind alert, going over their circumstances detail by detail over and over again. However, he found himself plagued only with questions, no answers. Whoever was keeping them here had a reason, but what? Why continue to give them food and water? he wondered. Surely, they had to know that eventually, searchers would find this place, free him and his friends, and whisk *them* off to prison for an extended stay. What was their plan? Did they even have a plan? Who was that scary guy who brought them their daily meals, and who was the kid he had heard playing outside? It stood to reason that everyone who lived here knew they were being held against their will and were somehow okay with it. It did not make any sense.

Conner jumped at a crack of lightning, and for a millisecond, the entire room lit up in a vibrant white flash. He heard Dickie moan, then go back to his snoring. The patter of rain grew stronger as the storm settled overhead, and he could almost imagine what the barn must look like from the outside, lashed with blankets of cold rain.

The next clap of thunder sounded farther away. The storm was heading out. Conner's father, like every other father, had shown him how to count between the lightning flash and the following rumble of thunder to determine whether a storm was coming or going. He thought of his father sitting in the green-belted aluminum lawn chair in the garage and watching the storms assault the neighborhood, wind lashing the limbs of the trees, the rain hitting the black pavement of the driveway in a relentless drumbeat. It was a vivid memory from his childhood but now seemed so far off, so distant, like it had been in another life. He lay back down and turned on his side, his right arm crooked under his head to serve as a makeshift pillow.

Sleep came.

Chapter 11

Little Henry, or "Bibbs," as his family called him (he had no idea know why), woke up shortly after dawn as he did every morning. The sky outside his dirty window was gray and bleak, and water still spotted the glass like tiny climbers clinging desperately to a steep mountain face. He sat up in his bed and looked out, dressed in the blue overalls he had worn the day before. The ground was wet, but on the bright side, there would undoubtedly be a few good puddles that would be perfect for jumping in or creating little marine battlefields for his toy soldiers. They would be storming the beaches today.

The toy soldiers were old, and some were missing body parts, like a leg or head, but this only added to their battle-torn realism. They had once belonged to his older brother, Derek, and Derek never let him forget it. One of his first memories was of finding the stash of soldiers in an old cigar box under Derek's bed, starting to play with them, and then Derek storming into the room, catching him red-handed. Derek had smacked the little figures out of his hand and pushed him right in his face, making him fall back on the hard plank floor and hit the back of his head on the edge of the bed with a stinging thud. He didn't cry. He never cried, at least that he could remember, but it scared him. Derek was like that. Scary.

Over the years, Derek's interest in the soldiers had waned, but he didn't let Bibbs touch them until this last year, when he seemed to forget about them altogether. Bibbs was ecstatic. It was better than anything he had ever gotten for his birthday, which was generally just a little car or horse crudely carved out of wood, or maybe a piece of white rock candy like he got last year when he turned seven. The soldiers were his now, though, and Bibbs was careful to keep them out of sight in case Derek should suddenly realize he missed playing with them and take them away again.

Bibbs pushed back the heavy quilt he slept under and put his bare feet down toward the floor. With a quick scooch forward, he bounced off the bed and landed on the cold floor with a thump, instantly mad at himself for the noise he had made. Long ago, he had learned that these early mornings were the best time—no one making him do extra chores or bossing him around—so he usually took care to make sure he didn't wake anyone up before he had a chance to play by himself outside. His chores were tedious and menial, feeding the scraggly chickens, scooping the goat poop out of their pen, and picking all the weeds from the small field of vegetables behind the barn. It seemed like he had to work all day long, and only got the chance to play by himself if Pa, Derek, and Mom were asleep or got distracted by some other task for the day.

Besides Derek, there was his sister, Mags, who was a couple of years older than Derek. She was a husky girl of twenty-three, with a thick mane of brown hair that reminded Bibbs of the tail on the old donkey they used to have before he got sick one winter and died—frozen dead like a big block of gray ice in the middle of the field. He liked the donkey, "Mr. Willies," as he called him, but that seemed to be the way around here for animals. Once he started to like one or the other, they died, or the family ate them, so he tended to avoid any real attachments to them if at all possible. He knew Derek and Pa had spent some time out behind the barn after Mr. Willies died, and he suspected that the sudden appearance of dark-gray, gamy-tasting meat at every meal was gruesomely related. He tried not to think about it. If Derek had caught on that it bothered him, he would use it against him every chance he got, maybe teasing him about Mr. Willies being tasty. He wouldn't put it past Derek to put a piece of the donkey, like an ear or its teeth, in his bed at night (he had done that once before with a chicken head that had belonged to a particular brown chicken Bibbs had been fond of). That was just the way Derek was…mean. Tormenting Bibbs was kind of his pastime, a living victim-based hobby of sorts.

In stark contrast, Mags barely ever acknowledged his existence, and for a brief time, Bibbs wondered if maybe by some weird turn of nature he was invisible to her most of the time. When she did acknowledge or speak to him, it was usually to tell him to fetch water from the well or use the broom and sweep out the dust and dirt from the kitchen floor. She wasn't mean like Derek, but she wasn't all that nice either, not like the happy people in the few storybooks his Mom had read to him when he was younger. Those families seemed to downright adore each other, often going on adventures and rescuing each other when they were in trouble. He certainly did not want to rely on Derek or Mags to save him from any danger, that was for sure. Derek was the danger. Mags…well, Mags didn't seem to care one way or the other.

Bibbs tiptoed to the door of his room and slowly opened it, trying to minimize the creaks and pops of the hinges as best he could. The kitchen was empty, four black chairs around the round, wooden table, pushed in neatly, in contrast to the general disorder of the rest of the room. There were yellowed curtains on the windows, and the sink was full of dirty pots and pans. The standard procedure seemed to be to wait for the moment when they ran out of absolutely every dish or bowl before washing. The rusted oil-barrel woodstove they used to cook on was coldly standing along the wall of the kitchen, no fire crackling or wisps of smoke emanating from its seams, a good sign no one else was up yet.

Bibbs made his way across the kitchen floor, deftly sidestepping the fat, gray cat sleeping on the threadbare carpet in front of the stove. He had stepped on Izzy's tail once by accident, and she had let out such a screech it had woken his mother up, ruining his time to play. Bibbs reached the front door and peeked out the window. Nobody in the front of the house that he could see. He slid the bolt and opened the door, then went out onto the small porch his father had made by hand with broken boards he'd scavenged. Most of the stuff here had been scavenged from somewhere else, although Bibbs had no idea where. His mother had told him once that the house and barn had been here when they arrived, abandoned and forgotten by its previous owners, and just like that, they had a new home. He had been just a toddler then, and couldn't remember ever having lived anywhere else. He had gone along on a couple of fishing and bird-hunting trips with Derek and Pa, but they never encountered any other people. Bibbs knew from his books that other people were out there, but he had never met any of them.

Until now, that is.

He stole a glance at the barn. He was under strict orders from Derek to stay away from the place, which was odd since a few of his usual chores took him in there to retrieve hay for the goats or nails for one of his father's projects.

He had been playing out behind the barn the day before, having forgotten about his orders to stay away from it, when he'd heard a voice come from inside. It had given him quite a start, and he'd peed his pants a little before he hurried away. Someone was in there, no doubt about it. He had also seen Derek and Mom taking food out there and had assumed they must be feeding whatever was inside. Until he heard the voice yesterday, he had just thought it was some animal they didn't want him to see yet, and he'd even started to hope that maybe it was a new dog or a replacement donkey that they planned to give him as a present for his next birthday. The voice was a complete surprise, though, and he didn't know what to think now. Derek and Pa had been gone the last a couple of days, and he noticed that Derek had brought more food than usual out there last night. Whatever was in there must be growing and getting hungrier, he had supposed.

After he had heard the voice, though, he thought about asking Pa or Mom, or maybe even Mags, about it, but decided not to. They might find out he had broken the rules and been playing where he shouldn't have been playing, and there was no way he was going to give his Pa any reason to lick him with his belt. For as long as he could remember, that was the one swift punishment his Pa dished out when he didn't listen or do his chores right away. It hurt like the dickens, but again, he didn't cry. Still, there was no way he was going to open himself up for one of those sessions.

Now that he knew there were *people* inside, he started to think that maybe they had something to do with the girl. His parents hadn't introduced him to her, but he'd heard some voices outside his room a couple of nights ago and peeked through the crack of his bedroom door. His mother was wordlessly leading a young girl into Mags's room. The girl had her head down, but he got a good look at her face as she passed by his door—her black hair, glowing brown eyes, and tan skin. She was pretty, and Bibbs had almost blurted out "hello, there" as she passed, but he sucked the impulse back down his throat. She had not come out for breakfast, lunch, or dinner either of the last two days, his mother bringing food into the room for her.

Still, now that he knew there was at least one other person in the barn, he knew something was up, but couldn't figure it out. If they were relatives, like cousins or something, he couldn't understand why Mom and Pa wouldn't just introduce them to him. It sure was weird.

Bibbs headed to the barn to do his morning chores. Work before play, Pa always said.

⅌

Bibbs walked over to the chicken coop with a silver pail of seeds clutched in his little hand for his chores. He shifted a block of wood crudely nailed in the center from horizontal to vertical and opened the wire mesh door. The chickens started clucking and moving jerkily around, knowing that a meal was about to be served. Most of the twelve or so chickens were already in the small open pen area, and only a few of the hens remained inside the shelter, probably guarding eggs they would never get to see hatch. Bibbs spread some of the feed around at his feet and chickens crammed in around his thin legs, jostling each other out of the way to get at the food. A few feathers flew up in the air as they fought for position, so Bibbs threw out a handful to the right side of the pen to break up the squabble.

After he had tossed out the last of the feed, he walked back out the door, the chickens too engrossed in their meal to notice his departure. He remembered to refasten the block on the door. One time when he had been daydreaming, he had left it open, and six of the chickens seized the opportunity to make their escape after he had left. His father and Derek had managed to round up four of the escapees, but two remained at large, gone forever. Probably eaten by coyotes, his Pa had remarked. The belt had come out again, and after that, he had never forgotten to secure the door.

Next Bibbs went over to the goat pen and let the four somber-looking goats out of their enclosure and into the pasture to feed on the weeds and grass that grew there. The garden where his mother harvested tomatoes, lettuce, carrots, and zucchini (he hated zucchini) was blocked off by a separate crude fence to keep the indiscriminate goats from feasting on their food source. The two white goats ambled out of the enclosure into the field, but the brown-and-white ones seemed content to stay near their pen. Bibbs took a flat shovel and scooped up the goat poop and placed it in the same pail he had used to carry the chicken feed. The chickens didn't seem to mind this breach of food hygiene, or at least they never refused to eat. He took it to the waste pile in the garden, next to another collection of clippings, egg shells, and vegetable scraps. Every few weeks, he was tasked with using a pitchfork to churn the unholy sludge, to be later spread on different parts of the garden.

Once he finished with his chores, he walked back to the front porch and retrieved the little bag of soldiers he had stashed in the weeds next to the steps. He picked up a small piece of firewood from the front of the house, took it over to one of the muddy puddles in the yard area, and set it down lengthwise next to the pool. His bare feet squished in the wet earth as he went, and then he sat down on the split wood, his feet marinating in the brown, muddy pool of water. It would be a water campaign today, and he tore off a strip of bark from the log under his rear and floated it in the water. He reached into the bag and retrieved four of the soldiers, balancing them carefully on the bark, which served as their landing craft. He removed six other soldiers and set them up on the perimeter of the puddle, their little rifles pointed out at the invading amphibious strike force.

"*Poosh!*" he exclaimed, tossing a small pebble at the bark, the four soldiers teetering but maintaining their footing on the vessel. "*Poosh!*" as he threw a slightly larger rock, this one hitting one end of the bark, sending three of the soldiers flying up in the air and then down to a watery death, the fourth landing on its back but remaining on the bark.

"Fire all the cannons! *Poosh!*" He tossed another rock at the bark, this time dislodging the one remaining soldier from the safety of the bark and into the water. "*Tat-tat-tat!*" He threw sand from the edge of the puddle onto the soldiers' positions in the water, simulating machine-gun fire.

"Well done, men!" he said, picking up one of the soldiers on the bank and moving it up and down, facing the others. "All enemies have been destroyed!"

Bibbs paused in his play, the soldier still in his hand, and stared over at the barn at the edge of the pasture. His thoughts drifted back to what he had heard the day before. Bibbs had no intention of going back there, at least not for the time being. If Pa saw him, he would be in big trouble. Still, it was curious. The voice he'd heard had sounded like a kid, a boy.

Turning back to the soldiers in the puddle, Bibbs launched three more campaigns from the water, the third and final assault successfully taking the beachhead and destroying the defenders' position. When he finished, he carefully rinsed the mud off each of the soldiers in the water, then shook them dry and placed them back in the bag, cinching the top closed. He got up, forgetting to retrieve the piece of firewood from the ground, and walked back to the house to put the soldiers back into their safe space, resting up for their next campaign.

※

Conner sat next to the wall, tapping rhythmically with the knuckles of his right hand, trying to get a response. Another day and night had gone by with no sign of the responsive taps he had heard a couple of days ago.

"You might as well just give up," Dickie said. "She's not there."

"You don't know that," Conner said, refusing to look over in Dickie's direction. "She responded before. She'll respond again."

"It was probably just a chicken or a goat, or something like that."

"It was not a chicken."

"Okay, then, keep it up. That guy is going to hear and come in here and beat you up or something, or even worse, beat the both of us up."

"Let him," Conner said. He wasn't afraid anymore. He was just angry. The fear and nervousness he'd felt the first night had faded away, replaced with something more tactile, harder, and red. He was going to get out of here, one way or another, even if he had to fight his way out.

As he continued to tap, the unlikely image of his parents' probable separation popped into his mind. It was hard to keep his mind focused—his thoughts danced uncontrollably, defensively attempting to avoid the grim reality of the situation in which he found himself. It seemed like a lifetime ago that he had been sitting in his house in Virginia first hearing the news, and also finding out about the plan to send him into exile in Maine. Those problems seemed so far away now. He didn't know Raylee or Dickie then, but oddly he couldn't imagine his life without them now. His mother had once told him that making friends was like having a baby: At first, it seemed foreign and strange to have a new little human being around, but soon the world before the baby faded into nothing, and it was as if it had always been there.

His mind jumped around some more, landing on the story Auntie had told them at her shop about the small boy who'd appeared unexpectedly in the town and was just as quickly whisked away by a stranger. He thought about the kid he'd heard playing outside the barn a few days before. Was it the same little boy who had appeared in town, and was this the same family that had scooped him up and disappeared into the woods? He didn't know, but something deep down inside told him there was a connection.

Conner heard a click and the jangle of a chain, then a door opening and closing, the solid click of a lock, and a quick bang on wood. The steps came back to the door of the room they were in and paused. He stole a glance at Dickie, whose eyes were filled with fear, waiting for the next terrible event to unfold. Conner thought he heard the breathing of someone outside the door, but he couldn't be sure. His mind had been playing tricks, and he was starting not to trust his senses.

After what seemed like an eternity, they both heard the sound of steps leaving the door and walking away. Dickie noisily released the breath he had been holding in his chest.

"See?" Dickie said, glaring at Conner. "You almost got caught."

Conner ignored the remark and started tapping again.

"What are you doing?" Dickie cried.

"Just shut up and be quiet," Conner said, his eyes focused on the wall.

He tapped more quickly and a bit harder than he had before. Then, faintly and some distance away, he heard what he hoped for: a couple of taps in response. His heart rate immediately sped up, filling his head with a rush of blood.

"Raylee!" he hissed, as loud as he could without breaking the technical bounds of a whisper. "Raylee! Is that you?"

Quietly, almost imperceptibly, a faint voice penetrated the thick wood wall. "Conner? Is that you?"

"Yes! Raylee is that you?"

"Yes, it's me. Are you okay?"

"Yes, I'm fine, and Dickie's here, too," Conner said.

Dickie, face frozen in shock, quickly rose up into a crab-like crouch and scurried over next to Conner. "Raylee?" he blurted, too loud.

"Shhh!" Conner said.

"Yes, it's me. Were you tapping the other day?" Raylee asked.

"Yes…yes!" Conner said, his heart settling into a slower, steady rhythm, relief and hope flooding his senses.

"I heard you, but I had tape around my mouth and head, and then they took me inside the house. I was there last night and the night before."

"You're a house guest now?" Dickie exclaimed incredulously. Conner shot him a fiery glance that cut off even the thought of further sarcastic comments.

"Yes, they had me in a room in there. I tried to get out, but I couldn't. Somebody nailed the windows shut from the outside."

"Who are they?" Conner asked, still smiling at the sound of her voice.

"I don't know. It's a family, though—a mother and father and three kids, I think. Derek is the oldest. I haven't met the other two; the mother just told me about them."

"Derek. Is that the 'top-top' guy?" Dickie asked.

"Yeah, I heard him say that. There's something wrong with him," Raylee said, her voice sounding stronger and more confident.

"No kidding, really?" Dickie blurted. "They're all freaking crazy."

Conner ignored him. "Did they say why they're holding us here?"

"No, not a word, and I was too afraid to ask. It was weird. The mother treated me like I was just part of the family. It was kind of creepy."

"We're going to get out of here," Conner said. "We're going to find a way."

"I hope you're right," Raylee replied.

Conner's world had suddenly gone from dismal to bright just knowing that Raylee was okay, at least for now. They continued talking about the events leading up to where they were and wondering what was going on. However, there were no answers or solutions, only more questions.

❧

"Bibbs! Get out here, *now!*" Derek yelled.

Bibbs's stomach seized up for a moment, hearing the call from his brother. He quickly stood up from the floor, left his bedroom, and went into the kitchen.

"Now!" a voice bellowed from outside.

"I'm coming!" Bibbs yelled.

Bibbs pushed out through the front screen door, the hinges straining and creaking as he went. Derek was standing a few feet from the front steps, rifle in hand. For a moment, Bibbs was alarmed. What was going on?

"Get your boots on, we're going hunting," Derek said.

Bibbs went back into the house and hurried over to the woodstove where his boots were. They kept all the shoes and boots behind the stove, using the heat to dry them after a day out in the fields. Bibbs quickly stuck his bare feet into the old leather boots, lacing them up as fast as he could. It wasn't often Derek took him hunting, and he didn't want to miss out on an opportunity to venture away from the house.

"Hurry up!" Derek yelled.

"I'm coming!" Bibbs shouted, and he ran back out onto the porch. "Where are we going hunting?" Bibbs asked.

"Over toward the creek; I saw some deer tracks there yesterday. Just shut your mouth and keep quiet. I don't need you spooking away any deer with your stomping around."

Derek turned and headed out across the pasture, Bibbs working his short legs furiously to keep up with his brother's long strides. It was sunny now, and Bibbs quickly felt the summer heat rising on the back of his neck as they went. Derek carried the old rifle low in his right hand, keeping it straight to prevent it from banging against his legs. Bibbs had shot it a few times, shattering a few old glass bottles off a fence post with satisfying pops. The rifle had kicked into his shoulder, kind of like getting a quick, sharp punch. Bibbs hit the first two targets he aimed at, but Derek wasn't impressed. He told him he needed to hold the rifle stock tighter in his shoulder, and to use his right eye to aim instead of tipping his head and using his left. Bibbs favored his left eye, which was strange, being right-handed. He had missed the third bottle using his right eye, and Derek just shook his head, telling him he wasn't wasting any more cartridges on him.

Derek headed through the pasture to a path leading into the woods away from the house, keeping a quick pace as he went. Small insects and grasshoppers were buzzing about in the field, landing and clinging to the growing wheat and oats the family would harvest in the next few weeks. Harvest time was hard for Bibbs. They worked the field from early in the morning until past dark some days. They cut the wheat with a hand scythe, then bundled it and stood it upright to dry for about a week or so. That part wasn't so hard, but once it dried, they had to spread it out on a tarp and beat it until the little grains separated from the stalks. Then they scooped up the grains and laid them out to dry some more before storing them in burlap bags. The whole process was boring and back-breaking. Bibbs hated the work but mostly hated having to work alongside Derek for so long, who continuously criticized how fast he was working, or said that he wasn't doing it right, or that he was just stupid, and on and on. If Derek had any big-brother instinct to mentor his younger brother, he sure hid it well.

On this particular day, though, Bibbs was in good spirits. Derek or no Derek, getting to go along on a hunt was something he enjoyed. Stalking through the woods up to the apple piles they left out for the deer and other critters, no talking, having to control every movement, even your breath, so as not to make the slightest noise. The strict hunting rules had been beaten into Bibbs by Derek during his formative years, but he enjoyed the hunts nonetheless. The excitement and building suspense of sitting and waiting for a deer to appear were enthralling. It left him feeling drained and exhausted at the end of each outing, but it was fun, even when they didn't bring home a kill.

Bibbs could see they were approaching the edge of the woods overlooking one of the apple piles, and he slowed his pace, knowing that at any moment, Derek would tell him to stay put.

"Stop here," Derek whispered, on cue. "I'll move to the right behind the old log; you move up the left to the mossy rock and sit there until I call you or you hear a shot."

Bibbs did not answer, knowing there was no need to make further conversation, and waited for Derek to move softly down the path, stepping carefully to avoid breaking any branches or twigs. There were no birds around, Bibbs observed, and no squirrels, either. That was good, as a red squirrel's chatter was just like an alarm bell for the skittish deer. They were like the watch guards of the woods. As soon as Derek disappeared around the blowdown of trees, Bibbs turned to the left and crawled up a little ridge to the large rock on the top. He could see parts of the field, but it didn't give him the best view of the pile, not that Derek cared. It was out of the way enough that Bibbs couldn't ruin the hunt with a careless movement or a cough.

Bibbs sat on the green, mossy rock and used a stick to pick the dirt from the treads of his boots. His mind drifted as the time passed, and he felt a faint rumble of hunger in his stomach. He could make out the top of Derek's head behind the downed trees, and he wondered for a brief moment if he could hit it with a small rock. There was just such a rock, smooth and gray, down next to his side. It was unthinkable, of course. How could he convincingly explain that it was an accident? However, it made him smile nonetheless. Derek was so mean; it would have served him right. He had a vague notion that his very name, Bibbs, had been conjured up by Derek in an attempt to belittle or make fun of him. Life was hard with Derek, no doubt about it.

Mags was less of a problem. He had vague memories that when he was younger, she used to play with him, but like all small animals and chickens, once they got beyond the cute puffball stage, they became less appealing, even repulsive, to adults, he supposed. Mom was the only one who was consistently nice to him. She still set out his morning porridge with a little dash of golden honey drizzled on the top to make it sweet, even though Pa said it was a waste of precious resources, whatever that meant. Pa, well, Bibbs was just plain scared of him, thanks to numerous encounters with the belt.

A crow landed on the branch of a pine tree about fifteen feet above Bibbs's head. It gave a quick, high-pitched call and tipped its head to observe him, white-gray eyelids blinking over its ink-black eyes. Bibbs always thought crows looked dirty, like they hadn't had a bath in months, or years. Their feathers always seemed somewhat disheveled, the odd black feather sticking out here and there. This one was no different. It looked like it had just woken up from a bad night's sleep or had just survived a cat attack. The crow seemed curious about Bibbs's presence in its domain, as though he was a trespassing and uninvited guest, here to possibly steal food from him. Bibbs made a face at the crow, sticking his tongue out in hopes of scaring it off. It was starting to get on his nerves. The crow did not oblige, merely shifting its feet on its perch on the limb. Bibbs decided it was best to ignore the ratty-looking thing.

His mind wandered back to the barn and their new guests. Why were they here? Were they relatives of some sort that he had never heard about before? That didn't make any sense. For as long as he could remember, it had just been Pa, Mom, Mags, Derek, and him. Sometimes at night when he woke from dreams, though, he could sense that he had known other people. It was mostly blurred images and smells, cookies baking, loud noise, and the scent of fresh-cut grass. But he couldn't remember them, and he assumed it must be just the weirdness of dreams.

After what seemed like hours had passed, Bibbs was starting to drift off into a dozy sleep when a sharp crack rang through the air, causing him to fall off the rock onto his right arm. Derek had taken a shot.

"Get down here!" Derek yelled.

Bibbs hurriedly got to his feet and headed down the hill, rubbing his elbow as he went. Before he reached Derek, he could already see something tan lying in the field next to the pile of apples, and he could smell gunpowder lingering in the air. A blue haze hung above Derek's head. Bibbs rounded the blowdown and skidded to a stop as Derek came into full view. Derek crawled over a log and headed out into the field. Sure enough, lying on the ground was a doe, a small black splotch on the tan and white hair just below and to the rear of its shoulder—a perfect shot to the heart and lungs. The deer was motionless, dead before it hit the ground, and its left eye was wide open and fixed with a look of terror.

Derek walked up to the deer and looked down, his rifle hanging low in his hands. "Well, not much, but better than nothing."

Bibbs said nothing. He was usually excited about a kill, blabbering on about wow, what a great shot, Derek, look at the size of that thing, and so on; but not this time. Bibbs felt oddly sad about the dead deer and wasn't looking forward to the gruesome gutting and hauling out of its still steaming organs. From the small pack he'd worn for the hunt, Derek pulled a few dark, wet-looking sacks for the heart and liver—which Bibbs would be carrying back to the house. Derek then set to work gutting the animal.

All Bibbs could do was watch, and stare at that fixed, dark eye, and think about the barn and its occupants. He couldn't figure out why, but he felt bad inside, like there was a black, tarry twisted knot in his stomach, churning and rolling.

Something just wasn't right.

❧

Granville stopped at the edge of the marsh and watched the red sun fading behind the trees on the horizon, dark shadows slowly spilling across the marsh grass. He would have to stop again for the night and make camp. Two days he had been hiking along the riverbank. Two days and no signs of the kids, the people who had them, the boat…nothing. He turned his back to the fading sun and made his way into the woods, soon finding a small clearing with a blanket of thick green moss to make his camp. It was not a spot he would usually have picked given the recent rain, which tended to linger in the sponge-like moss, but he was too tired to venture further to seek a drier and more elevated location.

He was tired and hungry. He was down to his last three power bars, two apples, and a blackened banana that had seen better days. He would have to eat the banana tonight, or it was likely to transform entirely into brown mush. He collected some dead branches and built a small fire, lighting it quickly with waterproof matches and a few of the cotton balls soaked in petroleum jelly that he carried in a plastic baggie in his pack. He relayed another message of his approximate location with the radio, but, as before, he got no response.

As the dimming sunlight made its terminal descent among the trees, the fire took on a more visible, glowing presence, and he knew he would be expecting a great deal to get even a couple of hours of sleep. Still, there was nothing else he could do right now, so he cut some pine boughs to lie on, propped his weathered canvas pack into a makeshift pillow, leaned his back up against it, and stretched his aching legs.

He reached into his top pocket and pulled out a tin container of small white quinine pills. It was hard to come by these days, but he had a source at the local pharmacy about a half hour from Morgan. Getting in good with the pharmacist was always a good thing; they often knew more about how you were doing and what you needed than even your doctor. The quinine helped alleviate his leg cramps, which he had been prone to since he was in his twenties, and they sure weren't getting any better with age. Sometimes his calf muscles would knot up into a ball of iron, and the pain would make him want to scream. He took a pill with a small swig of lukewarm water from his canteen and laid it down next to him. He couldn't afford those cramps sneaking up and hobbling him, especially now.

Granville reached in his pack and pulled out one of his remaining energy bars, unwrapped it, and quickly devoured it. It tasted vaguely like chocolate but was chalky and chewy. He followed it up with the mushy banana, tossing the peel back over his shoulder into the woods. Some little critter would appreciate it. He thought to himself that he was going to need some real protein soon or he would run out of energy to keep walking. If a squirrel or partridge presented itself tomorrow, he would take a shot at it and hopefully be able to hit it in the head. The .30-30 was certainly not ideal for small game, and it would blast it to shreds if he accidentally hit it center-mass. Ready-made hamburger, he thought.

Granville crumpled up the energy bar wrapper, stuffed it in his pack, pulled the rim of his hat down over his face to keep the mosquitoes at bay, and closed his eyes, quickly drifting off into a dream state.

His vision soon filled with terrible fleeting images of Conner and the other kids wandering around in the woods, dirty, scared, in danger for their lives. He could see them and was trying to call out to them, but no sounds were escaping his lips. They just kept walking away, deeper into the enveloping darkness of the forest, and there was nothing he could do to help them.

Chapter 12

Raylee sat on the bed in the room, examining the dusty old patterned quilt. Derek had wordlessly gotten her early this morning and escorted her back inside the house, giving her a slight push into the room and locking the door behind her. Two days locked in this room with her meals brought to her by the mother, one night in a barn, now back in this room again. She didn't know what to make of it. She didn't know whose room this was—it was decorated with a few old dolls, their dead black eyes staring out at nothing—and she felt sorry for herself. One in particular unnerved her; it was about two feet in length, had knotted blond hair with a blue bow, and was wearing a tattered red dress. Its face was dirty and scratched, and it was sitting on the dresser in the corner of the room, legs splayed out and wearing one black shoe. It looked like it might have been one of those dolls whose eyes opened and closed when you laid them down and set them back up again, but one eye was now frozen in a permanent half-closed position, giving it a menacing look. The open eye seemed to stare at her intently, menacingly.

"Are you decent?" a woman's voice came from the outside of the door.

"Yes," Raylee answered.

She heard the sound of a key scraping into the lock beneath the glass knob, and the door swung inward. A girl stood there, maybe ten or so years older than Raylee. Her hair was a light dusty brown, and she wore a blue dress with black trim on the hem. She entered, walked over to the one chair in the room, and dragged it scraping across the wood floor. She positioned the chair directly in front of Raylee and sat down.

"My name is Mags," she said. "I'm not much of a talker, not like there's much to say. I'm supposed to say hello, and that's what I'm doing."

Raylee looked up and met her gaze, her cold blue eyes, brow furrowed as if she had caught Raylee in a lie.

"Hi," Raylee said.

"Like I said, hello. We got that out of the way. Is there anything you need? I'm supposed to ask that, too, so I am."

"No," Raylee said. She paused for a moment, then asked, "When can I go home?"

Mags hopped up from the chair as if she received a jolt of electricity to her backside and turned toward the dresser. "Not up to me. I'm just here to say hello and see if you need anything, like I said." She released a huff from her lips and took a few steps over to the dresser with the doll resting on it.

"This is my room, but Mom told me I had to give it up for some company that was going to be staying with us for a while. I suppose that's you. I can tell you I'm not happy about it. I'm sharing a room with Derek right now, and he's disgusting. Farts in his sleep and doesn't care. It's gross, stinks like the dickens. Don't be getting too comfortable. I'm coming back here soon enough."

Mags went to the dresser and pulled out the top drawer with a wooden squeak. "There are some old clothes of mine in here and in the closet. I'm supposed to tell you it's okay to wear them." However, she didn't sound like it was okay.

"I see you've met Dizzy here," Mags said, poking a finger into the face of the doll on the dresser. "I've had her my whole life. She keeps a watch on things around here." Mags turned her face sideways to Raylee. "And she's going to keep an eye on you. Her good eye." Mags let out a curt laugh.

"Why are we here?" Raylee asked, feeling bolder and shifting herself on the bed.

"I already told you, that's not my business. I don't know why you're here. You and those two stupid boys. I haven't met them, but Derek said there's a skinny one, Dickie, with glasses, who's a little slow or something."

"No, he just does things his way. He's actually really smart."

"Well, Derek doesn't seem to think so. He thinks he's a little trouble-maker and warned Pa to keep a close eye on him. What do you think?"

"I don't know," Raylee said, gripping her knees with her hands. "I suppose he's just scared…like I am, and probably Conner, too."

"Conner? Is that the other one?" Mags took a few steps back to the chair and sat down.

"Yes, Conner. That's his name."

"How did Pa find you? He hasn't said much since you all came back here together."

"We went looking for Dickie. He got lost in the woods. We were following him when…" her voice trailed off. How much did Mags know? Did she know they had been attacked in the middle of the night and kidnapped? She didn't know what to say.

"And?" Mags said, her hands clasped in her lap, like a schoolteacher expecting an answer to her question.

"And, well, and we ran into your Pa and Derek, I guess, and they brought us here."

"Oh, well, as I said, they haven't said much to me. Mom only told me you'd be staying with us for a while, and that I should be nice to you and make you feel welcome. That's what I'm doing right now."

"Okay," Raylee said, feeling like she needed to respond in some way.

"If you're staying, you'll all get used to it. There's not much to do here, really, besides work and eat. Nobody comes here to visit. It's boring, actually." Mags took a long strand of straw-dry hair hanging in her face and tucked it behind her right ear. "Pa keeps telling us we should be thankful for all that we have, and that we're not out in the world where people will try to take what we have. I'm not sure what he means by that, we don't have anything—nothing I would want to take. I was in town with him once, lots of people walking around and working in their yards. It seemed like an okay place to me, but what do I know. That was years ago. Maybe it's changed, I don't know."

Raylee studied Mags's face, which was staring out the dirty window next to the bed. "Does anyone else live around here?"

Mags turned her eyes back to Raylee. "Not anymore. One of Pa's cousins and his wife and kids lived nearby for a while. They used to come over when it came time to dig potatoes, and we would see them every few months, but he and Pa got into an argument about some chickens once, and they don't come around anymore."

"What about the chickens?" Raylee said, not caring, but sensing that she needed to learn as much as she could about these people.

"I don't know. I think Pa had promised him some chicks one spring but didn't give them over, and they got into a fight. That was a few years back, and I haven't seen them since. They were stupid anyway and dressed like pigs. We're better off without them."

"It must get lonely," Raylee said.

"Oh, yeah," Mags said, pulling the same strand of hair from behind her ear and letting it fall back to the front of her face. "There's no one for me to talk to my age except for Derek, and I'd rather not do that for too long; he's a pig, too." Mags paused for a moment, then asked, "So what's the deal with those two boys? Are they your brothers or something?"

"No, they're my friends. Dickie and I live in Morgan. Conner is visiting up here this summer with his grandfather."

"Well, isn't that a bite! Comes here for a vacation, and now he's here. Oh, well. That's how it goes, I suppose."

"Mags, if you can, can you ask your mom when we can leave?"

Mags tilted her head to the right. "You can be a little stupid, too, can't you? Like I already said, that isn't up to me, I just came in here to be friendly, that's it. Ask her yourself if you want, but I don't expect she'll have anything more to say about it. If I were you, I'd make myself comfortable and leave it at that." Mags stood up. "Just not too comfortable in this room. As I said, it's mine, and I'm going to be wanting it back, and I don't like the idea of having to share it with you. No offense, but you should be out in the barn with your friends, I think."

Mags went to the door and pulled it open. "Anything else?"

"No," Raylee answered.

Mags walked out and shut the door behind her. Raylee could hear the click of the key in the lock, and then there was silence. It sounded like a jail cell door closing, and a small tear slid softly down her cheek.

❧

Mags walked into the kitchen and over to the sink where her mom was washing the dishes from breakfast. Mags couldn't stand her. They had been close when she was little, so close that Mags couldn't stand to be away from her mother's side for more than a few minutes without crying and wailing, but those days were long gone. Once she turned fourteen, her mother had decided that she was lazy and messy, and continuously picked on her from then on about this and that, her hair not being combed, her room being too messy, her face not being washed enough. It was endless, and it went on that way for years.

When Mags turned nineteen, though, she had felt a change within her; she was fed up with being criticized, and one evening when her mother had scolded her for not wearing her shoes in the barn, which seemed pointless, she told her to shut up. Her mother froze in place, her face blank of any expression. Then she slowly walked up to Mags and punched her right in the face. It caught her completely off guard, and she had fallen backward onto an apple barrel, sliding off to the right and crashing down hard on her side. In shock, she looked up at her mother, blood streaking down her chin from the corner of her lips, not knowing what exactly had just happened. Mom just turned around and walked back to the door of the barn, opened it, walked through, and closed it softly behind her. It had never been the same between them since. Mom didn't criticize Mags at all after that, and Mags barely spoke to her except in passing.

"I did what you told me to. I spoke to her, and she seems fine, but she doesn't understand what's going on or why she's here," Mags said.

"Good," was all Mom said, not even looking up from her dishwashing.

Mags sighed. "Okay, well, I'm not going to be sleeping in a room with Derek forever. I don't see why I had to give up my room for her. She can sleep in the barn with the other two."

"You won't be," Mom said, still not looking at her, continuing to scrub brown crust off a yellow plate.

Mags turned to look out the window above the sink. "Good."

Mags turned and walked out of the house onto the front porch. The sky was clear, and the sun was beaming down on the yard, warming the brown earth, and fat flies were zipping around the compost pail next to the steps. The goats were in their pen, bleating and aimlessly walking about in the small confines, looking for any little bits of grass to eat. Mags put her hands in front of her, her fingers toying with the fabric tie on the front of her dress, not remembering why she had walked out here in the first place.

She turned and went back into the house.

Chapter 13

Conner woke with a start, as he had each morning he'd been in the barn, looking around in a panic, trying to figure out where he was. It didn't take long for the realization to come to him. Dickie was uncharacteristically already awake in the corner, his back resting on the wall.

"You had a bad dream," Dickie said.

"No kidding."

"You were saying something, but I couldn't make it out."

Conner sat himself up and proceeded to brush the wisps of hay from his pants and shirt, not that it did much good in this room.

"Anything happening?" Conner asked.

"You mean like the rescue mission you slept through last night?" Dickie said.

"You know what I mean."

"Sorry, I'm getting even more testy, if that's possible."

"No problem. I know exactly how you feel."

Dickie then explained that he had woken up while it was still dark and couldn't get back to sleep. He heard the door of the house open a few times and footsteps outside the barn door just before the sun started to peek through the boards, but they had gone away without a word. Dickie said he had whispered to Raylee but didn't get a response.

Conner immediately pushed up and went over to the wall. "Raylee? Raylee, are you there?"

"Not so loud, they'll hear you!" Dickie hissed.

"I could care less if they hear me. Raylee?" louder this time.

Nothing.

"Maybe she's in the house again," Conner said hopefully...hopefully that was it, and not something worse.

"Maybe," Dickie said, yawning.

Conner realized to himself that he had begun to lose track of time. "How many days have we been here?"

"Well, I've been here a lot longer than you, but you got here about three or four days ago, I think."

"Raylee!" Conner said louder still, not wanting to give up, that she might be in there asleep. Still nothing in reply. He walked back over to the spot where he had slept, defeated, and sat down. "I just don't get it. What do they want with us? It seems like they're keeping us here for no reason. I can't figure it out. I've been thinking about it. I'm positive now it was one of them I saw that night out the window of the Farm. They've been watching us, I think."

"Watching us why?" Dickie asked.

"I don't know why. It just doesn't make any sense. They have to know that people will be looking for us. The police. My grandfather. They must be searching for us right now. How are they going to explain kidnapping us and keeping us here?"

"I don't know either, and I don't want to know. I just want to go home."

"Me, too."

"To Virginia?"

Conner had to think about that for a minute, startled that he was thinking about the Farm and his grandfather. When did that change happen? he wondered.

"Not really, I guess. I was thinking about my grandfather. He must be worried sick. I bet my parents are mad at him for not keeping me safe. He doesn't deserve that. It's not his fault."

"My parents are probably freaking out right now, too," Dickie said. "My mother is a worrier, that's for sure. This one time, I ditched school with this kid Herb to go fishing at Double Tunnels. The school called to ask her if she wanted them to send my homework home with Raylee, and she flipped out. She called the sheriff, the state police, the wardens, and darn near everyone in town, as far as I could tell. Boy, didn't I get it good when I got home."

"What's Double Tunnels?" Conner asked.

"Oh, that. It's this place up the stream that feeds the pond where the water goes under the old railroad tracks. There are two old, rusty tunnels there to let the water go through, and it forms a little pool on one side. The brookies love to hang out in the pool, and you can usually catch five or six, no problem."

"What, did you bring your fishing pole to school?"

Dickie looked incredulous. "No, stupid. Jeez…you *are* a city kid, aren't you? All you need is some line and a hook. We just cut up some fresh green saplings and dug up a few worms and grubs out from under a dead log and used that to fish."

"How were you going to explain coming home from school with fish?"

Dickie paused in thought. "Well, okay, I didn't think that far ahead, Mr. Lawyer. I was making the point that my mother tends to freak out about nothing. I didn't think I was going to have to mount a full defense of my actions."

Conner smiled. Dickie, despite being smart and seemingly sure of himself, sure was easy to rile.

"Sorry," Conner said.

"Besides, I didn't get it as bad as Herb. His dad drinks, and he came to school the next day with a red-and-black welt under his eye. It was puffed up good. I don't know how anyone can do that, hit their kid in the face. I mean, sure, I got my share of spanks over the years, but they never hit me in the face. Never an honest-to-goodness smack in the face."

Conner thought about his own family. He had never been spanked at all, so far as he could remember. It was almost unheard-of in his neighborhood. He thought to himself that was probably a good thing. Hit a kid in the Virginia suburbs, and it would likely trigger a full child abuse investigation.

"Top-top, don't stop!"

The biting words made Conner's fists tighten involuntarily. He looked over at Dickie, who was staring wide-eyed at the barn door. They heard the familiar unlocking of the small door, and breakfast arrived. Only when they listened to the footsteps fading away did they exhale the breaths they had been holding. The pan appeared to contain the routine breakfast they had become accustomed to, but neither of them got up to retrieve it.

"That guy is completely freaky," Dickie said, finally breaking the silence.

"No argument here."

"I wonder if they give Raylee the same thing to eat."

Conner sat and pondered his situation once again. If they could find a way out of this room, they could free Raylee and take to the woods, maybe after it was dark. What then? Conner realized they wouldn't even know which way to go. Heading south made the most sense. Gramp had said there were people south and not much north. He knew the sun set in the west, so he decided tonight he would follow its path through the boards of the barn and draw a crude compass in the dirt to point the way south. He wished he had the compass Gramp had given him. It would make things a lot easier, he thought. Still, it was all he could think of to do and not much at that. However, it was better than doing nothing.

"Are you going to eat?" Dickie asked.

"Not now. Not hungry."

"Okay, then," Dickie said, standing up and heading over to the pan. "I'll save your half for you."

Food was the last thing on Conner's mind. Dickie began his rhythmic munching in the corner where he sat down to eat, and Conner continued to look around the room for any items that might aid in their escape. Nothing except for what he had already seen. If only he had his knife to pry the door open. Conner couldn't imagine the lock on the door was any less rusty and old than everything else in the place. Still, he didn't have his knife, so it was a moot point. Next. He had tried digging in the dirt by the barn wall yesterday, using the hoe to chip, but the earth was so hard and pebbly that he had torn up the ends of two fingernails. He'd stuck the bleeding nails in his mouth, tasting an earthy mix of barn dirt and metallic blood. The two fingers throbbed for hours after, and he was worried they might get infected, so he kept sucking on them periodically. No good.

Conner stood up and walked back to the wall where he had talked to Raylee, but decided against calling out again—not with that guy having just left. He felt shaky, the kind of feeling he sometimes got running around on the grass in the humid Virginia heat. He felt a buzzing sensation in his ears, like little wasps were in there, and he put a hand out against the boards to steady himself.

He had better get something to eat, after all, he thought, and he headed back over to where Dickie was sitting.

⅜

The rest of the day passed uneventfully, other than having to watch Dickie use the corner bucket, which had made Conner's stomach turn. He had only used it twice himself since he had been here, and the very thought of it sickened him and made him feel dirty.

Conner made careful note of the direction of the sun rays as they sliced down through the barn boards. When they eventually began to disappear in the far corner of the barn, Conner had his bearings, and he drew two intersecting lines on the floor, marked with N-S-W-E. The one pointing to the W was aimed directly at the setting sun, and Conner added arrows to the tips of each line. He saw that south headed out straight from the back of the barn, away from the house. That was good news, finally. He took a small piece of dusty burlap and laid it carefully over the diagram, with plans to check it tomorrow. Now all they needed to do was break out. Easier said than done.

Just after the last light faded and the barn room took on a deep blue hue, Conner heard footsteps approaching the door. Dickie heard them, too, and looked in that direction, his brow furrowed into a tight pinch. Dinner? The little door did not open as expected; instead, a clink and a dragging chain sound came at the big door. It opened with a descending clump of fresh air quickly following, and Conner took a breath into his lungs.

Standing at the door was not the young man he had expected to see, but an older man with shoulders that looked as though he could balance a piano on them. His face was covered with a thick, curly black-and-gray beard, and he was wearing an old brown felt hat, his long, stringy black hair falling from its sides onto his shoulders. He wore tattered gray canvas pants, a shirt that had probably been red at one time in its life but was now faded orange, black suspenders with brass clasps, and heavy work boots. Conner stared at the enormous boots and thought for a moment they looked like the ones Frankenstein's monster had worn in that old black-and-white movie. They were scary-big.

"You youngsters get up and get a move on now," the man said in a deep raspy voice.

Conner and Dickie both rose to their feet, standing warily with their arms at their sides.

"Dinner's in the house tonight. Don't you try to run, or Derek will chase you down and give you a good thumping. He's as fast as a yearling buck, that one. I'd hate to see you boys get all stove-up for doing something foolish."

The man turned and headed away from the door, and Conner and Dickie dutifully followed. When they stepped over the threshold of the barn, Conner had the briefest instinct to take off in spite of the man's warning, but he couldn't leave Raylee or Dickie behind, he quickly thought, and resolved to do as instructed. There was still dim light in the yard, and he could make out a ramshackle chicken house made of wire and black wood, and a gate off to the right. He stole a quick look back at the barn, and it was as he had envisioned it, in a state of outward decay, its old gray boards rippling like a river going over a rocky streambed. He noted a second door down by the far end of the barn. That had to be the room Raylee was in. There was a double door with black iron hinges in the middle, probably hiding a larger space that separated the areas in which he, Dickie, and Raylee were held captive. It explained why it was hard to hear her through the walls.

The man continued to plod forward, his boots making heavy clumping sounds as he went, stirring up little clouds of dust. Conner felt sure he could outrun him, but the other boy was a different story. It was best to do as the man said for now. When they reached the three rickety steps leading up to the front porch of a small house—such as it was—the man walked up the steps and opened the screen door with a twang.

"Come on in, nothing to be scared of," he said, coughing.

Conner and Dickie paused for a second at the steps, as though each wanted the other to go first and make sure it was safe. Conner took the initiative and walked up and through the door, with Dickie following close behind, accidentally stepping on the back of Conner's sneaker as he went.

There in the kitchen of the house was a table set for dinner, the young man already seated next to a young boy, and Raylee, her head facing down toward the plate in front of her, but she glanced up at him with her eyes. Conner's heart leaped, and he almost smiled but held it back. There was an older, bone-thin woman with long gray hair tied in a ponytail over by an old cookstove, stirring a large pot of something. The room glowed from two kerosene lamps hanging from the walls and one in the middle of the table. Conner wondered briefly where they got the fuel from, as it didn't seem like this family went to the local market that often to buy supplies.

"Land sakes, if we don't have ourselves a full table tonight!" the woman exclaimed in a cheerful tone as she turned to look at them. "You boys just take a seat right there, and I'll get supper on in a minute."

Conner and Dickie pulled back the wooden chairs at the table and sat down. Conner was still looking intently at Raylee, relieved that she was okay, and he struggled to keep his emotions in check. He noticed she was wearing a frilly dress with short sleeves and a blue bow tied in the center of her chest. The dress looked like it might have been white at some point in its existence, but now it had a yellow haze to it, probably the effect of sitting for years in a drawer or closet somewhere, unworn and unloved. The table was set with mismatched plates and forks, with thick green glasses filled with water, and a brown- and yellow-stained cloth napkin laid next to each plate. Everything in the room looked like it had been abandoned by some-body else long ago, probably for a good reason.

"This-here is Derek, who you've met," the man said, gesturing to the older boy, "and Bibbs, he's about your age, I'd guess." Conner didn't think so at all; the kid looked about six or seven to him, but he didn't say any-thing. "Mags won't be joining us tonight; she's still got the runs." The mother flashed the man a furrowed-eyebrow look.

"You can call me Pa, and this-here is Mom," the man said.

Both Conner and Dickie nodded dutifully, but *Pa* and *Mom*? Not in a million years, Conner thought to himself. These people are crazy. He looked over at the young boy again, who was also staring intently at his plate but sneaking glances up at them with his eyes. The boy had short brown hair that almost looked like a helmet, blue overalls with no under-shirt, and dirt scuffs up and down his arms and on his left cheek, evi-dence of a kid having put in a hard day of work and play in the outdoors. The older boy seemed more confident of himself, staring intently at both Dickie and Conner, almost daring them to stare back, a slight sneer on his thin lips.

"We don't get much company up in these parts," Mom said, "so we're just as pleased as can be to have you all here with us."

Company? Conner's thoughts raced. Didn't she know how they got here? Was she mocking them? He couldn't make any sense of it.

Pa sat down at the table, picked up his napkin, and tucked it into the neck of his shirt.

"You youngsters are in luck tonight. Derek here got us a fine deer, and it'll be venison for dinner all week."

Conner didn't feel lucky at all. He was horrified by everything he saw here. Being forced to sit down to dinner with your captors, Raylee dressed up like some sad little doll, the whole thing was just surreal, and he felt his head begin to swim.

Mom hoisted the black pot off the stove by the handles with two thick rags and brought it over to the table, setting it down in the middle of a square wicker mat. Derek immediately reached for the metal ladle in the pot, and Mom abruptly smacked his hand away.

"Hey, what was that for?" Derek croaked, cradling his hand as if he'd snagged it in a piece of machinery.

"You mind your manners. We have company, they get served first. Didn't I raise you better than that?"

Okay, okay…sorry," Derek said, not sounding like he meant it.

"You go ahead, sweetie," Mom said, looking to Raylee. "Ladies go first in this house."

Raylee reluctantly grasped the handle, scooped up a ladle full of the concoction of brown meat chunks, yellow potatoes, carrots, onions, and gravy and plopped it into the center of her plate. She returned the ladle to the pot and looked down at her plate again.

"Don't you want more than that, honey?" Mom said. "There's plenty for everyone."

"No, thank you, ma'am," Raylee said, "this is fine."

"Well, okay, but I hope you boys brought more of an appetite."

After Conner and Dickie had ladled helpings of the stew onto their plates, the rest of the family served themselves. There was a short period of uncomfortable silence as they began eating, finally broken by Pa.

"Well, it's starting to get dark out early already. Looks like we're in for another banger of a winter."

"I hate snow," Derek said. "I'd rather have it be warm all year round. We should move again, further south this time."

"Aww, come on now, Derek," Pa said. "It's not that bad. Besides, we've laid down roots here. I wouldn't want to be anywhere else. We'd never like it down there. Snakes and bugs and all sorts of crawly things."

"We got bugs here, too," Bibbs said, startling Conner with his young voice. It was the same voice he had heard outside the barn a few days ago playing, he was sure of it.

"Sure, we got mosquitoes and black flies, but they got them cockroaches down south. Get into your food, into your bed—why, everywhere! You wouldn't like it one bit."

"I would," Derek said.

"Bet you a dollar after a year down there you'd be hightailing it back north. No, this is the best place for us. Folks down there are always getting into your business, telling you what to do, and people stealing your stuff. Bunch of lazy thieves, that's what they are."

Conner listened to the conversation and dutifully ate small forkfuls of the stew. He was surprised to find the vegetables were not that bad, but the meat was gamy and metallic-tasting, and it made his stomach turn a little. Pa explained during dinner that they had eaten the deer liver and heart because those were the parts that spoiled the fastest. The thought, far from helping, made Conner even more queasy. Conner, Raylee, and Dickie remained mostly silent during the meal, with the occasional yes or no to questions from Mom. When Bibbs had finished eating, he started playing with something in his lap, but Conner couldn't see what it was.

Mom pushed her plate aside and lit a cigarette with a wooden match, her long white fingers looking like weathered twigs, cradling it gently and flicking the ash into a cracked blue dish in front of her. Conner was struck by how pale and thin she was, but at the same time looking strangely strong and wiry. Her faded green dress seemed to hang on her tiny frame as if it was on a wire hanger in a closet. Her face was creased, cheeks pockmarked, and her teeth were yellow and stained, with black gaps where other teeth should have been.

Once they were all done, Pa stood up and told them they needed to be heading to bed. Derek rose up and led Conner and Dickie back out the front door, but before they went through it, he stopped short, looked them squarely in their faces and asked if they had anything to say to Mom.

"Thank you," they both said in awkward unison.

"You should thank me, too," Derek added, a cheerful smile on his face. "I shot the mangy thing."

"Thanks," Conner said, but Dickie stayed silent. He looked petrified.

As they were heading out the door, Conner noticed that Raylee wasn't joining them. Mom had whispered something in her ear just as they were getting up from the table, but Conner hadn't been able to make it out. He hated leaving her, but he didn't see that he had much choice, and soon they were across the yard and back in their makeshift prison in the barn.

Once Derek's footsteps faded away, Dickie let out a breath. "Well, that was freaking weird!"

"Yeah," was all Conner could muster. He couldn't stop thinking about Raylee and whether she was in any danger.

"Meat tasted like vomit," Dickie said. "I'm never eating liver again. Did you see Raylee? They had her dressed up. She looked scared. Don't you think?"

Conner didn't respond; he just sat down on the dirt floor and stared at the wall.

❧

The next morning, Conner woke up to find the sun already shining through the boards. He had heard the breakfast pan being delivered by Derek about an hour before, but he didn't move, just looked through the slits of his eyes at Dickie, who also didn't react. It was becoming painfully routine.

He pushed himself up with his arms and went over to check his makeshift compass. Sure enough, the east arrow was pointed more or less in the direction of the sun. Good. At least he knew he was on the right track. Now all he had to do was figure a way out of here with Dickie, collect Raylee, and get away without anyone in the house hearing them, then figure out where they were and get home…simple. Yeah, right, he thought. He was out of ideas, and he knew it.

Dickie rolled over and said something in his sleep Conner couldn't make out, but a bad dream was a safe guess. Then, out of nowhere, he heard a muffled voice from outside: "Hi." Conner's head jerked to the right at the sound. He glanced quickly at Dickie. No movement.

"Hi," the voice called again. It was a child's voice.

Conner tentatively got to his feet, one of his knees making a pop as he rose. It was coming from the back wall of the barn, low and quiet. He walked over to it and crouched down.

"Hi," Conner said.

"It's Bibbs," the voice replied. "Remember me from last night at dinner?"

"Yes," Conner replied. "I'm Conner."

"Oh, I know that. Dickie is there, too, and Raylee in the house."

"Have you talked to Raylee today?" Conner asked hopefully.

"Oh, no, I'm not even supposed to be talking to you. Is Dickie there now?"

"He's still asleep."

"Oh…oh well, okay. That's weird; does he sleep a lot?"

"I guess. There's not much else to do."

"Oh, don't worry, that will change soon. Pa said you all are going to help with the harvest the next few weeks."

The next few weeks? The words made the back of Conner's head prickle. "I don't know about that. I think we have to be getting home soon."

"Oh, okay. I like having you guys you here. It's kind of nice. Derek doesn't play with me anymore, and Mags ignores me."

"Mags, your sister?"

"Yeah, that's right. For the longest time, it's been just Mom, Pa, Derek, and Mags. Until you guys came to visit."

Conner thought about how to word his next sentence. He didn't want to scare Bibbs off. "Well, we're not visiting; we're kind of…kind of being held here."

"Held? Like a hug?" Bibbs replied.

Conner stifled a sudden laugh. "No, not hugged. What I mean to say is that we all have families of our own we have to get back to… Do you know why we're here?"

"Pa said you came to stay with us. He said you're sleeping out here in the barn just so you all can get used to the place, but soon one of you may be moving to live with us in the house and become part of our family like Raylee is now. He said you might not seem to like it at first, but eventually you'd be happy here, part of one big happy family."

Conner froze. Raylee and *one of us*? "I'm not so sure about that, Bibbs. I think we'll have to go home." What else could he say? "Why did your Pa only say one of us?"

"He said there wouldn't be enough food for all three of you. Raylee, she's staying. Mom likes her a lot; she says she always wanted another daughter, and Derek likes her, too. He's joking that she's going to be his wife someday." Bibbs laughed. "Can you imagine that? She's too little to be married, I said, but Derek said, for now, but she'll grow up soon."

Conner felt sick to his stomach. His head was starting to swirl again. "Which one of us is going to stay with Raylee?"

Bibbs paused for a moment. "Pa didn't say; just one of you, that's all. I think it's probably you, though. Derek doesn't like Dickie much."

"What about the one who doesn't stay?"

"Pa didn't say. One of you will have to go back to where you came from, I suppose."

Conner decided to take a risk, not knowing how long the conversation would last. "Do you think you could let us out of here?"

"Oh, no!" Bibbs blurted. "I'd be in big trouble if Pa or Derek even knew I was talking to you. I just wanted to say hi. Hi."

Conner gritted his teeth and looked at the ground, then relaxed and answered. "Hi… Well, Bibbs, I'm not sure we can stay here. We all have to get home."

"I hope Pa is right. I like the idea of having you guys here. You could play with me."

"Well, I suppose, yes, we could play with you. The thing is, we have families we miss and need to get home to."

Conner heard scuffling outside the wall. "Okay, well, I have to go."

"Wait, Bibbs," Conner said, putting his hand on the wall, "are you sure you can't just let us out, just for a little bit?"

"No, sorry. I wish I could, but I can't. I have to go."

Conner heard Bibbs's footsteps heading away from the wall. He sat back down, stunned, reflecting on what had just happened. *Part of the family?* Were they kidding? Raylee married to Derek? It was all too impossible and horrifying to even comprehend. Was that why they had Raylee dressed up like some little doll? His thoughts were escalating and roaring in his head like an engine revving. Also, what about the one who *wouldn't* be staying? What did that mean? It could only be bad. They couldn't afford to let one of them go home.

Just then, Dickie started to stir.

"Hey," he said, still half asleep. "I thought I heard you talking. Were you talking to yourself?"

"No," Conner replied, not looking at him. "That kid Bibbs was outside the wall. I was talking to him."

Dickie quickly shifted into a sitting position. "What? Where? What did he say?"

Conner decided instantly to only relay parts of the conversation. Dickie was likely to go berserk with fear and dread if he knew everything. "He was outside the wall. He said we are going to be out of here soon and go to live in the house, and that we were going to help them harvest food soon."

Dickie's eyes went wide, and his eyebrows rose, making his forehead crease into a ripple of little fleshy lines. "Is he kidding or something?"

"He didn't sound like it. He said we were part of the family now."

"No freaking way! He said that?"

"Yes."

"There's no way I'm doing any work for these monsters. I'm sure enough not going to be part of their twisted family!"

You have no idea, Conner thought silently. Work was the least of their problems. He shifted around to face Dickie. "I'm just telling you what he said. I asked him if he could let us out of here, and he said he couldn't. He sounded scared of getting in trouble with his father or Derek."

"Well no doubt—he lives with a bunch of backwoods freaks!" Dickie was almost out of breath.

"He sounded like he was glad we were here, and that we could play with him."

Dickie shook his head in disbelief. "Well if that little troglodyte thinks I'm going to play nice-nice with him, he's sorely mistaken."

Conner looked Dickie in the eye. "Look, you need to calm down and think. He could help us get out of here. If you start calling him names and scaring him, he's just going to tell them what you said or never talk to us again, and then we'll *never* get out of here."

Dickie paused. "Well…I guess, maybe. Okay, I'll play nice-nice if you think he can help us, but I'm not going to like it."

"I'm not asking you to like it, I'm just saying that right now he's the only one who doesn't seem to understand what's going on, and maybe we can get him to help us. He won't do that if you abuse him."

Dickie studied the floor and just nodded. Conner hoped he'd gotten the message and would be smart and keep quiet. Despite the horrible things Bibbs had innocently told him, it was the first glimmer of hope he had felt about getting out of this whole situation.

The sun's rays were coming through the wall cracks full force now, shining down on the floor in a vertical pattern and warming the air. Conner twisted the edge of his shirt into his fist until his fingers turned white and cold, and thought about what to do next.

⁂

It was late afternoon, the sun melting beneath the horizon and casting an orange glow across the field, as Bibbs finished up one of his favorite chores—potato-bug hunting. He carried a rusted blue coffee can to deposit his quarry in, already fifteen or twenty of the little creatures slowly crawling about in there, looking for an escape route. His Pa had taught him long ago how to identify the little pests, the larval bugs appearing dark red with a small hump on their backs, a black head, and two rows of black spots along their sides. The older bugs had alternating yellow and black stripes on their tiny wings. They left sticky orange globs of eggs in patches on the potato leaves, which he scraped off with a dirty fingernail when he found them. Pa had told him the bugs liked to eat the potato plant leaves, and if they damaged them enough, no potatoes would grow under the earth. Bibbs was a bit torn about this at first, killing the little families of bugs, although he didn't initially mind eating the yellow potatoes during the late summer and early fall. By the time spring rolled around, though, he would be sick to death of them.

Bibbs walked carefully so as not to step on the plants. His father inspected the fields every few days and would notice if he had been careless. Each time Bibbs spotted one of the little pests crawling lazily on a leaf, he grasped it with his thumb and middle finger and plopped it in the can. He was careful not to pinch too hard; the *snap!* sound of an accidental squish grossed him out. At least they didn't bite—that was a good thing. He hummed a tune to himself that his mother used to sing to him when he was little, something about working on a railroad, fee, fi, fiddly ay oh, and a kitchen for Dinah, whatever that was supposed to mean. It didn't matter. Bibbs loved it when she sang it, and he used to ask for it every night before bed.

He ambled down the last row of plants, looking sharp for victims for the cylindrical metal prison and ultimate death chamber he carried with him. He never participated in the executions himself, feeling somewhat guilty for having plucked them out of their mindless crawling and munching on the leaves. Derek took care of the grisly task of mashing them up, which for some reason, he didn't seem to mind. In fact, he gave Bibbs the impression he enjoyed it, using a small wooden dowel he had cut from an old broom handle to carry out the deed.

As he walked, Bibbs thought back to the conversation he'd had with the boy Conner earlier in the day. Even now, he couldn't believe he had ignored Pa's and Derek's warnings not to go near the barn. It had been on an impulse when he was playing with his soldiers in the yard. One minute he was coordinating an attack, and the next thing he knew, there he was, crouched next to the barn wall whispering to them. He was surprised to get such a quick response from inside. The one that answered, Conner, he liked. He looked nice. He didn't like Dickie, though; he looked kind of scared or angry. The girl, Raylee, had spent another night in the small bedroom in the back of the house, but Mom was in the house all morning, and he couldn't have talked to the girl even if he had wanted to. She seemed nice, too, and she was pretty. Smelled pretty good, also, as he noticed when she walked by him at the dinner table. He couldn't help staring at her when she was near him, but he was too scared to talk to her yet.

He thought more about what Conner had said. It didn't make any sense. Why wouldn't they want to be part of the family? What did he mean when he said they all had to go back to their families? Why were they here, then? It was strange. After dinner the other night, Pa had sat with him, Mom, Mags, and Derek and said that Raylee and one of the boys, maybe, would be part of the family now, and that they needed to make them comfortable. It wasn't so bad here, even though Derek could be kind of mean. It seemed strange that Conner didn't want to stay. He thought about it some more, but couldn't figure it out. Why did they come here in the first place, then? Conner was silly. How could they *not* want to stay here and be his new brother and sister? Also, the one not staying, Dickie probably, he would just be going back to where he came from, right? It was the only thing that made any sense.

Dark shadows began to inch across the field toward Bibbs, and he quickly finished up his pass of the last row, probably missing a few trespassing bugs as he hurried. They would have to wait for another day.

He didn't like the dark, not one bit. Derek had told him a few times all about loathsome things that came out in the night. Hideous creatures with long black mossy arms, clawed feet, thick crooked fangs, and red eyes that would scoop you up and take you back to their caves to rip you apart and eat you. His mother had scolded Derek once for making up lies and scaring him, so he didn't know for sure if the stories Derek told him were real, but he had no intention of finding out.

Chapter 14

Granville stopped at a small stream feeding into the river, knelt, took off his hat, and splashed cold water on his face and the back of his neck, rinsing away the dirt, pine needles, and sandy salt from sweat. It had been tough going the last six hours; the riverbank had closed up into thick pines and saplings, and he'd had to fight his way through to make a path, his feet occasionally sinking into wet holes formed by water. It would be smoother going up into the woods a few hundred yards, but Granville knew his best chance of seeing where they had exited the river, either on this side or the far side, was to stay close to it. Once he had cooled off, he retrieved a small orange bottle of mosquito repellent from one of the side pockets of his pack and reapplied it to his face and neck. The repellent trickled down onto his top lip, making it feel numb. Still, it was better than getting eaten alive by the little devils. In spite of the repellent, the skin on his neck was peppered with blood splotches and smashed insect bodies.

He tucked the wide-brimmed green hat back onto his head and looked up the river, noting that it went around a bend to the west just ahead. He was starting to doubt his decision to go upstream. He had been walking for days now. How far up could they have gone? If they were paddling or rowing, he would have found them by now, leaving the only possibility that they were in a motorboat, but he couldn't afford to dwell on it. He thought back to the trip up the bog he had taken with Conner weeks ago; this had to be the river he had visited with his grandfather many years before, and eventually, it terminated at a lake. However, that was at least another fifty miles or more, judging by what he estimated to be about twenty-five miles he had already covered. He usually could do five miles hiking in the woods in half a day or less, but that was on a groomed, well-marked hiking trail. It was different here, off the grid and in the wild. Once, he had taken his son, a few of his college friends, and one of their fathers on a two-day fishing trip down the river from town. After slogging their way through a thick blowdown, the father had succinctly summed up the experience: "Worse than Vietnam!" he had shouted, with a sweaty, red-faced laugh.

Most people who hiked national or state park trails would find hiking in this stuff a rude awakening. Still, Granville respected anyone who took the time to leave the relative safety of civilization behind and venture into the woods, marked trail or not. It was a spiritual experience, and those who understood the quiet peace that came with being out in the woods with only yourself and your thoughts were one step in front of everyone else, in his book. It was different this time. The joy he usually found being in the woods was starkly absent, and although he was sweating and hot, his insides felt cold, like plate steel left out in the snow. He had a constant acrid taste in his mouth, not from the exertion, but from worry and fear—fear that he would never find these kids, and that it was all his fault. He had not impressed upon Conner the gravity and danger of venturing into the woods on a foolish whim, and for that, he would never forgive himself.

His thoughts broke with the familiar chatter of a red squirrel alerted to his unwelcome presence, and with a grunt he started again, stepping on a muddy rock and forcefully thrusting the tree branches aside, violently snapping the weak ones, as if they were purposefully and maliciously holding him back from his objective.

❧

The afternoon had passed without incident for Conner and Dickie, and both were leaning against the wall of the barn when they first heard it—a voice, or voices, off in the distance. Conner jerked his head toward the door, but the voices were suddenly overtaken by the fast footsteps of someone approaching. The chain outside the door clattered roughly, and the door burst open, exploding particles of dust and hay in a violent, mini tornado-like swirl. Derek stood there, silhouetted by the fading sun, but he quickly entered the room and closed the door behind him. He walked briskly over to Conner and Dickie, who were stunned at the sudden turn of events, and crouched down.

"You two," Derek said with a sharp hiss, "you keep quiet, not a single word or sound, you understand?"

Conner and Dickie were too shocked to answer at first.

Derek's lip was tightly gripping his upper teeth. "I said, *do you understand me? Answer!*"

"Yes," Conner said, "we understand." Dickie's eyes were darting back and forth with adrenaline.

"How about you?" Derek said, looking squarely at Dickie.

"Yes," Dickie managed to croak, "I understand."

Derek stood up and looked down at them, two tiny animals entirely at his mercy. "The girl is with us. If I hear so much as a single sound come out of this room, I'm going to kill her dead. Is that clear?"

Conner and Dickie were motionless. "Yes," they said in unison.

Derek spun around and headed back out the door, shutting it tight after him and fastening the chain on the outside.

Dickie turned his head to Conner. "What's going on?"

"Shhh…be quiet, I can't hear," Conner whispered.

Muffled voices were coming closer now, and Conner got up as quietly as he could and went to the barn door. Once there, he carefully pressed his ear up against it, the rough wood scraping his skin.

More voices, but getting clearer; he could just barely make them out:

"Well, goodness, are we glad to see you! It seems like we've been wandering around for days without seeing anyone!" A strange voice.

"What can I do for you?" Pa said.

"Well, we were hiking on the North Camp trail, but somehow wandered off it, and I'll be snookered if we can find it. We tried to make our way back to our car but managed to get even more lost. Our GPS seems to be sending us all over the place. I don't know what's wrong with it—I just bought it last week. The darn thing is so complicated to work. Oh, I'm sorry, my name is Pete Vaccaro, and this is my wife, Nancy. We've already spent two nights in the woods we didn't plan on, and, as I said, you are a sight for sore eyes."

"Hi," Nancy said, a slight hesitation in her voice.

Nancy wore khaki shorts like Pete, with thick heavy socks and brown leather hiking boots with red laces. Her shorts and shirt were dotted with dirt and pine needles, evidence of bushwhacking through the forest.

"Don't know nothing about no trail, can't help you," Pa said.

"Oh, well…that's okay, we don't need to find the trail at this point. I know you're supposed to stay put when you're lost, but we came out on this trip on a whim and didn't tell anyone exactly where we were going. I know—stupid, right? They always say you should give someone your plans before you go on a hike. I can't get any cell service, and well, we hadn't planned on being out for more than a day and a night, so we sure are glad to find you."

"The way back to the roads and town is south, that direction more or less," Pa said, waving his hand.

Pete shrugged the red backpack on his shoulders uncomfortably. "Well, thanks, but I'm not sure I want to risk getting even more lost at this point. Can we borrow your phone to call for someone, or maybe you could give us a ride into town? I'd be happy to pay you something for your trouble."

"Don't have no phone, no car, and I don't need your money." Pa's eyes narrowed to hard slits. "You need to head that way. I can't do anything more for you."

Pete walked up closer to Pa, out of hearing distance from his wife. "Look, I understand, you live out here on your own, and you don't want to be bothered. However, I'm telling you, we are completely lost and…oh, is that your son?" Pete looked over at the house, where Derek stood on the porch, arms crossed tightly across his chest.

Pa glanced at the house. "Yeah, but as I said, I can't do anything for you… you best be on your way now."

Pa turned to walk toward the house, but Pete gripped his arm. "Sir, I'm begging you…we are completely lost. We need your help."

Pa turned his hard gaze down at Pete's hand, clenched on his right arm; this was not going to stand.

"Help us! Get us out of here!"

The scream was so loud in his left ear, Conner fell against the door of the barn, sliding down and landing with a thud on his side on the ground. Dirt flecks rained down on him like confetti. He'd been so intent on making out the conversation going on outside the barn, he hadn't heard Dickie pad up beside him and press his ear against the wall directly behind his head.

"No, Dickie!" Conner hissed through his teeth, looking up at him in horror. "Raylee!"

"What was that?" said a muffled voice through the wall next to his head.

Then, "No, wait, we're sorry, we're leaving!" anguished, stressed, volume rising.

Crack! Crack! The sharp, thunderous explosion of two gunshots rang out clear and quick, followed instantly by a woman's scream of terror and pain.

Crack!

The sound of the woman cut off abruptly, and then there was silence. Dickie recoiled from the wall as if it was a rattlesnake ready to strike. Conner looked back at the wall, his mind unable to comprehend what had just happened.

Then came a final voice, subdued and annoyed.

"Really, Derek?" Pa said.

❧

Heavy footsteps to the door, the rattling of the chain, and Derek stormed into the room, flinging the door hard to the wall with a crash. Conner and Dickie scrambled to their feet, backing away in unison from the looming figure of Derek, a wild, tight smile on his face as he swiftly came upon them. Conner saw for a split second the wooden grip of a single-action revolver tucked cross-draw into his belt. Before the word *sorry* could leave his lips, the swift arc of Derek's arm slammed into the side of his face, sharp pain blazing across his cheek as if he'd been struck by a rock…a flash of stars. For a millisecond, he thought how odd that was, just like in the cartoons.

He had no memory of hitting the floor.

❧

Conner opened his eyes to find the room almost completely pitch-black. It was night. How long had he been out? It was all just a blur; the visitors, the voices, those shots, and then the attack from Derek. He reached up to his left cheek, which felt swollen and raw, and he could feel a sticky trail of blood on his face. He looked around the room, trying to force his eyes to adjust to the blackness. "Dickie? Dickie are you there?"

Conner heard a garbled sound from the corner of the room. He pushed up onto his knees and started to crawl toward the sound. He didn't see Dickie lying prone on the floor before he bumped into him, collapsing on top of him.

"Aww, what happened?" Dickie groaned.

Conner rolled off to his side. "I'm not sure. I don't remember anything after Derek came in and punched me in the face."

Dickie shifted his head up, resting on both elbows. "I can't remember what happened after he hit you, either. You hit the floor like a sack of grain. I think he hit me, too; my glasses feel bent, and my face is killing me."

"It's killing me, too." Conner was surprised he had enough left in him to try to make a joke, especially since he could barely see Dickie's face in the darkness.

"Ha, very funny."

"You shouldn't have done that...I hope Raylee is okay."

Dickie sighed. "I'm sorry. It just came out. As soon as I heard that guy's voice, I couldn't help it. Really."

"It's not your fault. None of this is. I'm sorry if I made you feel that way."

"I keep thinking this is all because of that stupid knife."

"I'm not sure it is. I think they were watching us for a while. A couple of times in the woods, I had that feeling, and then there was that person standing in the field that night. I think they planned this somehow. You just gave them the chance to grab you sooner than later, and Raylee and I walked right into their hands trying to find you."

"Well, I appreciate that you guys did that. I was losing hope in this room those first days."

Conner pushed himself up into a sitting position, touching the blood on his face again. He tried to scrape it off with his fingernail, but that only made his cheek throb in spidery pain. "We have to get out of here. After what Derek did to those people, there's no way they are ever going to let us go." Conner hesitated. "There's something else, something I didn't tell you before because I thought you might freak out."

Conner saw the dark silhouette of Dickie's head shift toward him. "Bibbs told me that they're going to keep Raylee, and that's she's going to be his sister…and that they might also keep one of us."

"*One* of us? What did he mean by that…*one of us?*" Dickie cried.

"I don't know. Bibbs said something about there not being enough food for all of us."

"Oh, man. They're going to kill me, aren't they? I know it."

"We don't know that. All we know is that we have to do everything we can to get out. I know which direction south is—I've been following the sun as it shines through the walls. We need to break out of this room, free Raylee, and head south—*now*."

"How are we going to do that?"

"I don't know. Bibbs said he couldn't let us out, but if he comes back to talk to us, I'm going to try again. He has to know what just happened to those people, and he's our best chance. I need you to go along with what I say and not do anything stupid again."

Dickie hung his head in resignation. "Okay…whatever you say," he mumbled.

They didn't talk any more, but neither of them could sleep, staring at the ceiling until a faint blue light appeared from outside.

Another day, prisoners in a wooden cage.

Granville was walking along the edge of the river when he spotted the ducks floating lazily in a back eddy next to the shore. There were three of them, northern pintails, two males and a female. The males had breasts that radiated snow-white, with white lines stretching up their brown heads and necks. The female was less colorful but still beautiful, with brown and white feathers that reflected the sun like gold. He had always thought pintails were one of the more elegant-looking Maine ducks, more suited for the ball than the bar, as his father used to say. They were a rare sight in Maine, but he needed meat, and soon. He had consumed his second to last energy bar this morning, and despite keeping himself well hydrated, he was having spells of dizziness that he could only attribute to a lack of calories. He quickly and quietly crouched down, pulling his slung Winchester off his shoulder and cradling it in his arms. The water wasn't deep next to the shore—he could see the bottom—but it quickly dropped off about ten feet out, so he knew he needed to time his shot when they drew close to it. He had to wait ten minutes, but finally, one the males made its way up to the reeds to investigate something, probably an insect or piece of grain. Pintails were dabbling ducks and lived off aquatic plants, grains, and insects. They had a good flavor due to their mostly vegetarian diet, as opposed to diver ducks, like eiders and mergansers, which dined primarily on fish. Their taste had a noticeable fishy tang, which some people liked, but which turned him off. Not that he would have been picky at this particular moment in time.

As soon as the duck reached the reeds, Granville drew the sights of the rifle onto its head and fired a single shot. The duck instantly flopped over on its side in the water, one wing beating furiously and a tuft of feathers swirling into the air, the other wing splashing up water like a geyser. The struggle was mercifully brief, and aside from the ripples left by the other two ducks, who had immediately revved up their wings and taken off, the water was still. He could hear the thudding wings of the other ducks beating a hasty retreat as a paper-thin blanket of blue smoke from the shot hung in the air. Granville walked down to the water's edge and stepped directly into the reeds and the mud, which quickly took hold of his boots with a slurp. A few more steps into the water and he was able to stretch out his arm and retrieve the floating bird, noting that his shot had taken a goodly portion of the back of its head off, but had left the eyes and beak intact. It was grisly but necessary.

Once back on shore, he pulled his knife from its sheath, and with an expert hand, swiftly dressed out the bird, separating the heart, liver, and gizzard, and tossing the rest of the entrails in a wet red glob onto the mud. He pushed the saved organs back into the cavity, removed a plastic grocery bag from his pack, and wrapped the duck carcass in it, then stuffed it into his backpack. Dinner for tonight was covered, at least, he thought to himself.

Granville put his pack back on his shoulders, jacked a fresh round into the rifle chamber, expelling the spent one, lowered the hammer and re-slung it on his shoulder, then continued along the bank. When he turned the next bend, he stopped and surveyed what lay before him.

"Blast," he said out loud.

The ground in front of him rose sharply in a hundred feet or so, forming a rocky ridgeline that extended as far back into the woods as he could see. He weighed his options: either climb up and over it, or follow it back into the woods until it retreated into the ground and he could flank it. Twenty years ago, he wouldn't have hesitated for a moment. He had always been lean and wiry, and climbing obstacles was something he enjoyed. However, now, in his older years, he found his body to be less accommodating to his mental whims, creaking and stiffening up when he pushed it too far. Still, there were obvious handholds of small trees and protruding rocks to the top, and he figured it was something he could manage: Time was of the essence.

Using a technique he had learned from loggers he knew, he began his slow ascent, always keeping three points of contact with the rock face as he went. He gripped each handhold with care, testing it with his arm to make sure it was stable before moving upward. He reached the top quicker than he had expected, but a look back down to his right made him realize he was, indeed, taking an awful risk climbing like this, alone in the woods, with no hope of quick rescue if he fell. His pack seemed like it was purposely pulling him backward, almost wanting him to fall. To his relief, he pulled himself up over the top of the ledge and clambered to his feet, reflexively brushing off the bits of dirt, moss, and lichen that covered his pants. He stretched his back and looked at his palms embedded with pebbles, dirt, and grass.

"Well, that's one for the Gramp," he said aloud, imagining it might be what Conner would say if he were here.

Chapter 15

Raylee sat quietly in the room on the thick quilted blanket on her bed. Her sneakers were on the floor next to her, the socks she had been wearing for days now still on her feet. Small pine needles and brown dirt stains almost completely masked their once brilliant white color, and for some reason, this minor thing depressed her. She felt lost and alone and couldn't keep her thoughts straight. She dropped her hand down onto the bed, raising a mushroom cloud of fine dust particles that sparkled in the sun shining through the cracked, rippling glass of the window. The glass reminded her of the windows in her grandmother's house. Unlike the clear glass windows in most homes today, it had distortions and bubbles, a sure sign of being made a very long time ago. She had strained to lift the window the first night she'd spent in the room, but it was nailed shut and wouldn't budge so much as a millimeter. For her efforts, she received two red indents with dirty white caulk in the skin of her palms. She considered trying to break the glass but knew she would most likely not be able to make it through without being heard.

Raylee scanned around the sparse room. The small dresser of musty-smelling clothes and the creepy doll resting on top; a candle; a closet with no door but the brass hinges remaining, hanging precariously like two golden leaves on a tree. It was not as bleak as the room in the barn, but somehow it was even worse. Being this close to the "family" made her uncomfortable and twitchy, and she had reverted to an old childhood habit of picking the skin around her fingernails and the creases of her thumbs. Her mother had always hated her nervous habit, scolding her when she saw the fleshy red patches around her nails. Her mother had even resorted to bribing her, offering her a quarter for every week she left her fingers alone. Now they were as ragged and torn as they ever were, and a few times, she'd had to stick a finger in her mouth to stop the bleeding, the metallic taste of the blood flooding her senses.

She had changed out of the dress the mother had made her wear for dinner and carefully hung it back up in the closet, as instructed. She had on her pants and T-shirt again, and those dirty socks. Still, they were better than the dress and made her feel more like herself.

She thought about Conner and Dickie out in the barn. And about this family holding them here, Derek in particular. He frightened her with his incessant staring at her. Outwardly, the family appeared to be happy and friendly, with broad smiles and winks, but they were anything but what they seemed. She was scared for herself, yes, but she was even more scared for Conner and Dickie. As bad as this was, her instincts were telling her it was only going to get worse—if that was even possible.

The unexplained events of yesterday left her feeling even colder inside, and although she hadn't seen it, she had heard the sound of gunshots close by and feared that Conner and Dickie might be dead, leaving her alone in this awful place. Dickie was like her brother—she had known him forever—and Conner…well, she had just gotten to know him this summer, but already had feelings for him that confused her. She'd never really had much use for boys. They were loud, obnoxious, and, quite frankly, *smelled* sometimes. He was different. He had a caring way about him, and she had been close enough to him on some occasions to know that he didn't smell. He had a faint scent of something like shower gel, and in those moments, she had to resist the urge to wrap her arms around him and bury her face in his neck, breathing him in. It was unlike anything she had ever felt for a boy before, and the thought that now he might be gone was too much to bear. She told herself that they were okay; it was all she could do.

Raylee stood up and walked over to the window. The sun was bright outside, and it was a perfect day, except that it wasn't. A small brown-and-white bird flitted to the windowsill, taking in its surroundings with a nervous back-and-forth tilt of its tiny head, then flew off. She envied it. She went back to the bed and lay down on her back, crossing her arms in a tight tuck and staring at the cracked and water-stained ceiling. She had always been independent and prone to doing her own thing (sometimes to her detriment), not overly concerned with the judgments of her peers or parents. That inner strength seemed to be fading from her, though, like a slow leak of tepid, warm water from a kiddie pool. Soon it would be gone, and likewise, soon her hope and strength would evaporate with it.

She closed her eyes and tried to imagine comforting things; the kitchen in her home with a fresh apple pie, warm from the oven, on the counter. Christmas morning, the presents under the colorfully lighted tree, with white snow sparkling outside the window, the anticipation of what surprises might be concealed in the red and green wrapping paper. Conner. Conner, for the way he made her feel safe…safe and wanted. Stealing glances at her when they were alone that he probably thought she didn't notice, but she did. She saw everything he did, and she longed to be able to go back to the time before this ever happened. When they were happy and home.

❧

It was late afternoon when Granville finally reached the end of the ridge, which descended gradually, thankfully, back to ground level with the river. It had been a hot morning of hiking, and although he was still feeling depleted, last night's dinner of duck had filled his stomach, more or less, and given him renewed energy. After the exertion of climbing to the ridge-top, he had decided to make camp for the night and sparked a quick fire to cook his meal. It probably wasn't close to restaurant quality, but it was by far the best thing he had tasted in recent memory, roasted to perfection on a cut green branch over the fire. He saved most of the bones, little bits of red flesh and tendons still clinging to them, and wrapped them up in the plastic bag. Tonight, he planned to use them to make a stew of sorts, using the small tin cup that dangled from a rawhide string on the outside of his pack. He never went on an overnight hike in the woods without it. He could use it for cooking directly over a fire, boiling water for drinking—a veritable one-stop kitchen in a small package.

Even with the ready-planned meal ahead, he kept a sharp lookout for any more ducks, partridge, or squirrels. He had one energy bar left but was saving that in case of an emergency—an emergency worse than this already was, that is. A partridge right now would be a blessing, although he had noticed that in the last ten years the sighting of them had become more and more infrequent. They were good eating, tasted a lot like chicken (of course), but with a slightly stronger flavor. Making a successful shot with his rifle would be a challenge, but he knew if he flushed one, they tended not to go far, usually perching in a branch, their muted brown and white colors allowing them to blend in perfectly with the limbs and leaves, maybe giving him the opportunity for a shot.

In his youth, partridge had been abundant in the woods and along the logging roads, and more times than he could count, he had happened upon them by accident in the thick brush, their wings exploding into a thumping drumbeat as they took off, nearly giving him a heart attack each time. Usually he hunted them with his single-shot .410 shotgun. The .410 was a much smaller shell than a 12-gauge or even a 20-gauge, perfect for making sure the shot pellets didn't destroy the delicate meat. A running joke with newcomers to eating hunted partridge was to tell them they might want to check their meal for romets, a telltale sign being small black smudges on the breast meat. These marks, of course, would be evidence of the shotgun pellets having done their job, which was usually revealed to the eater after a significant level of concern about deadly north-woods diseases had built upon their faces. Of course, some people Granville knew had a streak of mischievousness that knew no bounds, and they would never reveal the innocuous truth. They would just as soon allow city folks to go on worrying about romets, mountain lions, and bears, or even more exotic species unknown to the zoological world: swamp-swishing stump crunchers (beavers), bushy-tailed tree squeaks (squirrels), and side-hill badgers, which, through evolutionary time, had developed the peculiar feature of their legs being shorter on one side of their bodies from living life on steep slopes. Jokesters like that populated the rural areas of Maine like black flies.

The woods opened up a bit, and Granville made his way over the branches and rocks with a quickened pace.

Relief. Just ahead, he could see the trees start to clear, and he took a quick step forward, but instead of finding solid ground beneath his sole, his right leg shot down into a hole with a sickening pop. The hole had been hidden by dead branches and leaves.

Searing pain shot up from his ankle and into his calf. Yelling in anguish, Granville slumped onto his left side and attempted to pull his leg out of the hole, only worsening the lightning bolts that fired up from his ankle.

Finally, on his hands and knees, he managed to pull his leg free, a glob of wet mud and twigs coating his boot, and he rolled over onto his back.

"No, no, no!" he screamed.

He lifted his torso into a sitting position and grasped his ankle. The pain was unreal, causing little reflective black dots to flood his field of vision. "No!"

He felt around his ankle. There was no protruding bone that he could find, but he could barely touch it without wincing in agony. The *pop* sound he had heard echoed in his head like a fading thunderclap, but he still couldn't accept it.

Taking some deep breaths, he calmed himself, and once his vision started to clear, he reached to the right, grabbed a small pine tree, and pulled himself up into a standing position using his left leg. Once he had his balance on his left leg, with just the toes of his injured leg barely touching the ground, he tried to put some weight on it.

The pain was immediate and almost as fierce as the initial injury, and he fell back against the pine and slid to the ground. Beads of sweat coursed down his forehead as he stared down between his feet.

Looking up into the tree canopy, he saw the sun piercing down through the tops of the trees, and although it went against his beliefs—and over the course of his life, he had often counseled others against doing the same in times of crisis or distress—he cursed God.

❧

Derek pulled Conner out of the barn just after daylight without a word. The door made its familiar rattle, and Derek entered as both Conner and Dickie looked at him with fear. He walked over to the prone Conner, grabbed his arm with a vise-like grip, and hauled him up to his feet, pushing him toward the open door. Dickie's head moved to follow him, but he remained silent.

Once out in the yard, Derek finally spoke.

"You'll be working in the field today, digging potatoes. You ever dug potatoes before, boy?"

"No," Conner replied.

Derek herded him toward the gate leading out into the field, where a rusty red wheelbarrow and a five-pronged pitchfork with a long handle rested against the wooden fence. The sky was cloudy and overcast, but there'd been no rain yet.

"Well, no matter, it's easy. Bibbs will show you which ones are ready to be dug up and what to do."

It was only then that Conner noticed Bibbs to his left, standing next to a small shed and holding a similar pitchfork with a shorter handle. He walked up silently beside Conner and led him into the field.

"Don't you try nothing, like running away or anything," Derek warned. "That wouldn't be too good for your friends." With that, he turned and walked away.

Bibbs spoke softly. "This way." Conner followed him.

"These two rows here, we planted early; we can get them now. Most of the plants won't be ready for a few more weeks. Try to get the fork under them so you don't spear them. You want to pull them up in one piece if you can."

Bibbs pushed his fork into the ground a few times to loosen up the dirt, then with a bit of effort turned over a plant and a sizeable chunk of earth revealing six dirt-covered potatoes. He picked up the plant and shook the dirt off, then carefully popped them off the root and laid them on the ground.

"We'll go around after with the wheelbarrow and collect them up," Bibbs said.

Conner dug his fork into the ground like Bibbs had shown him and was surprised to find five potatoes of his own on his first plant. There was a light breeze in the field that slid across the back of Conner's neck, and it created a slight chill down his spine.

"We always dig when the sun isn't shining. If you leave them in the sun too long, they turn green fast, and they aren't good to eat."

They worked silently for the next hour or so, depositing the small round spuds in a line along where they dug. Conner was surprised how quickly and precisely Bibbs dug for such a young boy. It was not his first time doing this. As they dug, Conner could feel the rough wooden handle of the pitchfork starting to raise a blister on the webbing between the thumb and index finger of his right hand, but he didn't say anything. Another hour passed, and Conner figured they probably had seventy or eighty potatoes on the ground ready to be picked up. Bibbs dropped his pitchfork on the ground with a dismissive clatter, went back to the fence, and brought the wheelbarrow forward, tipping it awkwardly a few times side to side before finding a perfect balance.

They collected the potatoes and put them in the wheelbarrow with echoing metallic thumps, Bibbs moving it every so often so that it always sat near them, ready to receive the spuds. As they finished the last stretch, Bibbs stopped and plopped down onto the ground.

"Come on, sit if you want."

"Okay," Conner said, taking a kneeling position next to Bibbs.

Bibbs reached into the front pocket of his overalls and brought out a small cloth, opening it to reveal a few sad strips of brown jerky and a little toy soldier holding a rifle above his head, mid-charge. He handed one of the jerky strips to Conner.

"Here, eat this, it's good. Pa makes it himself from deer meat."

Conner took a bite of the jerky, pulling it to one side to tear off a piece. It tasted salty and a little gamey, not like the kind his dad sometimes bought him in convenience stores, but it wasn't terrible.

"What's the soldier?" Conner asked.

"Oh," Bibbs said, "sorry about that. I have a bag of them, and sometimes I carry one of them around to keep me company. I don't think he hurt the jerky any."

"Was that what you were playing with outside the barn a few days ago?"

Bibbs gave a small smile. "You heard that?"

"Yeah, it sounded like you were having a good time."

"They're my toys, my friends. My only friends."

Bibbs munched away on his piece of the jerky, finishing it much quicker than Conner, who still had a few inches to go.

"Thanks," Bibbs said, his mouth still turning around a few pieces of the meat.

"Thanks for what?" Conner asked.

"For not telling Derek I was out there talking to you guys. He'd be mad if you did. Thanks for not telling."

"That's okay, no problem," Conner said, thinking hard about what he would say next.

"You seem like a nice kid, Bibbs," Conner said. Bibbs just grunted an acknowledgment and shrugged his shoulders.

"I didn't mean to scare you if I did; it's just that I want to get home to my family. Raylee and Dickie do, too."

Bibbs didn't respond but just finished chewing with an audible swallow. The breeze picked up a bit, and even though it was still only late summer, Conner began to feel legitimately cold.

"Did you think about what I said…about us needing to go home?" Conner asked.

"Yes," Bibbs answered, staring down at the ground.

"Well, I hope you know it's not you. Our families don't know where we are, and I'm sure they're worried right now. I'm sure my grandfather is just going crazy, not knowing where we are."

"But didn't you tell him you were coming to stay with us? That's what Pa said. He said that you all had decided that you wanted to get away from the dirty city and live out here in the woods with us."

Conner looked sharply at the side of Bibbs's head, which was still facing down toward the ground. The fact that he wasn't making eye contact made Conner think he didn't believe what he was saying.

"I don't know what your Pa and Derek told you, but we aren't supposed to be here. We came out into the woods for a picnic, Dickie lost his knife and went back for it, and then he disappeared. People were looking for him days and days, and finally, Raylee and I decided to go looking for him ourselves. That's when we ran into your Pa and Derek, and they brought us here."

Conner had decided to skimp on the details of the actual abduction, unsure of how Bibbs would process that type of information. "We didn't get to say goodbye to our families, and they don't know where we are. They probably think we're lost in the woods and need help."

Bibbs turned and looked at Conner for the first time since they had begun this conversation. "I don't understand. Why would Derek and Pa do that?"

190

"I don't know, Bibbs, but they did, and we need to get home." Conner shifted uneasily on the ground. "Bibbs? What happened to those people we heard yesterday in the yard?"

Bibbs turned his head away from Conner's eyes, staring back at the ground. "Bibbs?"

Bibbs let out a slight exhale of breath. "I don't know. I was in my room. I saw them out the window, but I don't know what happened. I heard Derek's gun go off. Pa and Derek came into the house, banging the door hard, and they were yelling at each other. I couldn't make out everything they were saying, but I was scared to come out of my room."

"Bibbs, I know it must have been scary," Conner said. "It was scary for us, too. Bibbs, I think Derek hurt those people, and I think you know that, don't you?"

"I don't know anything. I didn't see anything, and at dinner, Pa said that those people came here uninvited, and they were going to break up the family, and that what's done is done, and there was nothing anybody could do about it, and that I wasn't to speak of it again."

"Bibbs," Conner said, "is Raylee okay? I mean, after what happened to those people. Is she okay?"

Bibbs's dark eyebrows pushed together and formed a crease in his forehead. "Of course. Why wouldn't she be?"

"You're sure? You're sure she's okay?"

Bibbs grimaced slightly. "Yes, I'm sure. I spoke to her last night. Well, kind of. There are cracks in the wall between her room and mine, and last night I talked to her through one of them. Don't tell that to anyone. She's nice. I like her."

"I like her, too," Conner said softly, an enormous sense of relief flooding over him that at least Derek hadn't carried out his threat. He studied Bibbs's profile. There was a tension in his cheeks—he could see them rippling, as though he was grinding his teeth together—but there was no sound.

"Bibbs…the reason Derek hurt those people is that Dickie yelled out 'Help' to them, and they knew then that we were in there. That's why Derek did what he did. Bibbs, I know this is hard for you to hear, but I think Derek killed them."

The words seemed to echo in the air.

After a moment, Bibbs said, "I don't know, I just know that maybe they shouldn't have come here."

Conner took a deep breath. He sensed he needed to change the subject if they were to continue talking. He could see Bibbs's shoulders moving up and down slightly, tensing.

"Bibbs," Conner asked, "do your Pa and Derek ever leave this place, like to go somewhere you don't know about?"

Bibbs thought for a minute, his shoulders relaxing a bit. "Yeah, sometimes they go off and say I can't come. I wish I could. It's fun to go out in the woods."

"How long are they gone for usually?"

"I don't know. A couple of days sometimes, I guess."

Conner readjusted his legs to keep the circulation flowing. "A few weeks before we came here, I saw somebody standing in the trees near my grandfather's house. I couldn't make them out too clearly through the window, but they were standing there at night smoking. I think your Pa or Derek was watching my house, maybe planning to bring us here."

"That can't be," Bibbs said.

"Why not? You said they left for days at a time, and someone *was* watching my house."

"No, I mean it couldn't have been Derek or Pa. They don't smoke. They both say it stinks and makes them not be able to breathe right."

The implications of the words stabbed Conner in the chest. Bibbs was right; he had never seen Derek or Pa smoke…but he had seen someone *else* here do it.

"Bibbs, your mom smokes, doesn't she?" Conner's mind was reeling at the prospect of where this was going.

"Yeah, she does. She runs out of tobacco sometimes, but Pa always brings her a bag of it when he comes back from picking up supplies and stuff."

Derek's voice boomed from the field gate. "You two get off your butts and bring those taters over here *now!*"

Startled, both Conner and Bibbs almost fell over, but they quickly scrambled to their feet, Bibbs grabbing the handles of the wheelbarrow and Conner the two pitchforks. They hurried back to the gate and the brooding Derek. Bibbs turned to the left toward the wooden shed, and Derek reached down with both hands and jerked the pitchforks out of Conner's grasp. He kicked the back of Conner's leg hard, sending a little explosion of dust into the air with the stinging pain.

"And you...time for you to get back to your room."

Chapter 16

Granville sat on a wet moss-covered log, thinking hard on his injured leg as if he could wish it away. He had created a makeshift crutch out of a dead oak limb, breaking off the branches completely save for one at the top, which he left about eight inches long, forming a Y support for his arm. He attempted to go on walking, but only made it a hundred yards or so over the root-infested terrain before he had to sit down to rest. Despite the crisp air, salty sweat trickled down from the inside band of his hat and into the corners of his eyes with a sting. He didn't bother to wipe it away; it was the least of his concerns.

Daylight was fading fast among the trees, and he had to decide what to do. He could try to continue but didn't know how far or how quickly he could go. Then again, he couldn't go back, either. The radio, though it still had battery power, had proved entirely useless. He would have to draft a complaint to its manufacturer when he got back. The thought, so ridiculously trivial given his current situation, still brought a small smile to lips. It was a reminder that survival out here depended on many things—experience, skills, fitness, preparedness, knowledge of the woods—but probably the most critical and overlooked aspect was the right attitude. An attitude that you were going to make it, you were going to survive, it wasn't a question of *if* or *maybe*. You just *were*, and you had to face any obstacles with resolve and, if at all possible, humor. Laughter was the ultimate antidote for despair. Although he didn't have any real statistics to back it up, Granville believed that most people who died lost in the woods did so because they gave up. They blamed themselves for everything they did wrong to get them into the situation, and couldn't let it go. That wasn't going to happen to him. Not with the kids still out there.

A small boreal chickadee landed on a branch next to him, tilting its head and studying him cautiously. Granville looked at the bird but kept still, knowing that the slightest movement would cause it to flit off in a hurry. He'd always held chickadees in high regard. They had an inquisitive nature, and he had gotten into the habit of giving them some of the seeds earmarked for the chickens on occasion. After a time, they started to congregate in the leafy bushes next to the wire enclosure when he fed the chickens, waiting for a noontime snack. On impulse one day, he left the seeds in the open palm of his hand and held it out to three or four of the tiny, delicate birds. To his surprise, one flitted over almost immediately and perched on his extended index finger, dipping its head to snip out a few seeds from his palm. The bird was as light as air, the only physical indication of its presence being a slight scratchy feeling as its tiny black feet clamped onto his finger. That had started what had become a summertime ritual, feeding the chickadees by hand.

The chickadee suddenly flew off and disappeared behind the trees. Granville wished it well out loud. "Safe travels, little fellow." It felt good, if only for a few moments, to have some company.

So, no communication, questionable mobility, a bit of food, an endless supply of water, the other assorted items of his gear, and his attitude; that's what he had.

Well, if he really couldn't go on, he thought, the next step would be to build a fire. A big one. A massive one. Once it was blazing away, dump some armloads of green leaves and pine boughs on it. The smoke would be visible for miles, and he had no doubt the wardens would spot it eventually. He would build it out on one of the bends in the river clear of trees so its bright glow would be visible at night.

However, that would be admitting he couldn't go on any further, that he was giving up and seeking rescue for himself.

No, I'm not there yet, he thought. He couldn't even imagine himself ever being there. He would continue for another few hours, make the best progress he could in the fading light, and make camp. Although his internal fuel gauge was low, it wasn't empty yet, and as long as he could still push himself to continue, he would.

Conner sat next to the sleeping Dickie on the barn floor, watching Dickie's chest rise and fall with each breath. He moaned something inaudible on occasion but otherwise seemed peaceful. Conner was feeling nothing but awake. That awake you get when you're in a scary situation, when your adrenaline starts coursing and you see everything more clearly, sharper, in high definition. The walls of the barn appeared deep-blue in color, the moonlight reflecting through the boards in an almost comforting way. However, he didn't feel comforted. Not in the least.

They had all had dinner again in the house, every bit as strange and awkward as the one before. Mags had joined them, but she barely said a word and left immediately upon clearing her plate. She was a real joy, Conner thought. Unlike the previous dinner, his attention this time was focused almost exclusively on the mother. Could it be, as he now suspected, that *she* was behind all of this? Was it her standing off in the woods watching the Farm that night? He was sure of it now. The small clue about smoking made him confident that she was playing a much more significant role in this whole nightmare than he had previously suspected. Was she there the night Pa and Derek fell upon him and Raylee? He didn't think so, but nothing would surprise him now. Mom had been her usual overly friendly and accommodating self during the meal, again treating them like they were visiting with beloved relatives in the country, not like the prisoners she knew they were.

He couldn't quite get a hold of it. Why was she doing this? Moreover, what was the goal? He noticed that she treated Raylee with almost sickening kindness, catering to her when her water glass ran low, and offering her second helpings on the potatoes and thick stew they had for dinner again. Raylee, sounding meek and defeated, politely declined, saying that she'd had plenty, thank you very much.

Still, as Conner looked more closely at Mom during the meal, he did notice something he had not seen before. Her eyes. They were narrow and gray, surrounded by the deep weathered creases of skin and brow, and seemed to dart about from Raylee to Pa and Derek in an almost manic manner. For one instant, when he was observing, she looked directly into his gaze, causing a wave of tightness to seize his gut, and he quickly looked down at his almost untouched plate of food. He thought about a documentary he had seen on serial killers. Their faces sometimes appeared friendly and welcoming, but there was something in their eyes that was unmistakably hard and calculating—almost blank. She had those same eyes. The constant, unnerving smile on her face distracted from the true nature beneath the surface, but the eyes couldn't hide. They were the eyes of a predator sizing up its prey. When he picked up his fork with the pretense of eating, his hand was shaking slightly, and he quickly set it back on the plate with a louder clank than he intended.

"Not hungry, my boy?" Mom had said to him, with the ever-present grin.

"No, ma'am," was all he could muster.

"How many times have I told you, call me Mom!" she had said gleefully.

Conner couldn't remember her ever having said that, but he nodded his head to indicate his understanding.

Derek had also been noticeably quiet during the dinner, as if his mind was in some distant place, just where Conner longed to be. Perhaps most disturbing of all was Raylee. Her demeanor was understandably the same as his and Dickie's, subservient and quiet. She wore a faded yellow dress this time, with small roses on it. It wasn't her dress or her manner that weighed so heavily on his mind; it was her right cheek. He noticed right off that it was a more crimson color than the left side of her face, and was ever so slightly puffier. At first, he thought maybe she had been crying while resting her cheek on a bed or something, but the coloration did not fade during the hour or so he had been at the table.

She had been hit, slapped most likely; he was sure of it.

When this realization first came to him, he felt his cheeks flush with heat and anger. His first thought was that it must have been Derek, but then he quickly discounted that as an option. Surely his heavy calloused hand would have left a more obvious bruise. Mom's eyes had settled the debate going on in his mind. She had slapped Raylee for some unknown reason—or maybe no reason at all, other than to establish herself as the master of the situation, like some cowardly person hitting their puppy for a minor offense like chewing on a shoe. Raylee looked like a beaten animal. Beaten into submission, into subservience, to make sure she knew her place. He was enraged, but he held it inside as best he could. There was nothing he could do…at least, not yet.

Dickie stirred in his sleep, uttering the word *okay* in the dimness of the barn. Conner couldn't imagine what he was dreaming about, but if it was anything like his own dreams of late, it was cold and unpleasant. Just as he was about to lie down himself and try to get a little sleep, he heard the light padding of feet outside the back the barn. They were not the heaving, thumping steps of Derek or Pa, and he instantly knew who it was. Conner didn't say a word but listened until the footsteps came to a halt just outside the wall.

Finally, the silence broke with the small voice of Bibbs.

"Conner?" almost a whisper. "Conner, are you there?"

Conner pushed himself up with his hands on the dirt floor, speaking as he rose.

"Yes, I'm here." In a half crouch, he went over to the wall.

"Conner, I need to talk to you."

"What is it?" Conner said, realizing quickly that his voice sounded annoyed, the memory of Raylee's cheek still fresh in his mind. He had to be careful.

"Conner, I don't know…I don't know what to do."

Conner made sure his response sounded less sharp. "What to do about what, Bibbs?"

"What I should do. I don't know." More silence.

"You're going to have to tell me what you mean, Bibbs," Conner said.

Then, like a flood of words that had broken through a dam: "What to do about you guys. I mean, I'm happy you're here and all, all of you. You guys are nice to me, not like Derek and Mags. You like to talk to me. But I don't think you should be here. Maybe you should all be home with your families. I don't know what to do. I've thought about it and thought about it, but I still don't know what to do. There's nothing I *can* do. I mean, right? What am I supposed to do?"

"Bibbs. I know this is hard for you, and you're right, we need to go home. We all need to go home. We can't stay here anymore."

Conner heard a slight thump as Bibbs's shoulder leaned on the side of the barn, blacking out a painfully thin section of moonlight.

"Mom got mad at Raylee yesterday."

"Why do you say that?"

"I was in my room, and I heard Mom yelling at her. She said she was ungrateful, that she didn't know how good she had it here, and that she wasn't going to put up with her moping around and crying. I think she hit her, too."

Conner felt his insides seize up like a vise was suddenly tightened a turn or two in his gut.

"Is that why her face looked red at dinner?"

"I suppose. It's no big deal. Mom hits me sometimes when I don't do my chores or break something. One time I picked the tea kettle off the stove, and it was hot, and before I knew it, I dropped it on the floor and the handle broke off. Mom smacked me good for that one, but she doesn't mean it."

Conner put his right hand against the wall, right on Bibbs's shadow. "Listen, Bibbs. I don't know what to say. I need you to help us. We have to get home. I'm sure my Gramp is worried sick about us. Raylee and Dickie's parents, too. Can you help us?"

"What can I *do*?" he whined.

"You could let us out of this barn, for one."

"Yeah, but what then? Mom and Pa aren't going to let you leave."

"You need to let me worry about that, Bibbs."

Conner could almost hear the thoughts swirling around in Bibbs's head.

Bibbs didn't respond, and Conner heard his footsteps leading away from the barn. He immediately straightened up and wanted to call out to him, but he hesitated. He knew that if he pushed too hard, it might scare Bibbs off. At the same time, he didn't want to give up. Conner felt defeated and hung his head to stare at the ground. He stayed that way for what seemed like an eternity but was probably only a few minutes.

Then he heard the distinctive click of a lock and the quiet jangle of the metal chain pulling through the outside handle of the barn door. His heart sprang alive in his chest.

⁊

"Dickie, wake up!" Conner hissed in the dark.

"Wh-what, what's going on?" Dickie said, flailing at Conner's hands as if a wild animal had grabbed him.

The door to the barn opened slowly, Bibbs's small frame outlined in the dark. He just stood there, not saying a word, while Conner and Dickie just stared at him for a moment. What was happening didn't seem real. They were free. It was night, everyone was presumably asleep inside the house, and they were free. They could go now, run into the woods, and get away from this place, except for one crucial thing: Raylee was not here. Conner stood up and quickly went over to the open door, Bibbs standing there, shuffling from one foot to the other. Conner looked down and saw a lump on the ground at Bibbs's side.

"Is that my pack?" Conner asked, already knowing the answer.

"Yeah…I brought it. I took it out of the closet in the kitchen. I wasn't sure what I was going to do, but I got it just in case. I put some food in there, and your watch is in there, too. Derek's been wearing it, but he left it on the bench in the shed yesterday. I also got the key for the lock from the kitchen drawer. Pa doesn't know I know where he keeps it, but I do. I saw him put it in there through my bedroom door after he locked you guys up a few nights ago. He'd be furious if he knew I was spying on him. You should get going. Just head past the potato field we were in today. There's a path at the edge of the field that goes to the river. It takes a long time, so you need to get started if you want to make it to the river before morning. Pa's boat is there. It's got a motor; do you know how to work it?" Before Conner could answer: "Anyway, the oars are hidden in the woods next to the big tree if you can't. You know how to row a boat? You can use it to go down the river, that's where the town is—I've heard Pa say it."

"We can't leave without Raylee, Bibbs."

"Oh, yes, we can!" Dickie blurted out from right behind Conner's head.

Conner turned sharply and faced Dickie in the dark. "No, we can't, Dickie. Either we all go, or none of us goes." There was no doubt in his voice.

"But we could get away and get help. They could come back here and get Raylee and beat these freaks."

Bibbs winced at Dickie's words.

"Shut up, Dickie. You're going to do what I say, you got that?" Conner poked his right index finger hard into Dickie's chest, and Dickie instinctively drew back, as if he was afraid Conner might hit him, which he very well might have if he hadn't stopped talking.

Bibbs spoke up. "We can get her out. She's in the back bedroom. There's a window in her room facing the woods. Derek put some nails in the outside of the window to keep her from opening it, but I pulled them out with a hammer."

"Why did you do that?" Conner asked.

"I took the nails out after we finished digging the potatoes. Don't worry. They didn't see me. I put Pa's hammer back in his toolbox. I wasn't sure what I was going to do yet, but I thought about what you said in the field, and I've been thinking about it ever since Mom hit Raylee. They're going to kill me."

Conner reached down and picked up his pack, feeling the heft, Raylee's full canteen strapped to the side. Poking out the front pocket was the bone handle of his knife, which he quickly pulled out and started to fasten to his belt. "No, they won't. Bibbs, you need to come with us."

"Oh, I can't do that!" Bibbs said, too loud.

"Shhh, you idiot!" Dickie hissed.

"I told you to shut up, Dickie," Conner said. "Bibbs, you can go with us. I don't think you belong here at all. I heard a story about a boy that went missing from his family, and that a little boy showed up in town one day, but got taken into the woods by some man. I think that little boy might be you."

Bibbs shook his head. "I don't remember that. It wasn't me."

"You wouldn't remember it. The boy was only a few years old."

"Nope. I've always been here, with Mom and Pa. That's not me."

Conner realized he was losing precious time. "Take us to her window."

Quietly, the three of them made their way across the front of the barn to the shed by the fields. They approached the house from the north side, keeping next to the fence so their silhouettes would not stand out in the moonlight. They reached the edge of the porch and crept to the back. The air was crisp, a gentle wind rustling the leaves in the trees. It was a beautiful night, Conner thought to himself ridiculously. It was funny that in moments of the highest stress, ridiculous thoughts can pop into your mind, like an uninvited guest at a party.

Bibbs stopped at the corner of the house and pointed at the first window around the back. Conner looked at the window, raising his chin toward it, and Bibbs nodded his head in confirmation. Conner put his palm up to Bibbs and Dickie, motioning them to stay put, then crept over to the window, careful to avoid the branches and broken slats of wood that littered the back of the house. He reached the window and tried to peer inside, but the yellow crust and dirt on the window made it hard to see anything. Conner cupped his hands to the side of his head and pressed his face closer to the glass. There, in the dimness, he could make out a bed against the back wall with a lump under a patterned quilt. Carefully, he tapped his index fingernail on the glass.

No movement that he could see.

He tapped again lightly, afraid of scaring Raylee, and knowing that a startled scream would end all of this instantly.

Movement under the quilt. He tapped again. More movement, and suddenly the top half of the quilt flopped carelessly to the side of the bed. He could make out Raylee's lithe form as she turned to her side and looked over at the window. A few more small taps and he saw her sit up in the bed, looking intently at the window. He only hoped the moonlight was illuminating him enough that she would see who it was.

Raylee turned and slid her bare legs and feet off the bed, standing slowly, apprehensively. As she stood up, she could see a person at the window. The person gave a small wave. Conner! She caught herself before she blurted his name aloud. She crept quickly to the window on her tiptoes, quiet as a fawn on a moss-covered forest floor. When she got to the window, she could make out his face, and she smiled. Conner raised his hands and made a pushing up motion. How could she with the window nailed shut? she thought. Instinctively, she looked to the outside windowsill and saw tiny black holes where the nails used to be. How? It didn't matter. She could get out, and Conner was there.

Raylee grasped the middle frame of the window and pushed. At first, it didn't budge, but she pushed a little harder, and it slid up about an inch with a scrape. Immediately, she felt the fresh outside air flood in and surround her legs. She pushed again, but the window began to creak and moan louder, lifting higher on the right side than the left, out of kilter. She pushed a little harder on the left, and it mercifully leveled out. Inch by inch, the scraping sound making her teeth clench, the window finally opened about halfway. She knelt, and Conner immediately put his face in, almost kissing her by accident when he did. Certainly not the right time for that, she thought, as a great wave of relief washed over her.

"Raylee!" Conner hissed. "Come on; we've got to get out of here."

"But how?" Raylee whispered.

"Bibbs. No time to talk. Get dressed and get your shoes on; we have to go *now*."

Only then did Raylee notice the unmistakable figures of Dickie and the much shorter Bibbs standing off to the right of Conner. She turned quickly, went over to the battered wooden chair where she had left her clothes, and hastily got dressed. She slipped her bare feet into her sneakers, tying them fast, and went back to the window. Without a word, she hunched over and lifted her right leg through the window and started to slide out. Her shirt caught briefly on a splinter of wood, but it popped free with a little snap. Conner grabbed her midsection and helped lower her down, her left leg pulling out awkwardly through the opening. When her feet hit the soft ground, she turned and instantly hugged him as tight as she could, and he hugged her back.

"We're leaving, let's go," Conner whispered.

Back toward the front of the house, to the fence and the potato field. They were going home.

Chapter 17

Bibbs, Conner, Raylee, and Dickie walked through the field, staying on the dirt paths among the rows of vegetables. They walked in silence, afraid that any sound could alert those in the house of their presence outside. Dark clouds had begun to skitter across the sky, blocking out the moonlight at times. A solitary raccoon stopped its lumbering gait and stood on its hind legs, getting a better view of the creatures walking silently in the field. Its primitive brain registered no threat, and it resumed searching for discarded potatoes to bring back to its lair.

When they reached the edge of the woods, Bibbs stopped suddenly, and Conner had to seize up to avoid bumping into the back of him.

"I can't go any further," Bibbs said.

Conner faced him directly. "Listen, Bibbs. You need to come with us. You can't stay here."

"Listen to him, Bibbs," Raylee said. "It's not safe. They'll figure out it was you who let us out."

Dickie uncharacteristically remained silent, still stinging from the scolding Conner had given him at the barn door.

"Nope. I can't. I can't leave Mom and Pa. I can't, they need me. Remember what I told you. Stick to the path and make your way to the river, and take the boat downstream. I'm going to miss you guys, I am."

Conner looked at Bibbs's small body in the dark. His thin shoulders were firm and erect, with no give in them. He had a stance not usually exhibited by a child of such a young age. It said, *I'm not going to be moved on this, no matter what you say.*

Conner sighed, looked back at the house across the field, and then gazed at the woods. He had no options here—they had to go, and they couldn't force him to go with them. "Okay, Bibbs. Just know that we have to tell people what happened, and they'll probably come looking for you all."

"That's okay," Bibbs said.

Raylee walked over to Bibbs and embraced him in a tight hug. "Thank you so much, Bibbs. I'm so glad we got a chance to get to know each other. We'll see each other again, you'll see."

Bibbs hugged Raylee back as hard as his little arms could, then he pulled back and away from her. "You better go now. You need to be at the river before it gets light out."

With that, he turned and began walking back to the house, his small figure dissolving into the black night, then disappearing.

Conner felt tears welling up in his eyes, but he willed them back. There was no time for feeling sad now. Not until they were far away from here.

⁂

Conner paused on the path to adjust his pack more squarely on his back. Despite the intermittent moonlight slicing through the trees and their eyes adjusting to the darkness, it was rough going. Roots and holes littered the way, making for occasional stumbles and trips. The path cut relatively clearly through the thick woods, but Conner still feared he might venture off it at some point and get them completely lost, so he was taking his time. Raylee walked behind him and Dickie behind her, no one talking, all of them feeling sad about having to leave Bibbs behind. However, there was nothing they could do, and they knew it. Conner only hoped that once people came and found this place, they would be able to rescue him from this so-called family.

Once they had gotten a few hundred yards from the field, Conner dug through his pack in search of his phone. Yes, it was there, right next to the gold watch Bibbs had rescued from a life on Derek's dirty wrist. He pressed the power button on the side but got nothing. Dead. So, calling for help was out, and he begrudgingly accepted that fact. They were on their own again. He zipped it closed, and they continued on their way down the trail.

When they reached a clearing, they stopped to survey the path of dampened-down grass ahead.

"What say you, Chief, are we getting close?" Dickie asked.

"I think so…maybe. See how the woods are thinning out and the ground is getting wet?" Conner replied. "That must be a good sign."

Raylee looked back at the trail behind them. "I think we need to keep moving." Her voice trembled slightly.

Conner and Dickie both nodded, and they headed into the clearing. Halfway across in the open, Conner suddenly felt vulnerable. He realized the thick trees of the woods had made him feel protected, like a small animal hiding in the brush from ever-watchful predators in the forest that just wanted to run it down and feast on it. Out here, though, they were visible and vulnerable. He didn't start to feel safe again until they reached the far side a few minutes later. The path cut neatly back into the trees like the entrance to a dark cave. One by one, they entered its mouth, the branches of dead trees on either side rising around them.

They trudged on for another hour, each of them starting to feel more and more apprehensive, needing to see the river and the boat, hoping it would be there just beyond each turn, but each time, they were disappointed. The trail just went on and on, unhurried and patient.

Snap! The sound rang out sharply.

They all heard it at the same time and stopped in their tracks. They listened and looked back into the darkness behind them. The snap of a branch in itself would not have caused too much alarm, as branches creak and break in the woods all the time, but this one had come from behind. Directly behind, on the path where they had just passed.

"What was that?" Dickie whispered.

"Quiet," Conner said, listening for any more sounds. Moments that felt like hours passed, but nothing. Just the wind rustling through the papery leaves on the trees, and the breathing of the three of them, rapid and uneven as their heart rates increased.

"It's nothing," Conner said finally, breaking the silence. "Let's go."

Five feet, ten feet, twenty feet, they kept going forward, their pace increased involuntarily by the simple breaking of a branch. Fifty feet, sixty feet, they were going to be okay, Conner thought to himself, it was nothing…

"Top-top, don't stop!" rang out from behind.

The shout burst through the trees behind them, so close all three of them collided and fell into a heap on the ground.

"Run!" Conner screamed, scrambling to his feet and grabbing Raylee by the arm and Dickie unceremoniously by his hair.

Everything was moving chaotically now, and Conner gave them both a push forward, and they started running. Dickie's wail led the way, like a fire truck siren in the blackness. Conner would have done anything at that moment to shove a balled-up sock in his mouth. Their feet thumped hard on the ground, stumbling, breaking through small branches as they fled the unmistakable voice.

Conner had chanced a quick look back when it happened: The path veered sharply to the left, a turn both Dickie and Raylee had clumsily navigated, but navigated nonetheless, their sneakers slipping on the mud as they went. Conner's turning to look back proved a disaster. He barreled straight ahead, missed the turn, and crashed into a tree, its branches spearing into him like daggers, his vision flashing bright white, and then the sensation of bouncing back to the ground.

He looked up, and the world had gone full tilt. The dim blue light coming through the trees above seemed to drift from left to right like he was lying on the deck of a boat in choppy seas. Just as he attempted to sit up, the light above went dark, and he felt a crushing, rock-like pressure on the center of his chest. The pack on his back caused his head to land hard at an angle to the cold ground, tree roots sticking sharply into the back of his head. He could feel warm blood trickling down his scalp.

"So, thought you were going to leave, did you?" Derek said. His face filled Conner's view; the only thing he could see was the clenched teeth of a vicious smile. "Well, I'm sorry to tell you that isn't going to be the case."

Conner tried to breathe, but only managed a few small barking coughs. Derek's knee was pressed firmly in the center of his chest. Conner's nose was overwhelmed by the smell of body odor and wood smoke, and he struggled to move the weight off him by pushing up with his elbows, but he was pinned solidly to the ground. His mind raced, and Derek's voice, though unmistakably his, was hollow and buzzing, the way the world sounded when he tried to stand up after being sick in bed with a bad fever.

"They're coming back with me, but not you. I'm holding you responsible for this one, and you're going to pay. Time for lights-out, boy!"

The sound of his voice reverberated in Conner's ears. He started to turn over in his mind what Derek had just said when he felt a wrap of cold iron hands go around his throat, cutting off instantly what little air he was able to draw into his lungs.

Derek was going to choke him to death.

He tried frantically with his fingers to free Derek's hands from his neck, but suddenly his head was lifted up and then slammed hard back to the earth, and his arms fell limply to his sides. As he struggled to lift them back up, his right elbow hit upon a solid object on his hip. He bent his hand down and found it—the bone hilt of his knife. As his vision began to fade into a spotty blackness, he seized the handle with his backward-bent hand and ripped it from its sheath, and in a swift motion with his last ounce of strength, punched Derek's side with the blade. He heard and felt an immediate cough of splattering wet air in his face. A warm syrup enveloped his hand, and he felt the grip on his neck fall away. Conner clutched the knife handle and tried to pull it free to stab again, but it was stuck fast as if embedded in rock. He could feel Derek's raspy breath on his face and could smell something like rusting metal.

As if he'd suddenly changed his mind about what he was doing, Derek began to rise off of Conner's body, and Conner felt the handle slip out of his grasp. His vision snapped into focus, and as he still attempted to catch his own breath and cough, Derek's form rose to completely standing, turned, and took a few steps away, his back toward Conner.

"Son of a gun," Derek said, and then his body crashed face-forward onto the ground.

Conner's vision faded to black again.

※

Conner was lying in bed at home in Virginia, the ceiling black oil, undulating and rippling back and forth, back and forth. He couldn't hear anything, as if cotton balls plugged his ears.

Then, off in the distance, he could hear the voice of a girl calling his name.

"Conner, Conner, wake up, wake up!"

The blackness of the ceiling began to drain down the walls around him, and slowly a bluish light began to appear above like a beacon.

"Conner, wake up!" Raylee yelled, tears in her eyes and anguish in her voice. "Wake up...oh please, wake up!"

The world began to light up, and Conner saw Raylee's face.

"Hey," he managed to say.

"Are you okay?" Raylee cried, and she immediately and clumsily fell on top of him in a hug. Conner could feel her wet tears on the side of his face, could smell her sweet scent, and he felt a sense of peacefulness come over him.

"I'm okay," Conner said, wanting to rise, but at the same time not wanting to break with the moment.

Raylee clasped his shoulders gently and helped him sit up. It was only then that the reality of what had happened began to crystallize. He looked over to his left and saw Derek's crumpled body on the ground only a few feet away.

"Can you walk?" Raylee said. "We should go...the others might be coming."

"I think so."

With Raylee's steady arms holding his sides, Conner slowly rose to his feet. He felt dizzy, and the wetness trickled down the back of his head.

"Where's Dickie?" Conner asked.

"He's ahead on the path, hiding and crying in a bush. We have to go!"

"Okay," Conner said, and the two of them began to make their way down the path. Conner noticed that the sky was turning a slightly brighter shade of purple; dawn was coming. They walked in silence, partially because he kept losing his footing as she held onto his waist with one arm, but also because there wasn't much to say.

He had killed someone. Derek. He couldn't wrap his mind around the gravity of that fact. Derek, who'd tormented him, threatened him, had hit him, and then tried to choke him to death, was dead, and there was nothing that would ever change that. It was unreal.

Fifty yards down the path, they found Dickie hiding in a scraggly bush as Raylee had said. He crawled out from the branches and stood up.

"What happened?" Dickie asked, hesitation in his voice.

"Nothing to talk about now. We need to go," Raylee answered.

"But what about Derek?"

"Shut up. Walk now!" Raylee said.

Dickie did as he was instructed, but it occurred to him that a lot of people had been telling him to shut up lately, and he wasn't sure he liked it. Grievances for another time, he supposed.

They continued down the trail, pushing the occasional branch out of the way, Raylee and Conner leading the way stuck together at the hip, Conner's arm over her shoulder, and Dickie following dutifully behind. As Conner's dizziness faded, they began to pick up their pace, and soon they were almost running through the woods, letting the branches whip their faces and not caring. As they skidded around a rock ledge, Raylee saw the black form of a hulking silhouette right in front of them and let out a scream that echoed off the rocks, and they collided with the dark shadow like a brick wall, Conner and Raylee falling to their knees as two solid arms grabbed them in an embrace.

"Conner! Raylee!" Gramp bellowed as he tried to keep them from falling over completely.

"Gramp!" Conner said, standing up quickly, pulling Raylee up with him and burying his face in Gramp's chest.

"Kids, I can't believe it's you!" Gramp cried. "Dickie, is that you?" looking over the tops of their heads.

"Yes, Mr. Williamson, I'm here."

"Where have you been?" Gramp said.

Conner answered with a question, pulling back gently from his grandfather's arms. "How did you find us?"

Gramp was breathing heavily, the sudden encounter making his heart race. "I've been searching for you for days. I followed your trail from your campsite to the river but lost you after that. I've just been going upriver since then, and last night I found a boat in the bushes. This morning before daybreak, I started up this trail. I can't believe you're all okay. You're okay, aren't you?"

"Yes," Raylee answered, "but we need to get out of here, now. They might be following us."

The words hung in the air like a ball at the terminus of a kick, and for a second Gramp inhaled and started to ask what she meant, but then quickly clicked into his all-business mode. "Okay, we can talk later; right now, let's get out of here. It's about two miles back to the river. I can't move very fast; I sprained my ankle something terrible."

"I can help you," Conner said. "Just lean on me."

All four turned in unison and started down the trail, conserving their breath by not speaking as they went. An hour later, the trail led into a field, the orange beacon of dawn breaking on the horizon.

"Here…over here," Gramp finally said, breaking the long silence as he hobbled along, right hand planted firmly on Conner's left shoulder. As they pushed through the golden reeds, the river opened up before them, and there, lying on its side, was a battered aluminum rowboat with a small motor in the stern.

"Wait," Conner said. He ran to a large oak tree, retrieved two wooden oars, and slid them under a seat in the boat. Gramp looked puzzled but didn't say anything. Together, the four of them righted the boat and slid it into the water, their feet sinking into black muck as they pushed. Raylee and Conner were at the bow, and as soon as the water reached their knees, they climbed into the boat and sat on the front seat, facing the stern. Dickie climbed in next and sat on the bottom directly in front of them, and Gramp, favoring his injured leg, gave a hard push and clambered over the stern. The boat floated slowly away from the shore, and Gramp maneuvered himself onto the second seat.

He twisted around to the engine, fiddled with a few levers, and gave the pull-cord a yank. The cord made a rattle, but the engine didn't start. He pulled again and again, but still no fire. He reached his fingers around the engine cover and popped it off. Immediately, he saw that the sparks plugs were missing. Whoever the owner was, they weren't a very trusting soul, he thought. He pulled the oars out from under the seat, shifted to the center of the bench with his back to Conner and Raylee, and fixed them in the oarlocks. He looked over his left shoulder to get a bearing on the shoreline and dug the oars into the dark water, one of them popping out of its lock momentarily, which he reinserted, and then dug in again.

The sun was now higher over the trees and warming the air, a wake-up call for the small birds of the river. Conner hunched over in the seat. His eyes fixed on Gramp's back as he rowed them at an impressive speed down the river. Conner began to shake slightly, adrenaline still coursing through his body. He felt almost at the verge of a panic attack when Raylee's hand quietly slid under his elbow and found his cold hand, interlacing her fingers with his. Her hand was warm and soft, squeezing his fingers as if to reassure him that everything was okay, and would always be okay.

He exhaled a deep breath, a blanket of calmness enveloping him.

They were free. It was over.

Chapter 18

Conner woke to see the sun shining through the same tattered green shade on the window of his room at the Farm. It was already at a high angle, early morning a distant memory. He could hear voices and the clanking of dishes from downstairs, no doubt his parents and Gramp fixing lunch, and still trying to come to grips with everything that had happened. They had only been back two days, but it felt like weeks.

Conner's parents and two wardens were at the kitchen table when the four of them had come stumbling through the door, and there was a distinct pause as they stared, blinking, at them as if they were seeing ghosts. Conner's mother quickly smothered him in a hug as the wardens immediately started making frantic phone calls. In what seemed like only seconds, Raylee's and Dickie's parents burst through the door, along with two state troopers and Sheriff Summers. There were no snide remarks from the sheriff to Dickie *that* afternoon, none at all. He seemed as relieved as everyone else, and soon laughter and hugging and crying had filled the room.

After the initial shock had subsided, they all filed into the living room with food and drinks, the sheriff looking out of place sitting on the floor when they ran out of chairs to sit on. With everyone finally seated, Conner, Raylee, and Dickie went through the whole story. For Conner, it was a release to describe the events, as if living through them one more time would start to wash away the black effect they'd had on his mind. However, it drained him, and he could barely lift his arms to get off the couch when they finished. Afterwards, one of the troopers told Conner he would have to come by the station in the next day or two to meet with the detectives and give another statement—Raylee and Dickie, too.

Conner pushed back the covers and rolled sideways out of bed. Even though he had showered twice since arriving back at the Farm, his feet still looked a little dirty to him, as if the filth from the barn and that place refused to release its hold on him. Clothes were already set out for him on the dresser, no doubt by his mother, who had probably come in and out of his room twelve times each of the last two nights to check and make sure he was still there. Conner got dressed and was heading out of the room when he heard a car start. He walked back to the window and pulled the shade to the side with a crackle, peering out. His father's blue SUV was backing off the lawn and onto the road. Conner felt oddly relieved. As much as he loved his parents, the way they kept hugging and holding him was starting to make him feel claustrophobic.

He left the room and headed down the stairs. He could hear someone in the kitchen, his Gramp, he hoped.

Sure enough, there he was, standing over the stove, pouring pancake batter into the cast-iron skillet in little beige circles. He was still favoring his sprained ankle.

"Have a seat, my boy, breakfast is about ready," Gramp said, "although eleven is kind of late for breakfast on the Farm."

Conner sat down and stared at the plate and orange juice in front of him. The juice still looked cold, a slight frost hanging on the edges of the glass. Gramp must have heard him moving upstairs; Gramp didn't miss a beat, he thought.

"How are you feeling?" Gramp asked.

"Okay, I guess."

"Your folks are doing a grocery run to town. They'll be back in a few hours. Are you hungry?"

"Yes, thank you." However, he didn't feel hungry. He didn't feel much of anything. Not hungry, not relieved to be home, not scared or happy. Almost a blankness. It was as if some part of him had hardened like red-hot steel dipped in oil, and he was starting to wonder whether he would ever feel normal again.

Gramp flipped the three pancakes over, showing a browned, slightly burned side up, and reached into the warming oven above the stove, pulling out three pieces of crispy bacon and setting them on the ceramic plate that was warming off to the side of the frying pan.

"I have some blueberries for you, too. I took a package out of the freezer last night. I know you like them on your flapjacks."

"Thanks."

Gramp slid the spatula under each of the pancakes and set them on the plate next to the bacon. He walked over to the refrigerator, pulled the door handle down, and reached in for a small dish of blueberries. He set them next to Conner and then brought over the plate of food. Without asking Conner how he liked his pancakes—he already knew—he used a small knife to slice off a few pats of butter and slathered them over the pancakes. Then he picked up the glass syrup jar and drizzled it over the pancakes in a crisscross pattern. Conner ate in silence as his grandfather took the frying pan to the sink and rested it at the bottom to cool.

This routine had played out countless times over the course of the summer, but it was usually with a lighthearted mood, unlike today. Gramp would let the iron cool, then scrub it out with a brush, no soap. He had explained to Conner that seasoned cast iron had baked-on oil, and that you should never use soap on it because that would remove the seasoning and it would lose its nonstick properties and become vulnerable to rust. At first, Conner had thought that was strange; he couldn't remember ever eating off of anything that had not suffered a blasting of detergent and searing heat in the dishwasher, and it seemed unsanitary somehow. "That's the way cast iron is," Gramp had said. "People have been eating off it for hundreds of years that way without getting sick, as good a testament as you could wish for."

As Conner was finishing up his last bites, his grandfather came over to the table and pulled out a chair, its wooden legs making an unpleasant squeak on the tile floor.

"I have some things to take care of inside the house. I was hoping you could feed the animals if you're feeling up to it."

Conner looked up and met his grandfather's gaze. "Sure, no problem, happy to."

"Great," and with that, his grandfather stood up and limped into the dining room.

Conner sat for a moment and thought how lucky he was that his grandfather was so tuned in to him. He knew he didn't feel like idle chit-chat, and, unlike his parents, Gramp didn't seem to need or demand constant reassurance that he was okay. It was nice.

❧

Walking into the familiar barn gave Conner an immediate sense of relief and purpose. Animals to feed, chores to do. The routine of filling up the bucket with chicken feed was familiar, as it had been all summer long. He shook the grains around in the metal pail as he always did, then opened up the door to the coop inside the barn. The chickens reacted to his entrance with their characteristic flurry of excitement as if they were starving to death. Conner poured some of the feed from the pail into the small wooden trough along the wall, and the chickens immediately took up the most advantageous positions they could find for the feast. The phrase "pecking order" had never really made sense to Conner before, but it certainly did now. The bigger chickens bumped and bullied the smaller ones out of the way, even though there was more than enough food to go around. Alas, the little chicken brain didn't calculate such apparent facts, and they acted like they needed to fight for their food to the last tiny seed.

Conner opened the door leading to the outside pen, and right away, five or six chickens filed through it, knowing there would be more food, and maybe less competition, out in the clear air. Once outside, Conner began to sprinkle the feed on the ground, and the chickens took up a leisurely picking and nipping of the seeds in the dirt. When the pail was empty, he went back into the barn and through the coop door, turning the wooden block with the nail in its center to secure the door.

His entrance had also attracted the attention of the goats, who were eager to partake in the mealtime. Conner went to the steel trash can that held the veggie scraps not destined for the compost pile out back. He filled the pail with carrots, lettuce, some radishes, and a few weathered potatoes, then went outside and filled the goat trough with the mixture. The goats were fast on his heels as he worked, bumping his legs with their coarse, hairy haunches. They began to munch away at the mixture, and Conner set the empty pail on the ground and walked over to the fence, resting his elbows on the upper rail.

Just as he was about to head back into the house, he heard the heavy footsteps of his grandfather coming through the barn. He turned his head and saw that Gramp had paused at the door, looking at him, as if he was contemplating what exactly he was going to do next. Gramp came out of the barn, walked over, and rested his hands on the fence next to Conner.

"Nice day out," Gramp said.

"Yes, it's warm."

"I know. First, it was getting colder day by day, and then we get a warm spell that makes you think the summer is just beginning. The higher elevation here does that, but it's only a tease. Pretty soon, I'll be shoveling a path in the snow for the animals." Conner nodded in acknowledgment.

"Listen," Gramp said. "I need to tell you something. I just got off the phone with Sheriff Summers. The wardens and state police went up the river to the spot I told them to, and…well…and they found the body."

Conner felt a chill wash over him despite the warmth of the sun. Goosebumps rose on his arms.

"I don't want you to worry about this. You didn't do anything wrong. You probably saved Raylee and Dickie's lives, not to mention your own. The sheriff said as much, and I don't want you to worry that you might be in trouble somehow." Conner could only muster another nod of his head in response. "I can't imagine what you must be feeling," Gramp said quietly.

Conner was sure of that. How could he? Killing Derek had been the worst moment he had ever experienced, and he knew, just as sure as anything, that the images and feelings of that moment would be with him the rest of his life. The punch, the cough, the sick smell of blood. Derek was dead—for-*real* dead. He would never walk or breathe or see again. He was just gone, forever. His hands began to tremble slightly, and he let out an exhale of breath.

"You understand me, right?" Gramp said. "You're not in any trouble."

"I understand," Conner replied. "It just doesn't seem real."

"As I said, I can't imagine. A boy your age going through something like that. I would give anything to take it away if I could."

"Thanks. And thanks for coming to look for us."

"Conner...there's more. The wardens followed the trail up to the homestead. They found the house and barn. No one was there."

Conner looked sharply at his grandfather.

"What do you mean?" he exclaimed, taking his arms off the fence and turning to face Gramp. "What do you mean, 'no one was there'?"

"I mean they didn't find anyone. There were empty boxes strewn all over the house, the closet doors were open, and a few chairs were tipped over. There was nobody there...they were gone. The wardens found an old overgrown woods road that led from the house to the east. It turns out there had been a few small homesteads built there, back in the late 1800s, as near as they can figure, but the one you were at is the only one still fully standing. I guess everyone who knew about it is either dead of old age or just plain forgot they were up there. The woods road intersected with a logging road eventually, but the entrance was covered by thick brush and cut limbs like someone wanted to make sure nobody ever wandered up that way. I never heard about anyone living up in that area, that's for sure."

Conner felt his face flush red, pushing the earlier chill he had felt out of his cheeks. "How can that be? Where did they go?"

"They don't know. The wardens said they're going back with a tracking team with a dog tomorrow to see if they can pick up some sign of where they went, but for now, they don't know."

"But what about Bibbs? Where is he?"

"Son, I don't know what to say. He's gone with them, I guess. They must have all left after they found out you all had gotten away. That's all we can guess from what we know. Dickie told the sheriff that you both thought he might be the boy that had showed up here in town a few years back. They're going to get some photos from the missing-child report filed back then, and they're going to want you all to look at them and see if you think it's the same person. I expect they'll have them when they interview you. The sheriff said they're searching the area surrounding the house for the two hikers you described. They think they know who they are, or were. They were from New York, here on vacation, and were reported missing a few days ago. They've been out looking for them, same as you kids."

Conner turned back to the fence and put his chin down on his arms.

"There's one other thing," Gramp said. "On the steps of the porch, they found a line of antique toy soldiers, set up like they were guarding the place. It seemed odd to the warden who found it. Does that mean anything to you?"

Conner put his hands up over his eyes and held them there. "Bibbs had toy soldiers he liked to play with; he showed one of them to me once."

"What do you think that means?" Gramp asked.

"I don't know. I can't believe it."

Gramp turned and looked off at the woods and mountains beyond, the deep green of the trees starkly contrasted against the blue sky. "I know this is a lot to take in, but I want you to know I think you're handling this exceptionally well. Not like I would think a kid might."

It was a compliment, but Conner didn't feel better hearing it. The thought of Bibbs out there with those people, somewhere in the woods. Pa and Mom. What would they want to do to him, Conner, after they found out he had killed their son? The thoughts spun through his mind like a vintage movie reel, flashing brightly and hitching up as it went around and around with a flutter.

"Are you okay?" Gramp asked.

Conner leaned forward and rested his chest on the fence, his arms dangling over the side. "Yes, I'll be okay."

"Okay, Conner. I'm going back in. I'll give you a holler for lunch in a few hours. Your folks should be back by then." Gramp turned and limped back to the barn door. He paused just before he went through it and turned as if to say something else, but then he just turned back and disappeared.

The sound of the goats chewing away on the greens came back into Conner's ears, and he shook his head. The brown-and-white goat he'd named Charlie at the beginning of the summer looked up at him and gave a wavering bleat, a complaint about the dwindling veggies in the trough. Conner reached down and scratched the top of Charlie's head and looked out over the small playground across the road.

※

He walked down the hill toward the center of town, the warmth of the sun heating his black T-shirt, making him start to perspire. He didn't know where he was going. He just needed to walk a bit and take his mind off of everything Gramp had said. The cemetery was empty except for some sparrows flicking in the grass around the weathered gray headstones. It occurred to Conner that the birds had no idea what lay beneath the cold ground. To them, it was just a field with rocks in it, certainly not a place of sadness, regret, and reflection. It must be nice to have such a carefree existence, he thought, only concerned with eating and surviving and taking care of your young, nothing else.

As he reached the bottom of the hill, he noticed two familiar bicycles lying on the grass in front of Auntie's. Raylee and Dickie were there. He walked up the steps to the front door and peered in through the screen. Auntie's dog, Little John, was at his post, lying on the porch by the door, and gave a few thumps of his hairy tail in greeting. They must be out back. He opened the door with a creak and walked into the shop. All of the familiar trinkets were there, the teacups and teapots, paintings of waterfalls and lakes on slices of wood, the paint darkened over the years. The jack-a-lope was in its familiar spot on the wall, its dead, black glass eyes staring ahead with an intensity that had unnerved Conner when he had first seen it. He heard muffled voices beyond the opening to the kitchen and went through.

Auntie, Raylee, and Dickie stopped in mid-conversation as if they were school kids caught smoking cigarettes out on the playground. Raylee was wearing blue overalls and a white short-sleeved shirt. Her black hair was pulled into a ponytail in the back of her head. Conner felt his gut ball up into the knot he had felt the first time he'd seen her. She was beautiful; beautiful, fierce, funny, caring, and well, just perfect in every way he could imagine.

"Oh, Conner!" Auntie said with a smile, hefting her weight out of a rocking chair and coming over to him with a hitching step, a living testament to years of working in the fields. "I'm so glad you're here. I wanted to stop by the house to check on you, but I figured your folks would be smothering you with hugs and kisses and probably wouldn't take kindly to any visitors for a while at least." She drew Conner into her massive bosom, then pulled back and clamped two solid hands on his shoulders.

"I can't believe what you all went through. Raylee and Dickie, here, were describing the whole sordid affair. Are you doing all right, hon?"

"Yes, I'm doing okay, thanks," Conner answered.

"Hey, Conner," Raylee and Dickie said in characteristic unison.

"Hey."

"Well, if you're sleeping at night, you're doing a heck of a lot better than I am," Dickie said from his perch on a step stool near the back door of the kitchen. "Mom's heard me wake up screaming a few times from nightmares. I think I almost gave her a heart attack last night. She came running in and nearly knocked my door off the hinges. Pop, well, he's acting so pleasant it's starting to make me uncomfortable. He won't let me do any of my chores, and he keeps wanting to sit down and have 'talks' to make sure I'm okay. I wish he'd go back to the way he was, barking at me to clean up my room, take out the trash, blah, blah, blah."

"How are your folks doing?" Raylee asked, twisting a strand of hay she must have plucked from beside the front porch.

"Okay, I guess. You're not far off, Auntie, about the smothering. Sometimes I need to get away from them to relax."

"Well, I expect that will change," Auntie replied. "You need to give them some time; they've been through a heap, too. Your father went around to near every house in Morgan, asking questions. I got the sense he didn't trust the investigative abilities of our local sheriff much."

"I'll second that sentiment," Dickie said with a grunt.

"We were telling Auntie about Bibbs and what he did to help us. Have you heard about them finding the house?" Raylee asked.

"Yeah, just now, Gramp told me. They're all gone."

"Gone and good riddance," Dickie said, looking at the ground.

"Zip it, Dickie," Raylee said, glaring at him. "What about Bibbs? He didn't do anything wrong."

"Yeah, I guess," Dickie answered. "But there's nothing we can do about it. They're gone, and so is he."

Conner looked at Auntie. "Where do you think they went?"

"Well, I don't rightly know. However, as I told you way back when, there are people who make their lives up there that we rarely, if ever, see or hear. I guess if I had to guess, I'd say they went back deeper into the woods. They must have known the coppers would come looking for them for what they did, and they probably had someplace to go where they can wait it out and hope nobody finds them."

"Or Bibbs," Conner said in a low voice. "I still think he might have been that lost boy."

"I tell you, there are many people in town who've been speculating on that and feel mighty bad about not having done more when he showed up here. That's just the way it is around this place. Folks tend to mind their own business, and unless it's smacking them right in the face like a broom handle that something's wrong, they don't *think* it's any of their business."

"Do you think they'll ever find them, Auntie?" Raylee asked.

"Maybe. Maybe not, honey. I don't know. There's so much land up there, it would make you feel dizzy, and if those folks live in that world, it may be mighty hard to come across them. It's hard enough to find a lost person, as you know, and even harder to find someone who doesn't want you to find them."

Auntie shuffled over to the stove and picked two oatmeal–chocolate chip cookies off a round pan and brought them over to Conner. "Here, I just made these this morning. They're still warm."

Conner said thank you and held the cookies in his hand, not feeling hungry, but not wanting to offend Auntie.

"Well, I think you all best get going. I got chores to do out back. You come back anytime and visit old Auntie. I'll always be here, cookies at the ready."

They said goodbye and thank you, and headed back out through the shop to the front porch. Dickie put his hands on his hips and looked off toward the pond. "Well, I'd better be getting home. Mom goes into nervous shakes if I'm out of her sight for more than an hour or so."

"See you, Dickie," Raylee said, and Conner just nodded. Dickie walked down the lawn, picked up his bike, pausing briefly to pull a small clump of grass out of the chain, then straddled it and pedaled off singing something about a modern major general, whatever that was.

Conner and Raylee walked over to her bike, and she lifted it by the handlebars. As she got ready to climb onto the seat, she paused and looked at Conner. "So, I suppose you'll be leaving soon?"

Conner could see what looked like sadness in her eyes. "I guess so, yeah. I have to talk to the police tomorrow, and I guess I'll be heading home after that."

"Yeah, I have to meet with them, too—ten o'clock. You must be looking forward to going home. Not the summer you expected, was it?"

"Not really." Conner paused. "I mean, I'm not looking forward to going back. I kind of like being here."

Raylee gave a small smile. "That makes two us."

She pushed off, putting her feet on the pedals, gravel crunching under her tires, veering left to avoid a chipmunk that ran toward the edge of the road, saw her approaching, and did a quick about-face back into a bush. Conner didn't stop watching her until she turned the corner over the bridge and disappeared from sight.

Chapter 19

The interview with Sheriff Summers and two plain-clothes detectives from Bangor went mercifully smoothly, and Conner was glad to have it behind him. One of the detectives was lean and hard-looking, playing the part of a cop in a tailored gray suit with a gleaming silver badge fastened to his belt. The other detective was less impressive—shorter, with a stubbly beard and dark hair that looked like an out-of-control blackberry bush. His suit was tan and wrinkled as if he had slept in it the night before, and it didn't seem to fit him properly.

They still had not found any sign of the family or the hikers. Conner recounted as much detail as he could remember, with a Styrofoam cup of tepid hot chocolate languishing in front him and the fluorescent lights humming and flickering above unnervingly. When he finished, they seemed sympathetic and satisfied with his story. During their questioning, Conner noticed that his palms were sweating, and when it was over, he felt like he had run a marathon.

One detail revealed to him during the interview made him feel sick with confusion. The body of Derek, they explained, had been found in the woods next to the path Conner, Raylee, and Dickie had been following, but he was laid out on his back, his arms crossed over his chest. One of the detectives mentioned this fact to him after he had explained how Derek had fallen forward onto his stomach. Conner had answered, no, he had not moved the body and didn't know how he wound up that way, but that wasn't exactly the truth—he had a pretty good idea. It could only be Pa, or Mom, or both of them. They had found him, positioned him out of respect, and then rushed back to the house to make their escape. It seemed like the only explanation, and the thought that they were out there, knowing that one of the three of *them* had killed their eldest son, filled him with dread.

They also showed him a picture of the young boy, Peter Terrell, who had gone missing some years before in the nearby state park. The boy was only two at most, and Conner strained to discern whether it was Bibbs. The frame was smaller, of course; the hair was a similar color but much longer; and the eyes did seem familiar, but this little boy, pictured next to a fence sitting in a toy red fire truck, looked happy—beaming, in fact. He had never seen Bibbs smile like that. In the end, he said he thought it might be Bibbs, but he couldn't be positive. The detectives told him that Raylee and Dickie had said the same thing and disappointingly left it at that.

The disheveled detective seemed to sense Conner's growing discomfort and told him not to worry. They would catch them soon enough, and when they did, they would need Conner to come back and testify at the trial. Conner wasn't sure. The way Auntie had talked about it made him think they might never be found, always out there, wanting revenge.

That afternoon, Conner, Gramp, and his parents drove to the next town over and ate lunch at a diner called Sue's Café. The wooden booths were narrow and shiny, polished by the thousands of rear ends that had sat on them over the years. His father had ordered a cheeseburger and fries despite his mother's presence, his mother a grilled chicken salad, and his Gramp the luncheon special of meatloaf, gravy, and green beans, with a hot coffee. The turkey club Conner had ordered was good, but he didn't feel like eating. He kept thinking about *them*…all of them, out there, right now, in the woods.

That night at the Farm, Conner struggled to sleep. They were leaving the next day, back to Virginia, back to a world that seemed as distant to him as an alien planet. He wondered how he would be able to adjust to some normalcy. The only good thing that had seemed to come out of his kidnapping was that his parents appeared to be getting along. They hadn't spoken of separation or divorce in the time they had been here, and Conner could only assume that once they were home, they would all be staying there together, at least for the time being.

His other thoughts were about his Gramp, Raylee, and Dickie. It was like he had been born again into a new world, a world he couldn't imagine leaving—them or this place. Especially Raylee; he couldn't imagine leaving her.

In the last few days, he'd found himself always thinking of Raylee, worrying about her, and missing her when she wasn't in his presence. He wondered if that was what it felt like to be in love. Conner knew they would keep in touch, but it wouldn't be the same. He would be a thousand miles away, going to school, hanging out with friends at the mall, and playing video games, although he couldn't entirely accept that reality yet. Those things all seemed so pointless and trivial to him now, and he wondered if he would ever fully adjust back to his old life.

When he finally did start to drift off to sleep, the image of Mom jumped into his mind again. Her ratty hair, wrinkled face, and cigarette-stained teeth were looming over his bed, mouth opening wider and wider as if to engulf his whole head. He let out a small groan and closed his eyes as tightly as he could, willing the image to go away.

He worried it never would.

Chapter 20

Conner worked at the bench in the barn, tightening the screws on the birdhouse he had been working on before they had gone looking for Dickie. He retrieved the thin dowel he had sanded down and fitted it into the hole so the birds could perch and claim the small white house as their own. The wood made a squeak as Conner twisted the dowel into place, and he righted the birdhouse and surveyed his work. Looks pretty good, he thought to himself, particularly for a kid whose only experience with tools had been the occasional screwdriver and hammer he had used at home. He took an oil rag and wiped the birdhouse down, not hearing his Gramp approaching from behind.

"Hey, kid," Gramp said.

Conner jumped a little and turned around. "Oh, hey, Gramp. I managed to finish up the house. I think it's ready to put on the post."

"Looks good, looks good. I'll get it out there tonight before dinner, promise. You've done a great service to some family of homeless birds in the neighborhood."

"Thanks," Conner said, looking back at the little house.

"Listen, Conner…your folks have the car all packed up. They said they want to get on the road within the hour. They're going to try to make it to New York or New Jersey tonight." Gramp put his hands in his pockets. "Look, I just wanted to say I'm sorry this summer didn't turn out the way you thought it was going to. No young kid should have to go through what you all did. I'm sorry. Your parents trusted me to look after you, and, well, I feel like I failed."

Conner hadn't seen sadness on the weathered face of his grandfather before, tears forming in the corners of his eyes.

"It wasn't your fault, Gramp. It wasn't anybody's fault; it just happened. I loved being here this summer. I didn't want to come at first, and I was worried about my parents, but I wouldn't trade this summer for anything in the world."

The edges of Gramp's mouth turned up into a slight smile. "Raylee and Dickie are waiting at the playground to say goodbye. They look pretty glum about it." He paused, then said, "One a bit more so than the other, I reckon."

Conner felt a warm flush of embarrassment rise in his cheeks.

"Well, if you're not too gun-shy after all that," Gramp said, "I'd love to have you come back, maybe next summer if you think you're up to it."

Conner stepped closer to Gramp and hugged him hard.

"I would love that."

❧

Conner stepped out into the bright sun and crisp air, immediately seeing Raylee and Dickie at the playground. Dickie was on one of the swings, his swing, dragging his feet over the wood chips as he slowly swung back and forth, and Raylee was sitting motionless in the center of the merry-go-round. Conner walked past his parents' car and across the road.

"Hey, guys," he said. They both looked up at once. "So, I guess this is it. I'm out of here in a few."

Dickie was the first to move, sliding off the swing and walking up to Conner.

"Well, city boy, it's been an adventure."

Conner smiled. Dickie, true to form, looked like he had just rolled out of bed, his hair tussled up in sprigs like a juniper bush, glasses slightly crooked on his face.

"You can say that again," Conner replied.

"Okay, I will: it's been an adventure."

Conner smiled again. "You have my address and number. Text me and let me know how you're doing." He put his hand on Dickie's shoulder. "And try not to burn down any more garages while I'm gone."

Dickie laughed and rolled his eyes. "A wise guy to the end, I see!"

"You know it."

"Well, I have to be going. Mom's serving leftover pot roast for lunch; wouldn't want to miss it. 'Bye, Conner."

"'Bye, Dickie."

With that, Dickie walked over and straddled his bike. "Try not to forget us bumpkins when you go back to civilization."

"I won't," Conner said.

Dickie gave a push with his right foot to pick up momentum and started pedaling down the road. He shouted something that Conner couldn't make out, but he was sure that whatever it was, Dickie probably thought it was witty and hilarious.

Conner went to the merry-go-round and sat on the edge just as Raylee stood up. She looked down at the bars welded onto the round steel plate. "Remember that ride I gave you the first time we met?"

"Sure, of course. I was stumbling around for an hour after that one."

"Don't worry. I'm not going to make you go through that again. That was just your initiation to Morgan." She smiled her beautiful smile.

"Do you wonder about Bibbs?" she asked.

Conner looked down at his sneakers. "All the time. I'm so worried about him. I hope they find them soon, and that he can get away from those people once and for all."

Raylee sat back down next to him, putting her sneakers closer to his than she needed to. She looked into his eyes. "I'm sure they will. They *have* to. He doesn't deserve that kind of life."

Conner breathed out. "No...no, he doesn't. If it weren't for him doing what he did, we wouldn't be here right now. Hopefully, they'll find him."

Together, they looked up at the sky and the white clouds moving overhead. Conner heard the muffled voices of his parents coming through the screen door of the Farm, and he knew this was it. He was leaving. His mind raced to think of the perfect thing to say, but it just wasn't there.

"I'll miss you," Raylee said. "I really will. I can't quite explain it, but I know that your coming here was just about the best thing to happen to me. Like, ever."

She had done it for him.

"Me, too."

Without warning, she shifted her body toward him and put her arms around him, her lips pressing softly up against his, and Conner's whole body went numb as the tips of their tongues gently touched. Conner wanted that moment to last forever, but he knew it couldn't.

They shifted back, Conner wondering for a fleeting moment if his parents were watching them. He hoped not. This moment was his. His and hers, and he didn't want to share it with anyone.

Raylee stood up, and the two of them walked over to her bike, hands interwoven. They hugged again, and then Raylee lifted her bike and climbed on. She paused to glance over at the merry-go-round.

"Are you sure you don't want another ride?" she asked, smiling.

"Not a chance," Conner answered, shaking his head and smiling back.

"Let me know when you get home. I want to make sure you're safe," Raylee said.

She did want him to be safe, Conner thought. She always would.

"I will."

Raylee had started to pedal onto the road when she stopped abruptly, her feet scraping on the tar. She looked back at him. "You know what, Conner?"

"What?"

She tipped her head to the side, her black hair hanging across her tan cheek. "I think I just might be in love with you."

Conner grinned and let out a small laugh. "Well, Raylee Drew. I think I might be in love with you, too."

Raylee smiled. "Well, of course you are!"

She pushed off and picked up speed, rounding the playground and heading down the hill, her hair blowing back behind her.

Conner smiled, kicked a little stone with the tip of his sneaker, and headed back across the street.